DEATH IS NOT ALWAYS THE WINNER

DEATH IS NOT ALWAYS THE WINNER

A novel by David Landau

pureplaypress.com

ISBN 0-9714366-0-6

Printed in the United States of America

Ce n'est pas toujours la mort qui gagne.

—Georges Arnaud, *Le salaire de la peur*

This book is dedicated with love to all who gave it sustenance.
It is also delivered, in just measure, to its opponents.

DEATH IS NOT ALWAYS THE WINNER

A WARNING TO THE READER

No one wants you to know the story this novel tells.

It's a story about Cuba and the United States during the reign of Fidel Castro.

In the last days of 1958 Castro, a thirtysomething prodigy of politics, came from out of nowhere to vanquish the régime of longtime U.S. ally General Fulgencio Batista.

Once in power Castro not only punished his enemies but also proceeded to destroy most of his friends – people who had helped him to victory.

A group of Cubans, who saw the fate Castro was preparing for them, determined to topple him. They tried to make common cause with the U.S. government because they knew that American officials, for their own reasons, also wanted Castro gone.

These resistance fighters were quite different from other Cubans who had fled to the U.S. Many of the exiles were Batista supporters, while the anti-Castro fighters in Cuba were revolutionaries who had actively opposed Batista – and who had thereby incurred the displeasure of the U.S. government.

When the revolutionaries went to the U.S. for help in their fight against Castro, American officials were loath to support independent-minded people who a short time earlier had helped overthrow America's ally. U.S. officials chose instead to support the exiles and other Cubans who would do as the U.S. told them.

In April 1961 the CIA sent a military force of Cuban exiles to destroy Castro with an invasion at the Bay of Pigs, a remote place on Cuba's southern shore. Meanwhile, the CIA gave almost no help to the rebels inside Cuba. U.S. agents in Havana refrained from warning those rebels that an attack was on the way. As a result, Castro was able to surprise his internal opponents with mass arrests and cripple their movement decisively.

The Bay of Pigs was, for Castro, a victory of the most far-reaching kind. It solidified opinion in Cuba, in Latin America, and in much of the world behind his régime. It allowed him to bring a mortal threat to the U.S. in the form of Cuba-based Soviet missiles. And it paved the way for Castro's rule across half a century.

Castro and his comrades were well aware of the extraordinary gift they had received. At an international conference in Uruguay, *Comandante* Ché Guevara went so far as to thank the United States for sponsoring the failed invasion.

* * *

In decades to follow, Castro's régime handed the United States one debacle after another – even as it continued to draw sustenance from the idea that socialist Cuba was a victim of the U.S.

The aging leader, who wanted to keep his image as a rebel and an underdog, had no wish to emphasize how he repeatedly trumped the U.S. – while America's officials and opinion leaders, rather than draw attention to their successive defeats at Castro's hands, downplayed or ignored the damage.

Castro often spoke about the efforts at sabotage against his régime by Americans and Cuban exiles. Not so noticeable, and far more vital, were Castro's own initiatives in sabotage. For decades he spread irregular warfare throughout Latin America, while also welcoming guerrillas from around the world to train in Cuba. He continuously threatened other Latin governments and in places he helped overturn them. His activities also went beyond the region. Only months before September 11, 2001, Castro traveled to the Middle East and spoke with leaders of Islamic states about attacking the U.S.

Through Castro's reign, a single false idea held unwaveringly in the public mind: a mutual fiction whose protagonists were mighty America and vulnerable Cuba. The actuality, meanwhile, stayed as unnoticed as the falling tree that makes no noise because people aren't in the woods to hear it.

Written histories of Cuba and America during the Castro period have largely concurred in the mutual fiction, while the present work of fiction points the way back to the forest where a hidden history dwells.

Reader, beware. You have entered the forest just as a mighty tree is about to fall.

I.

THIS IS HOW YOU DIE

Rodrigo gripped the iron bars of his cell, his hands in fists, his shaven head bowed. Seconds passed like hours, hours like seconds – each one of them unbearable and precious.

Why am I not dead? Why are these people keeping me alive?

It was dusk, the loveliest hour of day and the worst for prisoners.

This hour bore memories of homecoming, of children and women, of nights bursting with music and laughter and love. For men in prison it was the hour of deepest sadness, crawling with the stench of other men and the joy of well-fed fleas.

Rodrigo knew he might die at any moment. They could take his life in the next thirty minutes or they could let him live another thirty years. Those whom they had sentenced to death, they often kept alive. As for the man they reprieved – the moment he drew breath with a free man's attitude was the moment he might lose his life.

He was dancing with a paradox that reached into infinity.

How many angels can sit on the head of a pin? How many human lives can palpitate under a sword?

Rodrigo knew the sword was over him. His was not the every-day sentence of death which all humans face. It was an exceptional sentence befitting his exceptional life. *Not good, not bad,* he thought. *Just exceptional.*

Be an exception. Join the conspiracy.

He repeated that phrase to himself like an advertising jingle.

What a ridiculous thing his humor was! At times he felt he had no right to it. He had had no special aptitude for quotidian life. He had never quite managed to hold a regular job. Much of the time he had had no idea what to say to his wife. His sense of direction was so poor he often lost himself in neighborhoods he had known since childhood.

Still, he had become a conspirator – and in situations that would make most people die of terror he didn't simply survive, he fooled around.

If you don't tell us what we want to know, we will send you to the firing squad! the chief interrogator screamed at him.

To which he had answered: *Sir, you have threatened me with death so often that if you put me in front of the firing-squad and ask how I feel, I will tell you what the Chinese gentleman said: "Una 'peliencia má!"*

As a boy Rodrigo had heard Chinese vendors along the Malecón, Havana's ocean boulevard, speaking in their peculiar accents. When he addressed his interrogators and said *Una experiencia más* – "One more experience" – in that pidgin accent, the interrogators grew cold with fury.

It seems you do not care about saving your life at all, the chief interrogator declared. *We have nothing more to discuss. The sessions are over.*

How insane to resort to humor at that moment! How could he have been so cavalier with his life? Even if he wouldn't protect himself, how could he have been so thoughtless to his wife and kids?

No! He mustn't think like that. Saving his life was not the game he had chosen to play. If that were his game he would now be wearing a grey suit, working in a *yanqui* law firm.

He reflected back to the moment that defined his life and prefigured his death.

It was a clear night in April 1961, pleasantly cool, with enough and not too much of a moon. He was sitting stone-quiet in a fisherman's shack, a hand on his rifle, an eye on the grenades and machine guns to make sure they were in reach. His comrade Alejandro was asleep on the floor beside him. They were waiting for their target to appear across the river. The trap was perfectly set.

In a while Rodrigo would sleep and Alejandro would watch. It was their third night in the shack. The prey might arrive any moment or might not come for three days more.

That man's movements were unpredictable. For almost a year, in vain, Rodrigo had tracked him. Then, by luck born of industry – as luck nearly always is – Rodrigo had learned of his very private, very brief, and rather regular meetings along this quiet stretch of river in Havana.

When security guards arrived to prepare the meeting-place, Rodrigo would see their faces. If some of them happened to cross the river they would see Rodrigo's. He and Alejandro would fire, and those guards would take the bullets and bombs for the one they were protecting.

With a bit more luck the guards would not come across.

For the one about to conquer, it had been a thrilling and terrible ride to this place. He had fought for seven years to undo a tyrant, only to see that his risks and pains had served to put another tyrant in power. So he began to fight again.

Through these two wars he had killed other men. He had caused the deaths of people close to him. His constant exposure to danger had brought grief and despair to the ones he most loved.

Now, with a gunshot, he would redeem the suffering – all he had caused, and all he had borne. He would put himself, his family, and his country to rights again.

The idea unsettled him.

How simple it ought to be, this trigger-pull. He had lived past the rough stuff – the missions he would never have accepted had he known how arduous they would turn out. All that was over. He was about to win. He should feel triumphant. Why didn't he? What was churning inside him?

"Hey! Remember us?" a host of feelings cried out from within. "We're your friends!"

Some friends!

Here he was on the verge of a new life, and the expiring one pulled at him more insistently than ever. Faces living and dead, situations that had been or might have been, feelings he'd admitted and others he'd ignored were dragging him under water.

His oxygen was gone. He was drowning. As the waters closed over his head he put his mind's ear to the tumult and the waves brought him a clear, unvarying message: "This is how you die."

II.

ENEMIES AND FRIENDS

By morning it was warm, and yesterday's icy snow had turned to city sludge.

It was a case of Washington weather. In this fickle climate, it could be the depth of winter one day and springtime splendor the next. After that could come a blast of tropical heat or, if the weather wanted, a return to freezing cold.

On this perplexingly bright morning of December 1959 the monumental quarter of the U.S. capital, under its coat of snow-dirt, looked like a grimy unwashed animal.

After a visit with his parents who had just begun a new life in exile, Rodrigo had one item of business before joining his friend Antonio Moreno for the return trip to Cuba. He must make a stop at the FBI.

In Rodrigo's brain-stem the carrier of *yanqui* power was the FBI. Through seven years of fighting against Batista, fear of America's police had been a taste on Rodrigo's lips and a constant nagging in his insides.

Cuba was an American protectorate, Batista was America's man and the Americans, with their indecently vast power, stood behind Batista's régime. Rodrigo and his fellow plotters had taken great pains to dodge America's FBI as well as Batista's SIM. If either police force got evidence against Rodrigo and his comrades they would be off to the SIM's torture chambers, where they must hold their tongues and let themselves die unspeakable deaths.

As it happened, neither the FBI nor the SIM ever got a clear fix on Rodrigo but both agencies knew who he was – and the FBI would remember him still. It was less than a year since Batista had made his astonishing flight from Havana in the face of Castro's advancing Rebel Army. To the Americans the fall of their man in Cuba had been a bitter setback, and they were bound to dislike Rodrigo for his part in it.

Now Rodrigo made his way among Washington's granite monoliths toward the FBI's front door on a mission unthinkable only a year ago. He would show his face to this most awesome of enemies and ask the enemy to consider him a friend.

* * *

Rodrigo was wearing business clothes, with a camera slung over his suit jacket. In the front lobby of the FBI building he joined some sightseers for a guided tour. When the group returned to the lobby and broke up, Rodrigo stayed put.

"Can I help you?" an attendant asked suspiciously. In this austere official place, people were quickly seen as loiterers.

"I would like to speak to someone in authority," Rodrigo stated.

Three or four more employees queried him with a rising sense of urgency. He repeated his answer, each time with more insistence.

A pair of uniforms appeared with an older man in a rumpled suit and bow tie. A small man with curious eyes and a strangely pleasant smile, he had the air of someone who had holed up in a box for years and then stepped out for this occasion.

"Is there something you want to talk about?" the man said to Rodrigo with evident sincerity.

"May we speak in private?" Rodrigo asked as the uniforms watched closely.

The other man clasped Rodrigo's arm behind the elbow and led him into an office area. They entered a sparsely furnished room. The man did not sit behind the desk. He informally took a chair facing the desk and motioned to an adjoining one.

"Please sit down," the man said. "My name is Ungerleider."

Rodrigo sat and quickly said: "Thank you, Mr. Ungerleider. I am here today because I am a Cuban, and because I have serious concerns about what is happening in my country."

"May I know with whom I'm speaking?" the American asked.

Rodrigo sprang back to his feet. "How rude of me! I beg your pardon, sir. Here is my card."

It was a simple calling card in script, giving his name and under it the word *Abogado*.

"Mr. Núñez," Ungerleider said, pronouncing the foreign syllables perfectly. "I am pleased to meet you."

"And I am pleased to meet you, Mr. Ungerleider!" Rodrigo exclaimed as he gave Ungerleider's extended hand a vigorous grip.

"I see you're a lawyer but you seem rather young for that," the American said.

"I am twenty-six years of age," Rodrigo answered as he sat again. "I have been an attorney for three years. And I see you speak Spanish."

"I recognize a few words. Tell me. What is your specialty?"

"Civil litigation," Rodrigo answered with a perceptible lack of interest.

"Well, I suppose it's not a legal matter you've come about, is it," Ungerleider said.

"I have come to speak about relations between our countries."

"Really? In what regard?"

"I believe that your government and my colleagues may have a mutual interest," Rodrigo said, trying to sound more sure than he felt.

"Who are your colleagues?"

"We are people who fought for change in Cuba. We felt a change was necessary. And now we do not like the change that has resulted."

"May I ask what has made you unhappy?"

"It's a bit awkward to explain," Rodrigo began. "As you have noted, I am a lawyer. You see, Mr. Ungerleider, I became a lawyer because I care about the law."

Rodrigo looked squarely at the other man and kept on. "I also care for justice and reason and fairness. It happens at times that justice, reason and fairness are luxuries the law cannot afford. By the same token, I am sure we would agree the law must always uphold itself. Am I speaking correctly?"

"You are."

"Tell me, Mr. Ungerleider. Did you by any chance follow the trial, earlier this year, of Batista's air force officers?"

"I did but not closely. Perhaps you would explain why you think it important."

"I would be glad to," Rodrigo said, hitting stride. "The situation is that some officers from Batista's air force – a group of some forty men – went on trial for bombing Rebel Army positions during last year's battles. In this trial the defense was able to show that, during the attack in question, the airmen dropped their bombs on empty terrain so as not to harm rebel forces. Quite sensibly the jury found the officers not guilty."

"Wasn't there a second trial?" the American asked.

"That's just the point!" Rodrigo exclaimed. "Castro rejected the jury's verdict. He went before the masses and said: 'Revolutionary justice is based not on legal precepts but on moral conviction.' Those were his words. And the masses cheered them!"

Rodrigo took a breath and went on. "Of course Castro knows better than that. He himself is a lawyer, but his purpose is not to uphold the law – not common law, not revolutionary law, not law of any kind. His purpose is to expand his power, and if law gets in his way he pushes it aside. So in plain violation of every legal custom he ordered the judge to convene a new trial. For a second time the airmen faced the same charges. The government showed no new evidence but all the officers got heavy sentences.

"*That* is the kind of thing which led us to change our minds about Castro! It doesn't matter to us how popular Castro is. It doesn't even matter what kinds of programs he puts into effect. What matters is that he makes a government not of laws and rights but of arbitrary will and force. And we reject that!"

The other man waited for some moments, then said: "What is it that you want from the United States?"

"Mr. Ungerleider, please excuse me if I sound presumptuous. The day may soon come for a partnership between ourselves and your government."

"In that case," Ungerleider said in an official tone, "I am not the person with whom you should be talking. Another agency now has the primary responsibility in this area."

"You mean the Central Intelligence Agency," Rodrigo said.

"Exactly – but if you knew that, why did you come to us?"

Rodrigo smiled. "From my father, who is a politician, I have heard of the FBI's interest in Cuba ever since I was a boy. So let's say I came here for sentimental reasons."

"In that case," the American said, smiling back, "it has been my pleasure to receive you."

That was the signal to leave. Rodrigo stood up.

"Thank you, Mr. Ungerleider. I have already taken too much of your time."

They shook hands and the visitor made an abrupt, theatrical exit.

* * *

Striding up to the Capitol, pacing himself to arrive on the stroke of twelve, Rodrigo chewed over every nuance and detail of the meeting.

The Americans used to be merely our enemies. How will it be when they look at us as friends?

III.

ABORIGINES

Rodrigo skirted the great domed structure of the Capitol and found his friend Antonio Moreno standing next to a shiny white Thunderbird, top down and red leather seats bursting with color in the midday light.

A white covering reached from the car's rear body up to the seat backs, giving a futuristic profile. The interior shone with stainless-steel detailing, and the rear flanks were molded into a pair of large round tail-beam assemblies that looked like rocket exhausts.

"Ho-HO!" Rodrigo exclaimed. "So this is where your lawyer's earnings for the year of 1959 have gone! Hey, it's not a car. *Es un singado SPACE-SHIP!"*

"¡Hombre!" Antonio answered excitedly. "Wait till you see what this machine can do! Under the hood, a 390 V-8! You start at zero on the bottom of the hill and by the top you are doing ninety!"

"What the hell did you pay for it?"

"Less than three thousand."

"*¡No jodas, chico!* Not even three thousand!"

"Yeah! I made a deal! Come on, let's beat it. We have twenty-four hours to make Miami."

Antonio powered up the vessel and, after guiding it across one of the Potomac's bridges, resumed his story.

"My cousin took me to a Ford dealership in the Bronx. We made sure to go yesterday afternoon, the end of a selling cycle, when they need to move cars off the lot."

"Good idea," Rodrigo said.

"My cousin had already mentioned me to the dealer. When we got there the man said: 'So you're the fellow who won the U.S. fencing championship at age eighteen.' " Antonio's voice filled with a perceptible disgust. "Then my cousin started in about the White House offering me citizenship so I could join the U.S. Olympic squad."

"Hey!" Rodrigo laughed. "I know how you are with that stuff! Even as a student you showed no interest when people praised you – but now you are really allergic! Let me ask you something, Moreno. Is it your advancing years that make you so averse to celebrity?"

"Well, Núñez, just wait and see how you feel at twenty-nine! But, you know, the people in this country don't really respect us." Antonio's expression had turned quite dark. "No matter who we are or what we do, they look on us as aborigines."

"Aborigines! Yes! That's the word!" Rodrigo interjected. "In their eyes we were black before *their* negroes were black!"

"Thank you, Núñez," Antonio said, lightening up. "It's just what I meant to say."

"*¡Coño carajo!*" Rodrigo kept dogging the idea. "It makes no sense! And we aren't the only ones they treat this way. They do it all over the world – then they wonder why so many countries greet them with expressions of national pride!"

"I believe you have just put *yanqui* foreign relations into a nutshell."

"You know, Moreno, it's almost enough – not quite, but almost enough – to make even me, a dedicated anti-chauvinist, glad of being an ordinary Cuban."

"Well, that you will never be," Antonio put in smilingly.

"What do you mean?"

"*Fíjate, Núñez.* You are a man of exceptional gifts but one thing you cannot be is an ordinary Cuban!"

"Give me a single good reason why not."

"Well – for one thing, Cubans talk in eight-syllable sentences. *You* talk like some kind of fucking German philosopher! The subject can be ice cream and coffee or taking out the trash. With you, everything starts in ancient Rome!"

Rodrigo lowered his head into his hands for some seconds and picked it up again. "You know, Moreno," he said slowly, "you have a point."

"There's no harm in it," Antonio said with humor. "Only..."

"Only what?"

"Well, if those people you just saw happen to think they are dealing with an ordinary Cuban, they are in for some surprise!"

"No more of a surprise than *you* must have given to the dealer who sold you this car! By the way, how did you manage the price?"

"The first thing was to go there knowing what the dealer's cost was."

"I see. You used a basic tool: aborigine research!"

"The dealer asked forty-five hundred for the car. That's an abusive amount – much more than he would have asked from an American."

"So?"

"So I played dumb. I told the guy: 'Look, I am sure you understand forty-five hundred is a lot of money for a foreigner. Can you help me out?' "

"What did he do?"

"He started lowering the price. I asked if he had seen Havana. I bragged about what a great city it is and told him to come visit me. After a lot more talking we signed on two thousand nine hundred and some – a figure very close to his cost. The guy said he liked my cousin so much and I was such a charming fellow that he was selling the car at almost no profit."

"Oh yeah? What about the financing?"

"Come on, Núñez! How many times have I asked you not to get ahead of the story? Of course he counted on profit from the financing!"

"He wanted you to pay aborigine interest!"

"When the guy produced the loan papers I took out cash: 2,937 dollars and 12 cents, right to the penny."

"You didn't!"

"I did! And you should have seen his face. He didn't have to say anything because he was talking through his nostrils! He wanted to take back the deal but it was in writing. So he just picked up his money and gave me the car!"

The Cubans raced across Virginia in a bubble of laughter.

In North Carolina they lost track of the sun as it vanished beyond the trees in a fiery glory of reds, whites and greys. The cold air of winter had returned and they were driving with the roof up.

It was twilight, the hour of ghosts and dreams. Names of places they had passed – Fredericksburg, Spotsylvania, Richmond, Petersburg – unavoidably recalled that massive tragedy, the War Between the States.

We men do not fight for happiness, Rodrigo thought. *We fight for duty or country, riches or pride, God or justice or vengeance or honor. We will fight to make someone else's life harder – not to make our own lives sweeter.*

Women are the ones who fight for happiness, but war is not their chosen instrument. Children are the carriers of happiness and they prefer not to fight at all, but they get caught up in the wars of men or the machinations of women.

My wars have turnèd my happy family into an unhappy one.

Rodrigo hated to think of that; but as he held the driver's wheel far into the night and came to that delicate juncture near sleep where phantasms leap into one's head unbeckoned, he kept seeing the pained countenance of his young wife.

Rodrigo stopped the car and shook his friend awake. "My turn to rest. You drive," he said.

Antonio took the wheel and Rodrigo fell into a deep, untroubled sleep. Next thing he knew, he was being shaken.

"My eyes don't stay open!" Antonio was saying.

Rodrigo looked at his watch. "You only started twenty minutes ago!"

"So what? If I drive I crash the car. You had twenty minutes. Please!"

Rodrigo was back in the driver's seat, and more phantasms came.

Now the face before his mind's eye was *Doctora* del Monaco, his mythology teacher in high school. *La doctora's* husband was a well-known surgeon in Havana. Her daughter Elena was a dark, deeply beautiful girl of eleven. After meeting the girl Rodrigo made sure to ask *la doctora:* "How is my future wife?"

La doctora looked at him quite clearly with the annoyance of a lady who is not the one getting attention.

Then it was just before his marriage to Elena. Rodrigo saw his mother in front of him, giving some awkward advice.

"This girl has had a certain kind of upbringing. You cannot treat her as you treat those other women."

He was quick to get his mother's point: Elena is no whore.

How had the old woman learned of his habits? The old man must have told her. How had the old man found out? No one in Cuba could keep a secret from *el viejo* though his son had surely tried.

Rodrigo had shunned those obvious places like the *Casa María* where some of the world's most beautiful women entertained his father's cronies. Instead the young man had a private procuress, a lady journalist by the name of Margot.

To almost all eyes Margot was a prissy older woman who would faint if anyone dropped a rough word near her. The big strong men who spoke mincingly around her would have been the ones to faint if they had known that Margot dealt in some of Havana's most desirable females.

Whenever a lady of a certain caliber was available, Margot called Rodrigo and said, "I have a case for you."

He left whatever he was doing and went to an apartment where he made the acquaintance of a woman as conservative in dress and appearance as a senator's wife.

Margot's women were well mannered, well spoken, and compellingly beautiful. Each of them was expert at making a man feel gentle, courteous and virile. Rodrigo relished these ladies, genuinely liked them, offered them his friendship, worked to conquer them.

The real romance, he told himself, *is not to seduce a nun. It is to seduce a whore.*

Why not? These ladies yearned for tenderness and repaid it many times over. The men who saw them as playthings would have done far better to find mates among them, for almost any would have been the catch of a lifetime.

Why wouldn't Rodrigo marry one? He never nudged himself to understand that. He only sensed his mother's advice about Elena fitting with him as neatly as the right puzzle-piece. His bride was not a plaything or a pal. She would bear his children, and maybe she would bear his lustiness too; but in other respects he would give her the deference and distance his mother got.

A banging at the door woke him up. His beautiful slumbering wife had inserted a leg between his. Rodrigo jumped off the bed, donned a robe and grabbed a pistol on his way to the door.

The busy face of his mother-in-law was peering through the crack.

"What time is it?" he asked.

"Six."

"Is something the matter?"

"There was a shooting at the Montmartre last night," *la doctora* said. "The head of SIM is dead."

He shrugged it off, but *la doctora* was good in her guess that he had been part of the nightclub attack.

Elena's mother disliked and feared what he did, while also prizing it. Hatred for Batista and his secret police was such that anyone who fought against them was a hero. It entertained *la doctora* and roused her womanly feelings to have a son-in-law in the battle; while Elena, going where mother went, fell even harder for her husband.

Years passed. Rodrigo's child-bride bore two children of her own. Batista lost the war and fled. Castro entrenched himself. The glory went out of rebellion while the risks only intensified. Elena, no longer the hero-crazy girl, wanted to turn her husband into a homebody.

Should it have been a surprise? Elena was a spellbinding eighteen-year-old full of qualities, and bursting with respect as well as love for her husband, but in her heart she was an old-fashioned wife. In bed she was still a girl, not a lady....

What was the harm? When he needed a lady he found one of Margot's. The lady did for him what Elena could not, and that allowed him to be oh-so-tender with his wife.

More troubling was *la doctora's* presence everywhere Elena went: in the kitchen, in the garden, with the children, and in the marriage-bed.

A certain kind of young woman, in the flush of sexual pleasure, is bound to exclaim: "Holy Virgin!" "Mother of God!" "Forgive me!" "I am not to blame!" On a man's ears these phrases fall sweetly indeed. When he heard them from his wife he had the disconcerting sense that they were meant not for God's mother but for Elena's own....

Enough of this! Rodrigo told himself as Antonio's Thunderbird rolled across the sunlit expanse of Florida. Again the car's roof was down. As the two men peeled off their winter clothes by layers, Rodrigo felt the hard truth of his domestic situation.

The problem of my marriage is right here, in myself. Elena is the kind of woman Nature designed to make any man happy. She cannot make me *happy because I am not any man.*

A new war for Cuba was on its way. Rodrigo knew it. His friends knew it. Castro had prepared for it. Sooner or later the U.S. would catch on. When that leviathan had roused itself, the waters would come alive; and Rodrigo would be swimming in them.

Rodrigo had no further say in this matter. It had been some time since he had jumped into a current far bigger and stronger than himself. Now the rushing stream was carrying him, feet first, toward the rapids, and those rapids would push him to sea.

Elena was holding his legs, pleading with him to get out of the water. If he stayed in, she was going to be dashed on the rocks. If he got out, he would be walking away from his life. How sad, that in his quest to be himself he must bring harm to his wife! How sad it was – and how unavoidable.

IV.

THE LABYRINTH OF GUILE

"*Señor* Bill Whitmore to see you, sir!" the secretary announced.

Still weary from that drive down the East Coast and ferry-ride to Cuba, Rodrigo took some moments to prepare for a visit from an old college classmate.

Bill Whitmore was a fair-haired Connecticut Yankee. His family had settled in Cuba after purchasing a *finca* in Oriente province. During freshman registration at Havana University, back in the summer of 1951, Bill had approached Rodrigo and asked for help in finding the Spanish literature department. The American was a blue-blood, his unshowy, refined manners clearly inherited from centuries of forebears. For all his distinction he was unaffected and winning. Rodrigo adopted him as a friend and they spent many charmed hours together.

General Batista's attack on the government of President Carlos Prío disrupted this friendship, as it disrupted so much else in Cuba's life. On that memorable day of March 10, 1952, the university went into an uproar against Batista's action.

"What do you think?" Rodrigo asked his American friend as they listened to student leaders urgently debating the situation.

"I think these people are pretty agitated," Bill answered.

"Why wouldn't they be? Batista is trying to steal their country away from them!"

"It's Batista's country too," Bill said. "Prío and his friends have screwed up. When Batista was President he put a constitution into effect. He enacted labor laws. Prío never did anything like that."

"That may be true, but no one has the right to subvert an election! It turns us into a banana republic! The Cuban people will not stand for it! Mark my words. If this coup succeeds, the people will be up in arms!"

Rodrigo, nearly shouting, caught hold of himself. Bill had unfailingly been a friend and a gentleman.

"Forgive me for losing my temper," Rodrigo said. "I understand that you and I are bound to see this matter from different perspectives."

"Please don't apologize," Bill answered. "I'm just a visitor in this country. I shouldn't be talking out of turn."

"Attention everyone!" someone announced. "We have important news."

All eyes turned to the young speaker.

"President Prío, Prime Minister Varona, Doctor del Cordobés and other ministers are now in the embassy of México."

A tremendous groan went up. Only hours after fighting had begun, Prío had quit the Presidency by taking refuge on foreign soil.

The speaker continued: "General Batista has proclaimed the formation of a new government. He has pledged to restore the Constitution within forty-five days."

Boos and catcalls greeting the hated name covered up the rest of the statement. It hardly mattered. No one in the room would have believed the tyrant's promise.

Through the long struggle that followed, Rodrigo heard nothing from his Yankee friend. At times he regretted the lapse but it had to be. Rodrigo had joined the political underground while Bill was a loyal American whose government supported the dictator.

Now it was a few days before Christmas 1959. Seeing Bill for the first time in nearly eight years, Rodrigo was stunned. The elegant man of manners was dressed in scruffy clothes and sneakers. His eye-sockets and cheeks bore a haggard expression that spoke of much travail. Before a word had passed between them, Rodrigo felt the awful sensation of tears building up.

"Núñez!" Bill exclaimed. "I'm glad to see you looking so fine."

"Bill! Please come inside."

When they had sat down, Bill told a story similar to many others Rodrigo had heard during "Year One of the Revolution."

"After college I went back to Oriente and helped run the *finca*. We had some great years. Then the guerrillas got strong. They came to our place and demanded money for the Rebel Army. They said that if we didn't pay their levy they couldn't guarantee the safety of our property. In other words they were going to burn our buildings, destroy our fields and kill our animals if we didn't give what they demanded."

"I am sorry," Rodrigo said, feeling a measure of responsibility. He had fought on the rebel side. Still, he had no taste for a perversion that inhabits the dead center of politics: namely, the idea that people deserve to suffer when they hold a viewpoint opposed to yours.

"That levy was just the start," Bill went on. "When Castro took power and made his land reform, soldiers came and threw us off the *finca*. They said we *americanos* had taken Cuba's wealth away and now the people were taking it back. My father asked what compensation the government would offer. The soldiers said it wasn't their affair. They wouldn't even give us a receipt for the property! We moved to an apartment in the city. It's not a very nice place but it's all we can afford. The *finca* was everything we had."

"Are you getting any help from your government?" Rodrigo asked.

"They're giving us their usual line. First they have to take the diplomatic route. They want reparations for all confiscated properties. If Castro refuses, they may go to other options. In the meantime we're not getting any help."

Rodrigo studied his friend once more; the sad blue eyes, the premature folds in his jowls, the tattered clothes and sneakers. Bill's hurt was genuine, but something else was also lurking there.

The one certainty was that Bill wanted Rodrigo's friendship again, and Rodrigo could only give it. So he opened his home to Bill.

Rodrigo was also playing host to his old pals from the anti-Batista underground who came by with increasing frequency to talk about the deepening of Castro's one-man rule. During the war these people had been comrades in the resistance group headed by Rodrigo's mentor, Benjamín del Cordobés.

Benjamín, as everybody called him, was a professor at Havana University and one of Cuba's most respected reform politicians. He had been a minister in the government of President Carlos Prío and had joined Prío inside the Mexican embassy on March 10, 1952. Returning from México "in black" – fully underground, with no identity in society – Benjamín had become number one on Batista's most-wanted list, a vaunted rebel leader.

Then Fidel Castro, a man not yet out of his twenties, made his rapid ascent.

In the amazing early hours of 1959, when Batista fled Havana and Castro's army was marching toward the capital, Benjamín was still collecting weapons for the uprising he had never managed to launch. He turned those weapons over to the new government as soon as Fidel demanded that the country disarm.

When Benjamín requested an audience with Castro the new ruler played the senior man just right. "No," Fidel said. "I cannot have you come to me. You were my professor at the university and it's my place to come to you."

A man of powerful charm and sheerest guile, Fidel knew where his interests lay and pursued them single-mindedly. Benjamín was among the first to come under surveillance by Fidel's secret police.

Toward the end of 1959 one of Rodrigo's constant visitors was Pablo Domínguez, a tall, thin black man whose African profile had led Rodrigo to call him "Watusi" in the privacy of his own thoughts. In earlier years Watusi had worked with Benjamín's group before going into Castro's July 26 movement. Now Watusi kept saying he disliked Castro and wanted to know how others from Benjamín's group were planning to act against the new ruler.

When Watusi appeared for one of these meetings Rodrigo's one-and-a-half-year-old daughter Yrene, who had fallen madly in love with the handsome visitor, bounded to the door and leapt into the tall man's arms, covering him with kisses. Watusi took a chair as Peleón Fernández, another stalwart from the old Benjamín circle, declaimed: "Those *hijos de puta* are selling us out to the Soviets!"

For his part in the war Peleón had won a job at the Ministry of Trade but had then turned against the government. Unlike the calm and matter-of-fact Watusi, Peleón was quite over the edge. Whenever he spoke about Castro his handsome features – a Clark Gable face without the spreading ears – lit up with emotions that turned him bright red.

"No Peleón, that's a mistake!" Rodrigo said. "Things may not look good right now, but we have to give this government a chance." In front of Watusi, whom he didn't know so well, Rodrigo wanted to sound bland in his views.

"I tell you they are Communist! and the Lady agrees with me." Peleón cooled down as he fondled the religious charm on his neck.

"Hey, Fernández! What do you want to do about those *hijos de puta?*" Watusi asked provocatively.

"I want to raise hell!"

"How would you do it? Do you have a plan?"

"It's not so hard! If we take several actions at once and turn up the heat..."

"Cut it out!" Rodrigo interjected. "That kind of talk is *much* too premature."

Peleón left like a dog who has been kicked away and will be back for another try, while Watusi stalked off like a frustrated sports fan at the end of a nothing contest.

Comandante Lázaro Menéndez had served as one of Ché Guevara's officers in the liberation war, distinguishing himself in the crucial campaign of Las Villas, which secured the center of the island for the Rebel Army. Now Lázaro had quit his government job, a move sure to raise attention from Castro's spies. Rodrigo's number-one comrade "The Moor" loved and trusted Lázaro, and in a short time Rodrigo had grown fond of him as well. In Cuba's new environment of deception Lázaro had a purity and a straightforwardness that were easy to admire.

At Rodrigo's home Lázaro spoke about doing to Castro what Castro had done to Batista. Contrary to what the new government was broadcasting, and contrary to what most people believed, Castro's movement to power had begun not as a social revolution but as an old-fashioned military campaign, with just a few dozen dedicated men under arms. Castro's signal achievement was to fuel this campaign by tapping into the grave discontent which he found sweeping across rural Cuba. Unhappy peasants eagerly joined the rebel band while other peasants gave food, opened their villages, gathered information or became rebel spies.

The grass-roots movement spread. Discontent mounted. Batista's methods became visibly ugly and the Americans withheld support from his army. That move gravely weakened the régime and added to the rebels' prestige. In a brilliant campaign Castro's ragtag forces humiliated Batista's military machine. The dictator took a plane from Cuba before a final showdown could occur.

Now, with Castro's government just a year old, Lázaro saw that many of Cuba's *campesinos,* particularly in the central region of the Escambray, were starting to grow unhappy with the new régime. Lázaro's idea was to gather a small force that could harness the anti-Castro feeling into much the same kind of movement that Castro himself had built.

When Lázaro talked of this mission his Nordic features – fair hair, grey eyes – lit up with a wholly Cuban excitement. Even in shirt and trousers he looked like a soldier, and he exuded a soldier's confidence. Rodrigo's wife Elena, who detested these meetings in her home, was gladly present for Lázaro. So was Rodrigo's friend Bill, who didn't hide his fondness for Elena.

"Do you have men ready to fight?" Rodrigo asked Lázaro in Bill's presence. "And please speak freely. My American friend has the same interests we have."

"The men are there!" Lázaro exclaimed. "The problem is guns. When Fidel ordered the fighters to turn their weapons in to the government, every one of us complied. Who knew we were going to have another war?"

"Fidel knew," Rodrigo said sullenly.

"Well, now those *hijos de puta* have all the guns and we have nothing!" Lázaro said.

"The solution to this problem lies outside Cuba," Rodrigo stated.

"You mean Miami?" Lázaro asked.

"No," Rodrigo said firmly. "I don't think we should try to work with the exile groups. Their motives are too personal. And many in Cuba distrust the ones who have left. This feeling about the exiles is much worse than anything Cubans have against the Americans. I think we can do better by going to Washington."

"Do you honestly believe the people in Washington will listen to us?" Lázaro asked as he and Rodrigo looked at Bill.

"They may have no choice *but* to listen," Bill said emphatically.

Elena came in, all smiles.

"You have a call," she told Rodrigo. "The journalist Margot. She says it's important."

"She might have a case for me. Tell her I'll call back."

When Elena had gone Lázaro asked: "What can we offer to the Americans?"

"We can be valuable to them," Rodrigo said. "In Cuba *we* are the ones with experience. Lázaro, you fought in the Escambray. I fought in Havana. We know how to do this. Do the Americans have anyone to do it better? I know the CIA is good, but not even the CIA can do in Cuba what we can. Your people can seize a territory and raise a flag. As soon as that happens the Americans have an excuse to send help. That prospect should be worth a few guns. Tell me, Bill. What do you think?"

"It sounds quite plausible," the fair-haired *yanqui* said.

"My wife will stay in Havana after I go to the country," Lázaro said to Rodrigo. "She will keep in touch with you."

Rodrigo felt a swirl of emotion when Lázaro stood up to leave. The main feeling was one of newfound resolve. Their group had gained a strategy.

Under Lázaro's command they would launch a military operation in the center of the island. To support this campaign, Rodrigo and Peleón – a genius at demolitions – would raise havoc in the capital with bombing attacks.

Rodrigo's next visit to Washington could get the guns and other materials they lacked for these operations. Bill, who clearly knew a lot about his government's posture on Cuba, thought well of Rodrigo approaching American officials. This was not a far-fetched scheme. It had a decent chance to work, and *that* was exciting.

The plan, however, did have a weak link, which also happened to be its strongest: Lázaro himself.

The expert commander had no aptitude for dealing with spies. On the battlefield he would be formidable; but getting onto the battlefield with Castro required escaping detection by his net of agents. If Lázaro failed to take the right precautions Castro's police would infiltrate his force and make arrests. Rather than have a chance to fight, Lázaro and his men would go to a firing squad.

The man's greatest asset, his unshakable confidence, arose from an inner decency that could be mortal to him in the labyrinth of guile that Cuba had become. As Rodrigo watched Lázaro walk away from his home, a sudden melancholy plucked at him and filled up his eyes.

* * *

Rodrigo's kids were opening their presents on Christmas Day when Elena called her husband to the phone.

"Say Núñez, is that you?" a familiar voice was asking.

"Bill! Where are you?"

"At central police headquarters. It seems I'm under arrest."

"On what charge?"

"Disorderly conduct."

"I cannot believe that."

"On top of everything these people are not letting me go to the bathroom!"

"I'm coming right away."

Rodrigo grabbed a box of sweets, jumped into his car and made for the center of Havana.

"My name is Núñez," Rodrigo told an officer inside the police station. "I am here to see a *Señor* Whitmore."

"*Señor* Whitmore," the officer echoed laconically. "A strange case."

"Perhaps it would not be so strange if the man were able to use a bathroom," Rodrigo said sharply.

"With respect," the officer answered, "we have invited him several times. The man is a lunatic. He just urinates all over his cell."

This was extremely disturbing news.

In the cell the odor was strong and Bill quite lucid.

"Say, do you think you could get me out of here?" he asked.

It was Rodrigo's old friend, the man of manners, talking.

A fast reflection told Rodrigo to hold off.

"Bill, I will do what I can. If I don't make your bail today it's because of the holiday. I will get you out of here tomorrow morning at latest."

The other man cheered up a bit.

"And please!" Rodrigo gave his friend the candies. "I know this isn't much of a place to spend Christmas but anyway, Merry Christmas."

Driving home, Rodrigo pondered. Was Bill mad? And if not, what *was* he?

People often act crazy to get what they want. What did Bill want? Friendship, and access to Rodrigo's house – which meant access to those meetings.

Could Bill be a spy?

If he were a spy he would want to come and go without giving reasons. A normal person can't do that. A madman can. Maybe *that* was the play.

Or maybe Bill was over the edge.

Next day Rodrigo phoned the station.

"Please officer, be so kind. May I know the situation of *Señor* Whitmore?"

"Is this Doctor Núñez?" the officer asked.

"It is," Rodrigo answered.

"I thought as much. *Señor* Whitmore went out yesterday."

"When?"

"Not long after you came."

"Who paid his bail?"

"Two *americanos.*"

"Do you know who they were?"

"No. They said they were friends of the prisoner."

"Excuse me for troubling you. Did they look like officials?"

"I had that impression."

"Thank you, officer."

"At your service."

No doubt remained. Bill's "friends" were relations of the man Rodrigo had seen at the FBI; and now those people had become Rodrigo's friends too.

V.

INHERITANCES

In February 1960 the vice president of the Soviet Union, Anastas Mikoyan, made an official visit to Cuba and concluded an agreement with Castro's government. Castro got money in the form of a development loan, while the Soviets got a trade mission that would clearly become a base for strategic operations in the hemisphere.

"You see?" Peleón exclaimed. "It's just as I told you. Fidel is a Commie! He wants to turn us all into Reds!" So saying, he turned red himself.

"Yes, it's bad, but this is not ideology. It's money," Rodrigo whispered. They were in a restaurant and he didn't want his voice to carry.

"What money can the Russians give Fidel that he doesn't already have? Every day he takes money from rich people here, and from the *yanquis.* He has built up quite some treasure chest!"

"I'm not able to count what he has," Rodrigo said. "I only know that he will keep looking for money. The day is coming when he will have no more to expropriate, and he will be asking for money instead of taking it."

"You think this business with the Russians is just money?"

"Of course! He cannot ask the Americans for anything. The Europeans will give him friendship but no more, because the Americans will not let them. So if he can't get money from America or Europe he has to go to Moscow."

"But doctor!" Peleón objected. "Fidel has kissed the wolf on the mouth! With him and the Soviets it's a case of love!"

"No. Fidel is no Communist and he is certainly no lover."

"What is he then?"

"He's an entrepreneur."

"An entrepreneur!"

"Yes. An entrepreneur in politics. He uses what works. When he goes to Moscow he is a Communist. If instead of using Communism he could reach his goals by embracing Catholicism, Buddhism or Zionism he would do it gladly. They are all the same to him."

"Please! Don't put Communism and Catholicism together. Communism is for *hijos de puta*. Catholicism is a sincere faith!"

"Communism is also a faith," Rodrigo said. "Communists are believers. They are sincere – and maybe more decent than some other people we know. Tell me. Would you rather deal with the Communists in Cuba or with Batista's henchmen in Miami?"

"What a choice!" Peleón exclaimed.

"Listen. I don't like Communism any more than you do but the problem here is not Communism. It's Castro. Castro is a *user*. He uses people, nations, politics, ideologies, all for himself. You're right about one thing, Peleón. The Russians are coming in, and they will try to dominate us because that's how they do business. What an irony! Castro the liberator promises to end *yanqui* domination of Cuba, and he opens our door to Russia, which is the last of the unliquidated empires! By the way, Cuba's Communists – the honest ones, I mean – will be out of power *the instant* Castro can gain by dismissing them."

"What makes you say that?" Peleón objected. "Where is your

crystal ball?"

Rodrigo touched his forehead. "In here. Communists love to love a leader. They will be Castro's enforcers and they will serve him to the utmost. Castro knows it. When he has no more use for them he will throw them away like fruit-skins."

"But it makes no sense! Those people are the best friends Castro has."

"That's how the Communists think. It's not how Fidel thinks. When Fidel looks at the world he doesn't see friends. He sees enemies and people waiting to become enemies. It used to be that 'friend of the President' was the most privileged position in Cuba. Today it's the most dangerous."

* * *

Friday, March 4, 1960, toward noon. If you had been anywhere in the main part of Havana on that day you would have remembered exactly where you were or what you were doing when the explosions occurred.

Rooms, walls, windows, sidewalks, whole streets and avenues were shaking. People felt the world fall apart. A city was in panic, and when it started to calm down the explosions began again.

In minutes the news was everywhere. A French cargo ship in Havana harbor, the *Coubre*, had blown up. The boat had been carrying munitions for Castro's armed forces. That was why the explosions had been so numerous and shattering.

Accident or sabotage? Almost before people could wonder, Fidel's voice was everywhere, accusing "international oligarchs" and "war criminals" in the United States. News broadcasts were soon carrying statements from Jean-Paul Sartre and Simone de Beauvoir, who happened to be in Havana. Those renowned French intellectuals had hurried to second Fidel's broadsides against the Americans.

"Tell me, Mr. Núñez. What do you think is Castro's real point of view in this matter?"

Benjamín del Cordobés, the professor and politician, was lunching shortly afterward with his protégé Rodrigo at the Chinese restaurant Canton.

"That's easy," Rodrigo said. "Fidel hates the United States."

"Yes, but *why?* In what *sense* does he hate the United States?"

"I don't understand the question."

"What comes into your mind when you hear the phrase, 'Ship exploding in Havana harbor'?"

"The *Maine* of course!"

"Does the *Coubre* remind you of the *Maine* in any way?"

"Let's see. In '98 the Spaniards accused the Americans of blowing up their own ship to give themselves an excuse to come here and make war. Now it is Fidel pointing a finger at the Americans. And actually he's not wrong. The Americans must have done it."

"Let's leave that aside. What role is Castro playing?"

"Role? I don't follow."

"Don't follow. Think."

"I'm thinking, I'm thinking. I don't have a clue."

"Let me give you one. Who was Fidel's father?"

"A prosperous landowner in Oriente, a real *bourgeois.*"

"That would be the Marxist analysis. Who was Fidel's father *before* he was a landowner? How did he come to Cuba?"

"He came as a quartermaster in the Spanish cavalry."

"And what does that make Fidel?"

"The son of a Spanish army officer."

"So who is Fidel when he faces the Americans?"

"Of course! That's it!" Rodrigo opened a palm and gave his head a good resounding crack. "Why didn't I see this before? Fidel is the son of a Spaniard! He is playing the outraged Spaniard who accuses the Americans of blowing up the *Maine!*"

"Spaniards have long memories," Benjamín said. "To them sixty years is an eye-blink. In their eyes the explosion of the *Maine* and the loss of Cuba are things that occurred yesterday."

"Yes!" Rodrigo chimed in. "And Spaniards are not proud. They are *proud!* To *this day* many of them take offense at what the Americans did in Cuba. This is not a Cuban feeling. It has nothing to do with an oppressed Latin people standing up to the *yanquis*. It's the vindictive resentment of a weak old empire against a young and strong one."

"In fact Cubans do not hate the United States," Benjamín said. "Mostly we love and admire the United States. At times we suspect or fear the United States. At times we are disappointed or angry. Almost always we are envious – but *yanqui* hatred is not in us."

"While it *is* in the Spaniards, and it is most certainly in Fidel! It's the seed that planted itself in his mother's womb."

* * *

Cuba and the U.S. were moving toward open enmity. American officials threatened to reduce purchases of Cuban sugar. Since the U.S. was by far the largest market for Cuba's leading export, such a measure would force Fidel to find other customers or preside over a bankrupt economy.

Using the American threat to give himself another platform, Fidel called his people to the colors.

At a huge rally in the Plaza Cívica he egged the crowd on until hundreds of thousands were chanting in unison: *¡Cuba Sí, Yanqui No!* In a grand outburst he extolled his relations with the Cuban people and asked: "What do we need elections for?" The crowd shouted back its agreement.

The atmosphere having grown extremely tense, Rodrigo braced up when a boy came into his office and gave him a note, scrawled in a childlike hand, that read: "3:22 p.m., near the Caballero de París."

The corner of Infanta and San Lázaro streets in the heart of the old city was the turf of a well-known vagrant called the Gentleman of Paris. The note had come from Rodrigo's closest comrade, "The Moor."

A senior prison guard at La Cabaña fortress, the Moor had conspired against Batista and had secretly served for years as Benjamín's adjutant. He was a simple man with notable qualities: a childlike love of justice, an unerring sense about people and their motives, and street-smarts to burn.

They've caught Lázaro, Rodrigo thought on seeing the Moor's note.

Rodrigo strode up to the Gentleman of Paris and looked around for his informant. The other man was not in sight.

"¡Moro!" Rodrigo exclaimed before he knew it. He was looking into the other man's face inches from his own. How could this massive man, with his memorably tough mug, appear from out of nowhere? *El Moro,* when he wanted to be, was ever so discreet in his motions.

Rodrigo asked with premonition: "What is it?"

"Your friend Domínguez is in La Cabaña," the big man said.

Rodrigo drew a sigh of relief. It was not Lázaro but the Watusi! "How did they catch him?"

"I don't think they did," the Moor answered. "He looks like an informer."

"Yes, I think so too. So they've posted him in the prison. What an ugly job!" Rodrigo paused. "Any news of Lázaro?"

"Already in the Escambray."

"Good."

"His wife had trouble with someone who recognized her."

"What happened?"

"Soon Lázaro will be a wanted man so Charo decided to go 'black.' She got another name and took a new apartment. A man from Lázaro's old office recognized her in the apartment building. Charo told the man: Look, I'm not supposed to be here, my kids are not supposed to be here, and if anything happens to me or my kids, it's going to fall on *you*. The man said back: Oh no, Charo, I would never do that!"

The two men broke into laughter.

"That woman!" Rodrigo blurted, letting off steam. "In her house they don't need a broom. She sweeps the floor with her balls!"

The Moor went solid. Cuban men use lots of racy language but not across class lines. The man of humble origins was put off by a piece of vulgarity from a social superior. Rodrigo caught his mistake instantly.

"*Moro,* please excuse me. I didn't mean to offend you."

"Oh no Doctor, don't say that!" the Moor answered considerately.

As the large silhouette receded, Rodrigo was touched by the idea that this rough-hewn man, who in the heat of a situation would break another man's neck without thinking, was possessed of such tact.

* * *

An unannounced visitor appeared on the walkway outside Rodrigo's home. It was the tense, athletic, purposeful figure of Benjamín himself.

He is leaving Cuba, Rodrigo thought.

As the older man strode toward the house Rodrigo's emotions took hold, and memories crowded into the present.

Watching Benjamín with his father, young Rodrigo was struck by the man's obvious decency and sense of authority. The boy was also curious about Benjamín's Jewish heritage. This was the first Jew he had known, and a lifelong fascination began.

Just after Batista's coup the student Rodrigo went to Benjamín and asked for a place in the fight against the dictator.

"What do you want to do?" Benjamín asked.

"I want to be in the place of maximum danger!" Rodrigo asserted.

"Well – one doesn't always know where that is," Benjamín had said wisely.

Then came a later and crucial interview. Benjamín was holding back from the insurrection he should have launched. Rodrigo brought to their meeting a copy of Lenin's *What Is to Be Done?*

"Why are you giving this to me?" Benjamín demanded. The older man had met the book during his own youthful fling with socialism.

"No special reason," Rodrigo answered.

With Benjamín now at his door, Rodrigo cringed at remembering that patently false answer. Lenin had known just when to start the Bolshevik revolt. A day too soon or too late, and the U.S.S.R. would never have come to pass. Rodrigo had been hoping that one or another of Lenin's phrases might inspire Benjamín to act....

And now the older man was closing his own book.

As they sat down Benjamín went straight to reminiscing.

"I never liked Castro. Even as a student he was mixing with those political groups that were more like gangster mobs. But what a remarkable character he turned out to be! He understood something that we, his elders, failed to see. We thought the way to get rid of Batista was to do what Batista had done. Batista made the perfect coup. Imagine. In the whole country, just one person dead! That's how we wanted it. We never wanted to make a mess. We kept waiting for a perfect moment. Castro got there because he saw that in order to get rid of Batista you had to make a mess."

"And now we must make another one!" Rodrigo said.

"My friends and I will help you any way we can. You will have to get help from other people too. Those people are not going to be easy to work with."

Benjamín was talking about the Americans.

"I've just been in Washington," Rodrigo said. "I expect to be going back soon."

"Remember that if you do certain things the Americans are the last ones who should find out; because if they do find out, your success will be the very thing that spells your failure."

That referred to killing Castro. It was the obvious goal. If you killed Castro you killed the government. You would also bring a host of enemies down on yourself. Most dangerous of these might well be the Americans. If Rodrigo and his group were able to kill Castro as part of an American operation, the Americans' next move would be to kill *them;* since in matters of assassination no one, and certainly no government, likes to leave accomplices.

Elena came in and greeted Benjamín warmly.

"*Mi cielo,*" she said to her husband, "your friend the lady journalist is calling you again. She must be in some kind of trouble!"

"I have to take that. It's a legal matter," Rodrigo said in excusing himself.

When he returned, Benjamín said: "Was it Margot by any chance?"

Rodrigo felt the blush in his face and saw the older man smiling.

Benjamín resumed. "If your activities help the Americans win, they should recognize you afterwards. Of course they will not want to do that. In the war of '98 they were bullying our leaders even before the Spaniards were out. I'm afraid history doesn't offer much comfort in this regard."

"But we are trying to change history!" Rodrigo said.

"Yes, you are – and you fight for something essential. The Americans fight for influence, power, money. You and your friends are fighting for your native ground. The Americans have interests in many places. Your interests are all here. If you lose this battle you lose everything, and you lose forever.

"One more thing about the Americans," Benjamín kept on. "As a nation they don't always fight with honor. In their revolution and civil war they did, but since then they have only known how to win. That is a serious defect. If men or nations cannot lose, they cannot really win. Castro instinctively understood this. He knew how to fight with risks. That's why people love him no matter what kind of government he brings. You and your friends have a task even harder than our own. We fought against Batista and the United States. You fight against Castro and the Soviets and you must work with the United States. That means you have to fight against all three! In the course of your efforts you will meet many Americans who have all the attributes: courage, selflessness, pride, and honor too – plenty of it. Do not however be deceived. Their government will show you no honor because it has none to spare. This honor you will have to find for yourselves."

Benjamín paused and said: "Anything you wish to ask of me, now or in the future, please ask it. I am at your disposition."

The younger man was stupefied. *I am at your disposition.* For the first time Rodrigo felt the burden resting on his shoulders. His mentor, one of the important men in the history of the Republic, was counting on *him.*

Rodrigo thought back to the day his parents went into exile. As they boarded their plane *el viejo* looked the shadow of a man, beyond exhaustion. *La vieja* was firm and youthful, not showing anything, tough as always.

"Head high," she told her son.

A fine thing: *they* were leaving their home and his mother was telling *him* not to be dejected!

Only now did Rodrigo grasp what his mother had meant. Just like Benjamín, his parents needed him to be in high spirits because they were counting on him.

Inheritances are not given. They are taken. The statement fell into Rodrigo's head from out of nowhere and wouldn't go away. Where did it come from? Who could have said such a thing? It was something between trite and grandiose, the kind of verbal trick that French aphorists love to play. Maybe it was something that a famous thinker had dropped in a Paris café. When he said it, all the pretty ladies oohed and aahed – while the pundit himself or a follower found the phrase important enough to set down in writing.

As a boy on the grand tour of Europe, Rodrigo had sat in those Paris cafés. He had watched café-scholars command the attentions of women and he had felt envious.

Now he felt angry. He didn't like the idea that some philosopher might be telling a rapt audience: I have come from Havana, bombs were exploding, Fidel and I spoke about it, and we agreed one must combat imperialism in all its forms.

For European thinkers and others who lionized Fidel as heir to the world's great liberation movements, Cuba's leader was an ideal type who fit their needs. Those thinkers would not recognize the power-driven man, bent on subduing a proud nation for his personal ambitions, that Fidel plainly was. Rodrigo, as he looked at Benjamín, understood that inheritances are neither given nor taken. Inheritances, authentic ones, belong to those who accept them with honest, open hearts. Next to Castro's inheritance, Rodrigo's was puny; but it was honorable, and with Benjamín's parting words it had become solidly his.

At 1:28 a.m., where the bread chases the dog.

Another message with an odd minute-number – that was the conspirator's way. On the hour, half-hour, quarter or even the five was for businessmen or spy novelists. A plotter had to be on time to the odd minute or miss the meeting.

At the celebrated hamburger shop whose immense neon sign portrayed a bread-roll trying to capture a dog, Rodrigo watched the Moor emerge naturally from the mass of strollers along the still-busy rotunda.

"Doctor, it's bad news."

Who has been captured? Lázaro? Charo? Peleón? Rodrigo braced himself.

"Your brother is under arrest."

"My brother! What for?"

"The charge is stealing money from the National Bank."

Rodrigo was astonished. His younger brother Alberto, an economics professor and businessman, had gone to work as Ché Guevara's assistant at the National Bank. Rodrigo had put this move down to opportunism; but he would never have guessed his brother foolish enough to try stealing from Fidel and Ché.

"Where do they have him?"

"In a private residence."

"He is dead," Rodrigo said. "What else is there to say?"

"He is not dead yet. He is talking."

"Talking! About what?"

"About you. About Benjamín. He has spoken of Benjamín!"

This was dangerous. Benjamín was still in Cuba.

"But my brother knows nothing of our activities!" Rodrigo exclaimed.

"It doesn't matter. He is trying to save his life. He even mentions your father and his friends."

"*¡Coño!* My father knows thousands of people!"

"Your brother is giving those names. No one has ever heard so many names. The interrogators cannot keep up with him. Doctor, I tell you. That man will say anything to stay alive!"

Rodrigo's innards felt like lava ready to disgorge.

"*Moro*, we have a situation," he said with all the calm he could muster.

"Don't worry Doctor," the Moor said coolly. "For situations we have remedies."

VI.

THE WALL

"If I don't get out of here they are going to kill me!" Rodrigo's brother was screaming to him. "You have to help me out!"

They were sitting alone in a small, barely furnished room of the impromptu prison, a building that Castro's police had converted from a family home into a jail. A militiaman was listening through a grille-window in the door.

"That's absurd!" Rodrigo said. "I have no influence in your situation. It was all I could do to get this visit. Why not ask your friends to help you? What about Ché?"

"Ché is a very pure man. He is a foreigner who does not understand how things work here. Besides" – Alberto lowered his head – "he is the one who ordered my arrest."

Arrested by Ché! Rodrigo thought. *My brother is dead for sure.*

"I made a mistake! I know it!" Alberto was close to tears. "I am willing to go to jail. I can rehabilitate. Let them ask me for anything – but no! They only want to put me at the wall!"

Wide-eyed and unshaven, his clothes badly crumpled and seeming oversized, Alberto looked like a forest creature who has been cornered by animals much bigger and tougher than he. Rodrigo felt moved. He also felt constrained. He was a conspirator. Spies from two countries were watching him; and here he sat within the grasp of Castro's police as he talked to a brother who had become the state's enemy.

"They are going to punish you, Alberto." The older brother was trying to sound objective. "It's unfortunate but no one can prevent it."

"Punish? No! *Kill!* They are going to kill me! And for what?" Tears were falling. "Because I took a few dollars?"

"Alberto, you stole!"

"What of it? How many people do *you* know who have done that? You remember Dad's stories – like the time he went to see Batista's vice president?"

"I remember," the older brother said with distaste.

Alberto continued, whining. "The man just sat in his vice president's office counting out thousand-dollar bills. 'Come on in, Núñez, take a chair.' The man hid nothing. The stacks of money were right there on his desk. He kept counting out those thousand-dollar bills!"

"Why do you bother to justify yourself?"

"You want to know why? Because if they shot people for what I did, half the country would be dead!"

Alberto had a point; and Rodrigo, who was rare among strong-headed people for his ability to listen, took a reflective pause. Under the old régime, which was openly corrupt, Alberto would never have faced a death sentence or anything close to it. Fidel's régime was quite another matter. It portrayed itself as not merely another government but as a new order; and thanks to Fidel's genius for public relations, almost everyone agreed. Not just in Havana but in Chicago, Paris, Hong Kong and Timbuktu, the press carried photos and stories depicting those bearded young men, ardent and strong, who had vowed to remake a fallen society. The world was in love with them, and they with themselves. Rather few noticed the complement to their triumphal glory: a self-importance that made the old régime look lighthearted by comparison. While Batista's torturers had been merely cruel, Castro's people multiplied their strength with the heady motive of conviction. They took your property, they stuck you in jail or even killed you, and in so doing they were not henchmen or enforcers. They were avenging angels, ministers of grace. Rodrigo, as he dwelt on the matter, grew more and more uneasy. What doomed his brother was not a moral offense. It was caprice pure and simple. Alberto would not die for stealing. He would die for having stolen from the wrong people.

"Perhaps we still have time to work something out before they put you on trial," Rodrigo said, trying to sound hopeful.

"Oh no! I might not even get a trial! In this place they shoot anyone when they want – trial or no!"

Rodrigo lowered his voice to a bare whisper. "I have friends in the prison system. I will speak to them – but you must stay calm. If you tell the interrogators too much, they will only get madder at the idea of how many enemies they have. Please do not make things worse than they already are."

"Things cannot get worse! I am trying to improve them – and until *you* do what *you* should, *I* will do what *I* can to save my fucking life!"

Alberto was shouting at the top of his voice. Rodrigo turned away, disgusted at his brother's weakness.

The militiaman opened the door and told Rodrigo brusquely: "You must leave now!"

Rodrigo stood up, fixed his eyes on his brother and managed to say: "Alberto, take care of yourself."

* * *

"Doctor!" the Moor told Rodrigo on a busy street-corner. "Lázaro needs you to go and see him."

"When?"

"Saturday afternoon. Someone is coming down to meet you in Topes de Collantes" – a sanatorium town in the center of the island.

"Fine. Tell Charo I will go with a woman."

"What woman can you take? It's a hard climb up to the camp."

Rodrigo made a quick reflection. *One of my whores? No, I need a woman whose breeding any cop will smell a mile away.*

"I might take my wife," Rodrigo said.

"Do you have to?"

"She would be the perfect cover."

"Whatever you decide." After a pause the Moor said: "We must speak about your brother."

"Go on." Rodrigo knew what was coming.

"The man keeps making trouble for us."

Rodrigo drew a long breath. "Listen, *Moro.* Can you put a weapon into his hands and make sure he uses it properly?"

"I can – but what if he refuses to turn it on himself?"

"Tell him that if he doesn't do it, you will."

"Agreed," the big man said, and went.

Alone on the street, Rodrigo felt a void open up inside himself.

It's a law school question. If a man has jumped from a building to certain death and you shoot him as he falls past your window, are you guilty of murder? You are.

What if the falling man is trying to pull you out of the window with him? In that case it's self-defense.

What then do you tell yourself if the man you have just shot in self-defense happens to be your brother?

* * *

"Mi amor," Rodrigo said to his wife, "I have something to ask of you – and you must feel completely free to refuse."

"What is it, *mi amor?"* Elena answered her husband.

"Lázaro is in the Escambray. I have to visit him and I need a companion for the trip. Would you be willing to come?"

"Of course!" the young woman exclaimed.

"Think about it. The trip will be hard. Not only must we drive into the center of the island. We must also hike to the camp. For the hike we will have a guide but much of it is through jungle, and for several hours we will be walking uphill."

"I can do that!" she said robustly. "I'm fond of Lázaro and I would like to feel better about what you are doing with him. Maybe if I go with you I can do that."

Rodrigo still didn't quite like the idea but his broader purpose overrode that hesitation.

Starting out from Havana before dawn, they were well on time to the mid-morning rendezvous with their guide.

The hike began gently enough. The Escambray hills did not have an overwhelming sheerness or a forbidding density. In places Rodrigo and the guide had to use machetes to clear a path but the blade-strokes went quickly, and the uphill seemed to be not much harder than a brisk weekend hike.

If nature in its frank and savage innocence can be said to have a quality like cunning, here is where it lies: in the complacency it lends to an unwary traveler, so when the loan falls due, and nature's unkind immensity shows itself, the traveler gains an abrupt inward sense of how hopeless the situation is.

At a certain point in her climb, Elena cast her eye along the hill that kept sloping into the distance. She measured that vision against the waning strength in her lungs and limbs. A throbbing field of heat, reflecting the heat of sky and earth, had built up between her ears. The landscape had merely paused to sigh on her, and she was overcome. She cried out with a baby's lung power and then wept with a grown woman's devastating conviction.

"Shall we rest for a moment?" Rodrigo said, working to restrain himself.

They sat down like people ducking away from a downpour until

Elena was calm.

"Let's go," the guide said.

They resumed. A few minutes later the storm broke out again.

"Do you need more time?" Rodrigo asked his wife, now showing a bit of impatience.

As soon as she heard that impatience her sobs grew more convulsive.

"I am sorry, *mi amor*, but we must continue," Rodrigo said, his voice crackling with barely suppressed fury.

Across a trio of hours they mounted the hill – Elena weeping, Rodrigo pulling her along, and the guide spending most of his energy trying not to notice.

At the camp they got a tremendous greeting from Lázaro and his band of two dozen men, who looked every bit as selfless and heroic as the poster-images of Castro's guerrillas.

"Doctor! Take our picture!" some of the men cried when they saw Rodrigo's camera. He needed no urging, for he had come ready to snap photos that he could use later on.

Lázaro invited Rodrigo and Elena inside a shack to take them out of the heat. They sat on rickety metal chairs as a number of men squatted on the earthen floor around them. The simple dwelling, though pleasantly cool, quickly filled up with the stench of men and their unkempt life. Elena, feeling revulsed, began to cry again.

"Our popular support is developing," Lázaro said. "People are giving us food and help of all kinds. Many are now saying Fidel cheated them. Kids who went to Havana in the Rebel Army are coming back. They are complaining about Communist indoctrination and anti-American propaganda. I tell you, these people are ready to fight against Fidel. All we need are the guns!"

Rodrigo found it hard to concentrate because of Elena's weeping, which distracted everybody. From time to time Lázaro stepped over and gave her a tender embrace, to no avail; and though the other men kept up a chivalrous attitude they were clearly discomfited, as men always are by a woman's tears.

"What are your needs?" Rodrigo asked Lázaro.

"Arms for a hundred and fifty, and fast."

"We do not have that kind of supply in Havana. I have to go abroad."

"Abroad," as they well knew, meant Washington.

"Carry your shortwave," Lázaro said. "Andresito will send our news over the radio."

Andresito, a comrade from Havana, was sitting by. He started to whistle a popular Spanish opera tune belonging to a character named Pichi.

"Andresito, when you broadcast be sure to call yourself Pichi so I know it's you," Rodrigo said. He turned to Lázaro and added with emphasis: "Don't worry about those guns. You will have them soon."

As the visitors were about to start back down the hill, Lázaro came to them leading a horse by the reins. "Here. Take him with you."

"Lázaro, keep the horse," Rodrigo said. "He will not be able to return by himself, and you cannot spare him."

As Rodrigo made his gesture of refusing the horse, Elena once more burst into tears. The horse, who understood he would be going downhill, didn't like it and started to neigh.

"Don't worry," Lázaro said. "Someone in town will take care of him. We'll get another horse."

Lázaro's offer was so considerate, and Rodrigo so inwardly glad of it, that he could only accept.

Hardly a word passed between husband and wife as they rode the horse to town – and hardly a word more during the seven-hour drive back to Havana.

* * *

By the time they reached home the city had stretched her feline limbs and fallen into a cat's delicate sleep.

Rodrigo found a note from the Moor asking him to meet at some minutes past 4 a.m. He put Elena into bed and drove to a main intersection that was as quiet as a meadow.

The Moor pulled Rodrigo into an arcade where the odd passing vehicle would not see them. The big man was in a militia uniform.

"What is it, *Moro?"*

"Doctor, your brother is done."

"When?" Rodrigo was jolted by a force of feeling he had not expected.

"Last evening."

"How did it happen?"

"I entered the house while the militiamen were changing shifts. They took me for one of the new guards. I found your brother and told him to come with me. We went into a side-room where no one else would hear. Your brother asked about his regular interrogators. I suppose he had gotten used to them and felt comfortable with them. I told him that this time I would be interrogating. He didn't like that at all.

"I said I wasn't going to fool around with him as the others had. I said they were only going to drag every last piece of information out of him and then send him to the firing squad. 'But they promised me a deal!' he exclaimed. I said that was just a trick. As soon as they had gotten what they needed, he would go to the wall."

The Moor paused out of consideration for his comrade.

"Go on," Rodrigo said evenly.

"He asked me why I was telling him this. I said: 'Look, do you want to let them string you along and shoot you when they want? Or do you want to die by your own hand as a free man does?' He said: 'That is no choice at all!' Then he asked me: 'Who are you, anyway? You're not really an interrogator, are you?' I told him someone outside the prison wanted to give him a decent death. I showed him the weapon and said: 'A friend sent this for you so you can die like a man instead of a sheep.' He said: 'It's my brother, isn't it. I ask my brother to help me get out of here, and this is how he helps me!'

"I said: 'Enough talk. You are not leaving this room alive. You can do it yourself or I will do it for you.' I tapped my weapon so he would see it. He started screaming for help. I went closer and said: 'Don't bother. I can kill you this minute and no one will say a word. The only reason I am talking to you is that I want to let you die well.' Then something strange happened."

"What?" Rodrigo asked.

"He trusted me. I don't think it was easy for him, but at that moment he trusted me. He said: 'I got myself in a fix, didn't I?' I said: 'I am sorry for you.' He said: 'I guess I'm not going to get out of this one, am I?' And I said: 'I'm afraid not.'

"He asked: 'Is the gun loaded?' I said: 'Of course it is.' He said: 'Then give it to me!' I handed him the weapon and tapped mine again, just to make sure he realized he couldn't shoot me. 'May I cock it?' he asked, and when I nodded he said: 'What do you think? Just aim against my head?' I told him the head was not a good idea because he might slip and wound himself, which would be very painful. He should put the gun into his mouth.

"He asked: 'Will you tell my brother I took my life?' I agreed. He said: 'Please give him every detail.' It was a dying man's wish, and I promised. He took the gun with both hands and put it in his mouth. I said: 'You can close your eyes if you want.' 'No,' he said, 'I will keep my eyes open.'

"He was ready to shoot, and nothing in the world would stop him. He opened his eyes really wide and the gun went off. The guards came running but I was out of the place before anyone saw me."

"How can we be sure they don't give you trouble over this?"

"No one examines prisoner suicides. Actually the guards enjoy suicides because they look like confessions and they are more convenient than executions." The Moor paused. "Your brother – well, Doctor, I didn't like him at first, but he died in a good way."

"Thank you, *Moro*. I will be going out of the country soon."

"I will be here when you return."

* * *

Driving home, Rodrigo started to chew over the Moor's last comments. Could it be that in giving the order to finish Alberto he himself had actually done Fidel's bidding?

No. Wrong. The question doesn't fit this line of work. Hard situations call for fast responses. Under absurd pressures you do the best you can; and whatever the choice you made, you don't look back.

VII.

THE PURCHASE OF MANHATTAN

Washington, June 1960.

"I want to speak to someone about Cuba!"

Rodrigo, having entered the CIA by the front door, announced himself at the top of his voice. People stared in astonishment, and it was just the effect he wanted to produce: a madman, hardly a spy.

"Can we discuss this quietly?" someone said.

Rodrigo felt a voice coming from his shoes. A tiny human was speaking up to him.

This was a perfectly shaped man, with jewel-like features. At well under five feet, he just happened to be abnormally small.

Not so much walking as gliding like a figure skater, the tiny man led Rodrigo into an office. Rodrigo gave his name and presented his calling card. The other identified himself as "Nathan."

"Now, what would you like to tell us?" Nathan said.

"Thank you," Rodrigo said. "I will be as brief as possible. If I were able to impress only one point on your government concerning Cuba, it would be this: In the present situation the only anti-Castro activists who have the trust of their countrymen are people who fought against Batista. If you want to gain the favor of Cubans you *must* ally yourselves with those fighters. As of now your most important ally in Cuba is the Movement of Revolutionary Recuperation. The MRR people are honest and courageous but they are novices. They never fought against Batista, people do not know them as patriots, and they lack experience. For example, they do not see basic undercover ploys. Almost certainly Castro's agents have infiltrated them. Do you disbelieve me?"

"I neither believe nor disbelieve you. I am only listening," Nathan said as he took notes.

"Your government is also giving help to a group in Miami whose leaders are former President Prío and Prime Minister Varona. My father is a friend of Prío and I have warm feelings for Prío as a person, but he and Varona have reputations of exactly the wrong kind. No Cuban forgives them that day of March 10, 1952, when they gave the country to Batista with barely an argument."

"How can we help you?" Nathan said with an appealing shrewdness.

"I am here to inform your agency that my comrades and I have laid plans for an uprising against Castro. We want to work with you. I have evidence of what we have already done and I am ready to discuss the matter in detail. What questions do you have?"

"This is enough for the moment," Nathan said. "Let me pass it along. Someone will get back to you."

For an official response this was not bad but it put Rodrigo in the position he most disliked: the position of one who waits.

It was a captivating spring afternoon. At any other time Rodrigo would have pursued a young man's course. Before being a man, however, he was a son. He must accompany his parents through that sadness which is the worst a parent can endure; and he bore an extra burden for the secret part he had played in Alberto's death.

Riding a metro bus to Arlington, where his parents lived, Rodrigo again felt troubled by his failure to raise "Pichi" on the shortwave. He had tried before leaving Cuba, and then from several points along the road. At the designated frequency all he heard was noise. The thought of it gave him no cheer; but he felt so bad for his parents that he almost enjoyed the distraction of worrying about Lázaro.

Rodrigo felt further dejected on entering his parents' humble apartment in the blue-collar Barcroft neighborhood of Arlington. It was a perfectly decent place, but a far cry from the El Vedado mansion that *los viejos* had given up when Castro's reforms put Rodrigo's father out of a livelihood. The veteran *político*, having helped thousands of people in his prodigious life, had found himself at age fifty-four with no means of his own. In the end his best choice was to come to the United States, where he couldn't speak the language and where – after a quarter-century of being on good terms with Cuba's presidents – he took a job as a busboy in a Washington hotel.

His parents were happy when Rodrigo came in but then they could scarcely look at him; for when they laid eyes on flesh of their flesh, a horde of memories raised themselves and mournfully invoked the one they would not see again. *El viejo*, the more tender of the parents, more expressive of his love for his sons, could hardly glance at Rodrigo before he grimaced with tears and had to turn away.

His mother played tough and *was* tough. "*¡Hijos de puta!* Why didn't they just get their money back and give him a jail sentence? Did they think he was the first person who ever took money from a government? Why, people at the ministries used to carry money away in suitcases. No one ever died for that!" And then *la vieja*, even *la vieja*, let emotion overcome her.

Rodrigo disliked what he heard from his mother. It sounded like the baseness in Alberto. The evening before, he had had to sit through a memorial service organized by *la vieja* at which a few family friends living in Washington extolled Alberto as an enemy of Communism. To Rodrigo it was odious. Alberto's life had been empty of principle. More than that, he had been an ungrateful son and an indifferent brother. The old ones had never seemed to care. Anything they got from Alberto, they justified. Indeed, for Alberto's very roughnesses they had seemed to love him the more; and every time Rodrigo pondered it his mind came to a dead stop.

Rodrigo was not one to skate over life. Even with his "don't-look-back" credo he was impelled to think and re-think who he was, how he acted, what he believed. A comment from the Moor had led him to wonder whether he had made a mistake in causing Alberto's suicide. As Rodrigo stood before his parents it was his innards instead of his reflective sense that posed the question. If he had plunged his dearest ones into such a sorrow, how could he have done right?

A day and an evening went by, then another. At about seven on the third morning *la vieja* called him to the phone.

"Nathan here. We need you for an interview at ten o'clock. And bring your suitcase. We might have to put you in other lodgings."

The call from the CIA snatched Rodrigo out of depression. His life was back in focus; he had a destiny once more. *The unhappy man is a happy warrior.* The phrase came into his head and lodged there like an insistent melody.

The meeting address was a townhouse on Capitol Hill. A pair of G-men answered the door. They led Rodrigo upstairs to a room with a lie detector.

"We hope this doesn't offend you," one of them said.

"Of course not," Rodrigo answered forthrightly. "You have to be sure."

He wasn't lying. As the men wired him up, disdain was what he felt. These people ought to have surer methods of testing someone's loyalties. A well-trained agent could beat that machine.

There emerged a stream of questions that showed the extent of the Americans' information. They threw Rodrigo a curve about one of his father's old ministerial positions. They brought up Antonio Moreno's legal work for U.S. corporations in Cuba – work in which

Rodrigo had shared. They even asked about Moreno's contests at the U.S. fencing championships ten years before. *That must be the baseball question,* Rodrigo thought.

Then came the central items.

"Are you working for Fidel Castro?"

"No."

"Does Benjamín del Cordobés know you are here?"

"Yes."

"Did Benjamín del Cordobés ask you to come here?"

"No."

They pronounced Benjamín's name with evident dislike.

After a few questions more they unwired Rodrigo and showed him to another room.

"Please take a seat. Someone else will be calling for you. It may be some time."

"It's fine," Rodrigo said, holding back his elation. He was sure he had passed their test.

An hour or so later he was immersed in a novel he had brought along when one of the G-men called him to the phone.

"Nathan here. Take a taxi to the Madison Hotel on Fifteenth Street. I will meet you in the lobby."

At the Madison twenty minutes later, Rodrigo's eye went straight to Nathan, who struck him as the most graceful one in sight. They took an elevator to the third floor. Nathan knocked at the door to a guest room. A tall, slender man in his late forties opened it.

"From now on this is your contact," Nathan said. Rodrigo gave the new figure a good straight look. Then he saw the tiny man was gone and felt a twinge of regret.

"Please come in and take a seat," the tall man said. "You can call me Thor."

Rodrigo remarked the same inborn manners he had known in his friend Bill.

"I'm glad to meet you, Thor," he said as they shook hands. "Please call me Rodrigo."

"Very good. Shall we begin?"

Rodrigo launched into an account of the Cuban situation and the activities of his group. Knowing how good the other man's information would be, he had resolved on candor, only omitting the business about Alberto. After showing the photos from Lázaro's camp, Rodrigo finished with an item that gave no pride or pleasure: his failure to find "Pichi" on the shortwave.

"We'll look into the Lázaro matter ourselves," Thor said. "May I keep these photos?"

"Of course," Rodrigo said. At that moment he saw Thor giving him a sly once-over.

"What did you tell your wife about your coming here?" Thor asked.

"I said I was going to look for work in the U.S. and would be visiting law firms between here and New York."

"Excellent!" Thor smiled broadly as he slapped a knee. "It's going to be Baltimore."

After the trip to the Escambray, Rodrigo had decided to use cover stories with his wife; and by a neat coincidence this one matched the front that the CIA had designed for him. Rodrigo got a box of handsome calling-cards that carried his full name, the title "Associate," a law firm with a string of *yanqui* names and an address and phone number in Baltimore.

"We would like to offer you a contract and an agent's salary," Thor said.

On its face the proposal was flattering and ample. In essence, however, it was a snare. If he accepted, Rodrigo would lose all claims to a piece of Cuba's future and would become a *yanqui* in Hispanic skin.

"I appreciate it," Rodrigo said, "but I prefer to work alongside you. My people and yours have many interests in common. With weapons in our hands, we will have what we need to reach our common goals."

"The weapons will be there," Thor said. "Have no doubts. First, however, we need to have forces in place."

At once Rodrigo was on edge. "Thor, you have seen from those photos that we already have a group in the Escambray. Another group is about to form in Pinar del Río. We are still preparing our offensive but we need weapons *now*. Otherwise we cannot recruit more men, and the men already there are vulnerable to attack or capture."

As Thor listened, his face remained impassive but Rodrigo could feel the man's anxiety.

"You do your part and I'll do mine," Thor said. "In the meantime don't worry about funds. Whatever money you need, you'll have."

Careful! Rodrigo told himself. *Yanqui weapons would give us power. Yanqui money gives the yanquis power. The minute you take their money they have claims on you.*

"Our material needs are not great," Rodrigo said, "but if we are going to work together I want your word on something."

"What is that?"

"Our people are putting everything at risk in order to bring about a result that is going to serve your interests as well as theirs. They and I need your word that our forces will have political support from your government in the event we succeed."

"Yes," Thor answered without hesitation. "That I can give you."

"Thank you, Thor. It will mean a lot to our people in the field."

Rodrigo knew this kind of promise was inherently unreliable – even if Thor could speak for the U.S. government, which of course he could not. Still, the CIA was the powerhouse of American diplomacy; and to Rodrigo's eye Thor looked like a person of some stature. Even in the muddled and cheating world of politics, the man's word had its uses.

Thor extended his hand. "I have to go now. Please make yourself comfortable. This is where you'll be staying."

It was a handsome room but comfort was the last thing on Rodrigo's mind. He ordered a bottle of red wine, drank nearly all of it, and went out for a walk.

The radar of a man who is fond of art, music and pretty girls brought Rodrigo face to face with a young female clerk in a Georgetown bookstore. She had raven hair, blue eyes, marmoreal skin, and the robust attitude of a Nordic heroine.

"What is your stock?" he said.

"Do you want to know what's in the store?" The girl's cultivated speech was delectably lilting.

"No! I mean, what is your ancestry?"

"Mine personally?"

"Yours personally."

"Scottish, with a wee bit of English and Irish thrown in."

"A noble lineage!" Rodrigo said with genuine admiration. "And such a handsome, civilized country, too."

"So you have been to Scotland?" she said.

"No I have not, but I know about it. For a long time writers and artists from many different countries have had a fascination with Scotland."

"Have they now!" she threw back at him skeptically.

"They have," Rodrigo answered. "Just to mention one thing: an Italian opera, based on Walter Scott's *The Bride of Lammermoor,* contains perhaps the most beautiful duet that any man and woman have ever sung...."

"Yes, but in *Lucia di Lammermoor* Donizetti strayed far from the spirit of Scott. And the Italian composers only wrote about Scotland because the censors wouldn't let them write about Italy!"

This interrupting new voice came at Rodrigo from over the shoulder. It glittered with sensuality and had a powerful undertow. Rodrigo turned to find a well-dressed mulatto woman in her mid-twenties, pertly smiling as she went out the door. Her face, while it did not possess the classic beauty of the salesgirl's, had the kind of attractiveness that no man resists and almost all other women resent. Her skirt pulled at her to reveal a slightly oversized bottom, just the kind Rodrigo liked. Through the window he watched her walk away, and felt a rush when she glanced around to see if he was looking.

By the time Rodrigo turned back to the girl, she was gone. *Well, leave it for later*, he decided, and left.

Rodrigo had little to do but read, go for strolls and practice yoga – a cherished discipline – until Thor contacted him. His impatience, never far from the surface, was multiplying itself. At home history took a new shape every minute, while in Washington he sat like a kept woman, waiting for the phone to ring.

After several days Rodrigo received a summons to a hotel room in the Foggy Bottom neighborhood. In the upstairs room Thor was on the phone.

"I'm ordering lunch. What's your drink?" the CIA man asked him and said into the phone: "I need a double martini."

"Red wine," Rodrigo answered.

"And a glass of your best red wine." Thor put down the phone and said: "We have Lázaro."

"What do you mean, you have Lázaro?" Rodrigo said incredulously.

"Castro's troops raided Lázaro's camp. That's why you couldn't get through by radio. The troops captured almost everyone but not Lázaro. The army launched a manhunt for him. Our people went into the Escambray, found him, and brought him out of Cuba."

Lunch arrived. As the waiter set up their table Rodrigo had a few moments to let the story sink in. Castro's spies had beaten Lázaro. The Escambray force was gone. More notable still: U.S. agents in Cuba had tracked down a man that Castro's own forces couldn't find, and had whisked him off the island. It was a sensational maneuver, and it put an icy terror into Rodrigo's soul.

The Cuban collected himself and asked: "Where is Lázaro now?"

"Not far from here. I've already met him."

"Is that so!"

"A remarkable man. Actually he doesn't look Cuban at all. He's more like a British serving officer."

Thor had caught the fair-haired, grey-eyed Lázaro in a phrase.

The question that jumped into Rodrigo's mind was: "When can I speak with him?" It was a question he must not ask. The facts of the matter were hard enough. Lázaro's operation, the centerpiece of Rodrigo's strategy, was now in the hands of the Americans who had picked up the pieces with formidable spy-work. The CIA man had to be feeling proud. Rodrigo would not add to that pride, or diminish his own, by asking this *yanqui* to let him see his comrade. He took another approach.

"Castro's army was able to destroy the hideout because his spies had infiltrated there. Lázaro failed to prevent it because he does not think like a conspirator. He is a warrior. When the battle begins, no one will fight better than he. For the present, however, this is an intelligence war; and it's obvious that Lázaro's was not the only group that Castro's people have infiltrated. They have also infiltrated the MRR."

"Don't worry about that, Rodrigo," Thor said, defending the CIA's favored friends in the Cuban underground. "We know what we're doing there."

Rodrigo had used a piece of verbal judo. By admitting Lázaro's weakness, Rodrigo was able to "flip" Thor by imputing the same weakness to MRR. It had worked; the American had gone on the defensive. Instead of having to hear Thor speak down to him, Rodrigo was on top and pressing his attack.

"May I make a suggestion? Since Lázaro and I are both here, we should use our time to work on battle tactics. Can you put the two of us in military exercises where other men will be firing on us?"

This deliberate piece of *machismo* caught the CIA man further out. After a pause Thor said: "No, we don't have a facility where we can do that, but you can use our rifle range."

"That will do," Rodrigo answered.

"I have to go," Thor said, adding with a smile: "You'll find Lázaro waiting for you at your hotel."

That was a big point for Thor. "I appreciate it," Rodrigo said, shaking the other man's hand with an almost excessive vigor.

* * *

At his hotel Rodrigo went straight to the lounge; and from somewhere in the darkened room Thor's epithet flew at him almost before he could see the back of his comrade's head. The British serving officer was loading up at the bar.

Lázaro fell into Rodrigo's arms. "Hey, man! How you doin'?"

This was not quite Rodrigo's comrade. The greeting was an offense against dignity that *his* Lázaro would not have committed.

"Lázaro! We are in Washington!" In other words: Get hold of yourself. Here we cannot show anything but our best.

"*¡Sí! Aquí estamos.* It was not my idea to come, you know," Lázaro said cogently. The soldier had needed just a few words of his own language to snap him back into form.

At that moment Rodrigo saw what the man's ordeal had been. Lázaro's troubles from Castro's forces were a part of the soldier's burden, and Lázaro could bear it. Having the Americans pick him up and becoming, in a way, their captive was something else. For the past few days Rodrigo himself had been a man in a box. Lázaro's plight was more extreme. He was a tiger in a box, as hard-put as any wild creature to cope with the dismay of losing his ground.

Worse was coming. From Thor's comments about sending weapons *after* forces were in place, Rodrigo guessed that the CIA would want Lázaro back in Cuba double-time. For his own part Rodrigo was sure Lázaro must not return until the battle was imminent. To send him back in anytime sooner would be putting the tiger on ground where hunters with sighted rifles were waiting.

In the CIA's perfect world Lázaro and Rodrigo would serve as advance men for the Americans, risk their necks to secure some tactical positions, and then disappear. If Thor believed he could promote U.S. interests by sending Lázaro and his men to certain death, he would do it in an eye-blink. Rodrigo's job was to make

Thor see that this perfect world did not exist; that the CIA needed to work with Lázaro and other Cubans instead of just using them. In this task of suasion Rodrigo knew he had two assets and two only: his verbal skills, and the incompetence of Castro's other enemies. As in his war with Castro, Rodrigo must wage and win his war with the CIA by wits alone.

For the moment Lázaro was out of place in Rodrigo's war. A tiger who is your friend, and who is feeling sad, has no use for wits or words. "A bottle of your best red wine," Rodrigo directed the bartender; and the comrades, like British serving officers, drank side by side without speaking a word.

* * *

Next day, in handsome country, the Cubans began training at a CIA rifle range. Lázaro was back to his neat, clear self, the tiger finding his way on new ground. Rodrigo was the one glutted with feeling: annoyance at the Americans, impatience at not getting what he needed, sorrow for his parents, dislike of himself. *The unhappy man is a happy warrior.* That phrase had become his *leitmotif,* a tune given out by an adamant viola that the massed music of an orchestra could not suppress.

"Hey!" the rifle-range instructor snapped at Rodrigo. "You're not supposed to fire that weapon a round at a time! It fires in bursts!"

"Yes," Rodrigo said with coiled energy. "I am familiar with the Browning automatic. This is how I train for concentration and develop rapport with the weapon."

Then, like a virtuoso musician who plays a repeating note *tempo presto,* Rodrigo continued firing round by round, the intensely agile trigger-work bespeaking a world of emotions that he had drawn from the rest of his body and conveyed into a forefinger.

"Well I'll be darned!" the instructor said.

Rodrigo's next summons from Thor came sooner than expected.

"The instructor at the rifle range told me he would like to have the two of you with him when he goes into combat – you especially."

"Thor, I'm waiting to move. We have not yet put our pieces in place, not by a long shot, but even now we can do things to hurt Castro."

"Do you have a proposal?"

"Let me go in and take Huber Matos out of jail. It's 90 percent intelligence work. I could do it almost alone. The Matos case is a political treasure-trove. International attention has focussed there. Castro has taken a lot of hard publicity for jailing one of his best *comandantes*. If we free Matos and bring him to the U.S., we will have a public relations victory in solid gold. Fidel will feel so angry and humiliated that he will be eating his liver. We can use that situation to create chaos in his government."

Thor was laughing and Rodrigo's displeasure was visible.

"I'm sorry, Rodrigo. For once your impeccable English has let you down. The way you say 'focussed' sounds very much like 'fuck us,' which has quite a different meaning."

"Thor, excuse me! I will take care with that word – and thank you for saying so!"

"Not at all. As for what you proposed, it's an interesting idea. Let me think about it and get back to you. In return I have something for you to think about."

"And that is?"

"Castro himself."

It was the unmentionable, unavoidable subject.

"What about Castro?" Rodrigo asked as evenly as he could.

"I mean, an attempt."

"That is a very difficult matter."

"How do you see the difficulties?"

"Castro presents no target," Rodrigo said. "He has no patterns. I mean, *no patterns*. He has no office. He has no residence. He never does anything the same way twice. He moves with other men and always carries a weapon. An attempt would require many men. It would require a detailed getaway plan which would have to include the elements of an uprising to throw Castro's forces into confusion. Without a high degree of planning and a still higher degree of luck, it would be a suicide mission."

"You've obviously given thought to this subject."

"Many people have. So has Castro."

"Well, think about this: We're prepared to offer you twenty thousand dollars for a successful attempt on Castro."

Rodrigo did not move a muscle in his face. Thor put his right thumb on the tip of his nose and pointed the hand upward like a knife.

"TWENTY ... THOUSAND ... DOLLARS," the CIA man repeated in boldface, while snapping the knife-hand toward Rodrigo on each word.

"Let me get back to you on that," Rodrigo said, echoing Thor's answer to his proposal.

From the meeting Rodrigo went straight to a bar.

My friend Antonio had it right, he thought. *To these people we* are *aborigines. Twenty thousand dollars for killing Castro! Is it any more than the twenty-four dollars they paid for Manhattan? Surely it is not, and that's their trouble. They have never recovered from the purchase of Manhattan. They think they should be able to buy the world for nothing.*

VIII.

HISTORY IS MADE AT NIGHT

"If it isn't the man from Italy!"

Rodrigo was standing before his Lady of the Lake, the Scottish beauty of the Georgetown bookstore.

"What makes you think I am from Italy?" he asked.

"Aren't you?"

"No."

"Well then, what is *your* stock?"

"Guess."

"I don't know! Hungarian?"

"Sorry to disappoint you. I am from Cuba."

"Cuba! An absolutely brilliant country. I have always wanted to go there. The natural beauty is supposed to be unrivalled. I know you have music and I suppose you even have art. You must be immensely civilized!"

The girl was mimicking him and so deftly, too. Before he could answer he felt himself go completely hard. What to do before she saw? *Imagine something repellent. Castro sodomizing President*

Eisenhower. Fidel's beard tickling the back of Ike's bald head. In a moment he was back to conversing size.

"Do you speak German, by any chance?" he asked. Rodrigo had two foreign languages: English for business and German for pleasure.

"No," the girl answered, "but I am learning. I want to be an engineer. My dad says the best place for me to study is a German university. The language is interesting, though I don't find it at all pretty."

"You don't! Well, how about this?

"Eile denn zu meinem Lieben,

Spreche sanft zu seinem Herzen;

Doch vermeid ihn zu betrüben

Und verbirg ihm meine Schmerzen."

The girl took it in. "That sounds like poetry."

"Yes! It's by Goethe."

"Well then, I guess German poetry can sound rather nice!"

"Is your father a scientist?"

"Yes. He works at one of the technical ministries in Edinburgh. For about a year he's been in the embassy here."

On an instinct Rodrigo glanced around to see if anyone was watching. "So that's why you're in Washington," he said to the girl.

"Yes. And what are *you* doing here?"

"I am on a business trip, staying at the Madison. Ny name is Núñez. *Encantado,*" he said, extending his hand. When she took it, he raised her hand to his lips.

"Ooh! Pretty name. I'm Veronica – Veronica McBride. Pleased to meet you."

"Why don't we spend some time together? Would you like to have a drink with me?"

"That would be lovely. I'm not old enough for the bars here but we can have tea. I'm off in just an hour. Can you come back?"

"It will be my pleasure," he said with ceremony and exited.

The keen afternoon light had begun to soften. Rodrigo cased the surrounding streets for a tea-room. He found a charmer set among townhouses on a quiet side-street. Anyone who spied on him there would be visible, and the place had a back exit.

At the one-hour mark he went into the bookstore. Veronica was nowhere in sight. Rodrigo did come upon a bow-tie who was clearly in command of the store.

"Excuse me, sir. Will you be so kind? I am looking for a young lady by the name of Veronica."

"Veronica had to leave." The man's voice and face were as neatly pinched as his tie.

"Do you happen to know when she is coming back?"

"She is not coming back."

Damn! I should have gotten her address and phone number.

"Have you seen any good operas lately?"

It was the mulatto lady. What a relief to find her! And the coincidence felt natural. It had often happened that at the moment of his being let down by a woman, another somehow appeared.

"For me there is only one opera," Rodrigo said without missing a beat. "*Carmen*. Next to it, almost all the others feel underpowered or overproportioned."

"So! Have you seen any good *Carmens* lately?"

"Not since Georges Thill."

"My goodness! I haven't heard that name in a long time!"

"How do you know it?"

"Just as you know the name of General Pershing. It is part of my history."

"Pershing is not part of my history. Antonio Maceo is a name from my history."

"So you are Cuban," she said.

"And you are French," he answered.

On second thought – how natural is *this? Why has Veronica disappeared? And why is this woman in her place?*

"I was born in Paris but we left when I was quite young. I've spent most of my life here – in the U.S., I mean. My parents talked often about opera. They greatly admired Georges Thill. I didn't know he had sung in Havana."

"In truth I cannot say he did. The only place I ever heard that splendid voice was on my father's hand-cranked gramophone."

"What a charming story! About *Carmen*, by the way, the French would disagree with you. For the French, *opéra* is Wagner. It is also Mozart, Rossini, Meyerbeer, Verdi. *Carmen* on the other hand is *opéra comique.*"

"What is the difference?"

"*Opéra* is well staged and well sung. *Opéra comique* is well delivered and well meant."

"Well said! My name is Núñez."

"Nathalie Margalit."

He took her hand and kissed it. "*Enchanté, chère mademoiselle* – or is it *madame?*"

"It would be *mademoiselle* but please call me Nathalie."

"Listen," Rodrigo said. "I know a very pleasant tea-room close to here. May I invite you?"

"Delighted."

* * *

"So tell me, Mr. Núñez. What brings you to Washington?"

"I am here on business."

"What kind of business?"

"Perhaps you can guess."

"Let me see. I don't think you are in commerce. You have an artistic personality but you seem to be more an *aficionado* than someone who lives from art. You might be a teacher, but that would not make you come to this political town. You could be from the government but you don't have an official air. Let's say you are a politician with other skills, or more likely a professional man with an interest in public matters."

"That is remarkable!" he exclaimed.

"Not really. I know many people like yourself who are finding life difficult in Cuba today. Probably you are here to look for a way of settling in the U.S."

"Right again! And now, why don't you tell me what you do that enables you to make such rapid and accurate judgments."

"Why don't you guess?"

"All right. Could you be a psychoanalyst? Probably you are a bit young for that. A student in psychology? Classes at Georgetown, with time to browse in bookstores? No. You have the feel of someone who is beyond being a student. You combine an extensive knowledge with an aptitude for art, and you seem to know things in an up-to-the-minute way. That would make you a journalist, although I think journalism has only a limited interest for you. Perhaps you are a more serious writer, or a journalist who does other things. For example, you could be a spy."

"If only I were! The pay *has* to be higher. You are right about the journalism part, though."

"Do you work for one of the newspapers in town? Or do you wait in Georgetown bookstores for stories to come to you?"

"Both, actually. I do freelance work for a number of newspapers. I even send stories to my old college paper, for fun of course."

"Where did you go to college?"

"Barnard."

"Impressive. And you write about politics?"

"Mostly. When I write about anything else I have to get out of here."

"Where have you travelled?"

"I go often to New York but that's not travel, it's commuting. I also go to Paris but that's not travel, it's more like home. As for travel, let's see: Hong Kong, Tokyo, Berlin, Vienna, Yugoslavia. There. *That's* travel. Oh yes! I have also been to Cuba."

As the woman reeled off these names, a bolt of understanding struck Rodrigo.

¡Caramba! This woman is a spy. And finding her in the bookstore was

no coincidence. My "friends" put her there in place of Veronica. This is the woman they wanted me to meet.

"And how do you think of Cuba?" Rodrigo asked.

"It's fun! I have never enjoyed myself so much anywhere in the world."

"Yes," Rodrigo said with melancholy. "That's Cuba. By the way," he put in coyly, "it sounds to me as if you are an expert in the Cold War."

"Why do you say that?"

"Because every one of your travel-spots is a strategic location between East and West."

"Yes, I suppose so. May I ask you something?"

"Surely."

"Why do you admire *Carmen?* Men like *Don Giovanni,* or Verdi, Wagner, Puccini – almost anything but *Carmen*. They don't care for a piece that shows a strong woman. Even that most progressive of Englishmen, Bernard Shaw, spoke of it with revulsion."

Of course she wants to change the subject.

"I agree with Nietzsche on *Carmen,*" Rodrigo said. "It's clear and pure and beautiful and true – in a word, Mediterranean. And Carmen's power *is* the power of woman. This business of the 'weaker sex' I don't buy. In all the fundamental areas, women have it decisively over men; so much so that men have taken political and military power as a kind of compensation."

"Really!"

"Yes, and something else I like about *Carmen.* An old-fashioned custom, which you see in most melodramas, is that when a man discovers his woman with another man, he kills the man. I don't think anyone should kill for love; but if you kill, might as well be fair about it. The man who makes love to your woman is not the one who betrays you. It is your woman who betrays you! In *Carmen* a man kills a woman when she betrays him. That act, far from being an insult to women, confirms how strong they are; and it also gives the character of Don José a power that no Don Juan could hope for."

"Fascinating! Tell me, Mr. Núñez. Are you married?"

"I am."

"Excuse me for being forward, but it goes with being a journalist. If your wife betrayed you with another man, would you kill her?"

"Surely not. As I said, I don't believe in vengeance."

"And if you betrayed her with another woman, would you grant her the right to kill you?"

"No. To kill for love, even for fidelity, is a waste of life. Besides, in some marriages infidelity can be a safety-valve."

"Is it so in yours?"

"Are we speaking for the record?"

"We are just having a pleasant conversation."

"In that case, why don't we speak about relations between France and Algeria?"

"*Touché!* If you like, we can return to your favorite opera. I happen to have a record of *Carmen* made at the *Opéra comique*. Interestingly, it restores the original dialogues that some editors took out of the piece after Bizet died. We could listen to it because I live rather near here. You must however promise one thing."

This woman has a genius for conversation – moving from theme to theme like a composer. "And that is?"

"You must promise not to kill me!" she declared.

"To a woman of your charms, no man could promise that."

The brilliant young lady had no idea how sincere he was.

* * *

What is the most formative part of a romantic encounter? Each man and woman has definite ideas; and to speak of each man or woman still is not enough. The Cuban man and the Latvian man are bound to differ, just as the Frenchwoman and the Inuit woman are. For the French, who have laid claim to a certain expertise in these matters, the element of taste is paramount in at least two senses. One of these is taste as a sense of proportion, a feeling for beauty. Another, more common, is the sense of mouth-feel, which one pursues as avidly in person-to-person contact as in the enjoyment of food and wine. A signal romantic gesture becomes, then, *le baiser*. *Le baiser* has many forms. Most touching, perhaps, is that basic one which the English-speaking peoples, in a tribute to their Gallic sisters and brothers, have called the French kiss – a first intimate exchange between lovers to whom it conveys, even more than pleasure-in-itself, the sublimely happy feeling that more is on the way.

Cubans do not kiss in quite the French manner, any more than the skies over Havana empty themselves as the skies over Paris do. The rains that fall on Place Vendôme and Saint-Sulpice are not the ones that inundate the Prado and the Malecón. Cuban rains are heavier, stormier, more impetuous; and so in their way are Cuban kisses. The kiss that Nathalie bestowed on Rodrigo was a sensory preview of banquets to come – while Rodrigo's brought a hurricane, in one swift motion, to Nathalie's chambers.

He began to kiss her in a region well below the mouth.

"Why are you doing that?" she asked. "Don't you want to have me?"

"Of course! But first I am introducing myself."

Rodrigo in lovemaking was not one of those men who sprint toward satisfaction and then beach themselves like giant turtles. When it came to women, Rodrigo swam in all the currents. The act of love was everything to him. It was flesh and heart, casual and meaningful, urgent and thoughtful, momentary and eternal. It was at once grossly selfish and nobly selfless. That central paradox was one in which Rodrigo delighted. He went toward his pleasure by first seeing to the woman's. To take his own before giving to his partner was unthinkable. Apart from violating the most basic of etiquettes, it would have been, for him, a casting off of his manly prestige and power. A man who threw himself onto a woman and quickly finished in her, as many men did, became an appendage of the woman, hardly more of a man than an infant can be. That was a slap in the face to life and an insult to the act of love, which even as it brings a man into the deepest contact with a woman also separates him from her in an emphatic, triumphal way. The basis of life is differentiation, and Rodrigo's impulse was to stand apart. From that impulse had come his adamant libertarianism as well as his aesthetic refinements; and the centerpiece of his life-artistry was the pleasuring of women.

For *his* lover he needed a woman who could receive the pleasure he had to give. Elena had not come close to that. When marital tedium set in he used to imagine that if a yearning for liberty had not nudged him into politics years earlier, then perhaps a heightened longing would have done so now. There it was, that plaintive melody on a viola: *The unhappy man is a happy warrior*. The music was with him like a charm, soothing his mind, making things right. What would he hear if he listened to the part of himself that made the music play? What were politics to him, if not the expression of an inmost drive to keep free? Where had his path to freedom begun if not in the primordial struggle of his first days and hours – the ineffable urge to be other than what a woman wanted him to be? If not from that most formative of places, then from where had his manhood come?

Caressing this woman's lower lips with his tongue, Rodrigo made a meal out of her ample capacity for pleasure. Nathalie reached her plateau and gave him a sign that she had had enough of the "pink kiss." At this moment the ordinary lover of skills would have raised up his chin, touched his lips to the lady's neck or cheek or mouth, and pressed his loins upon hers. Rodrigo felt for another route, the one he'd envisioned when the lady had thrown out that sassy first comment in the bookstore. The crystal Arlesian light of Bizet's music was now quite far from his mind; he sought a darker, heavier place. It was the specialty in which he and his fellows had taken some careful schooling: a lust for ladies' backsides.

He flipped Nathalie onto her tummy, whisked her legs apart, and as she oohed with surprise he went toward the discreet aperture that can be a gateway to a man's intensest physical joy. Something however gave him pause. A premonition? An air?

Nathalie would admit him in any place he chose; and yet he knew that taking her by the backside would disorient her, especially at a first meeting. When a man knocks at a lady's rear entrance he announces: "I am here for my pleasure only." Yes, it *was* his turn, but he did not want an overblown selfishness to be his calling card. Rodrigo did not have to think through this. Like a musician who has absorbed a piece of music down to the toes, he played by concentration alone.

With a soft motion of his index fingers he pulled her hips back until her front entrance turned up to him, and he plunged into it. His body swooned; and as he looked down along her back, remarking its ample beauty, he did not regret the choice he had made. Indeed this was feeling *too* good. Nathalie was turning fluidly under him and in mere seconds had pulled him to the very edge. From among her gasps he could hear the words: *Tu peux venir.* This invitation in French was a strong stimulus. Even so, the man in him preferred to finish on his terms rather than hers. The exquisite sensations of the rearward position were going to bring him off much faster than he wanted; so he took hold of her left foot and arched it over his head, causing her body to twist in midair and drawing a yelp of astonishment as he kept firmly inside. He pinned her on her back and plumbed her, treading on the surface of his own pleasure, using his mind to mix up feelings of lust and disinterest, sweetness and mischief, so he could keep going, torture her to one climax after another, until she took his finale from him and he let out a roar of joy and indignation.

"C'était très bien!" Nathalie said and lit a cigarette.

* * *

On his way back to the Madison he stopped to take some red wine and a glass of soda water. After that heavy meal he wanted to settle his stomach. As the wine and water-bubbles took hold, he felt his appetite come up once more and relished the prospect of another feast.

Nathalie Margalit. Nathalie Margalit. Rodrigo resumed his walk and breathed the woman's name into the sweet summer-night air.

A woman with the intellect of a scholar, the perceptions of an artist and the talents of a courtesan. The perfect spy with a perfect cover – like Margot but different. Margot gives you an honest product. Nathalie gives herself but the whole thing is not on the table. Of course, what is *on the table is very good.*

The CIA served me a mulatto woman. Cuban men love mulatto women. Those people know it. They want me to get attached to her. Where men make love, they attach. Nathalie is a wonderful lover. She is an even more wonderful talker. That *is her inspired quality. Plenty of people can love. Rather few can talk.*

They want Nathalie to talk to me and they want me to talk to her. I think I can work with that program. Actually I should write a thank-you note to my friend in the CIA.

There you go again, Núñez – horsing around when you should be serious. Get busy! As they might say in Hollywood: History is made at night.

IX.

IN THE SAFE HOUSE

"*¡Cojones!* If I could send Thor a note from this cage I'm in!"

Rodrigo sat motionless in a Havana apartment. He had started for Cuba the day after his meeting with Nathalie, as soon as Thor had given him the dreaded piece of news: Lázaro was going back into action.

"No! That's a mistake!" Rodrigo had answered. "Our force is not ready for the battle. If Lázaro goes now he is dead. Please! Don't kill him!"

"We won't," the CIA man had answered. "We have a plan for re-assembling *and arming* his force."

"When do we get the guns?"

"As soon as men are in place."

"We have done this one already. Why do it again?"

"We need Lázaro there. We need you there. And we don't have time to discuss it. Lázaro has agreed. He is on his way. You will need to stop in Miami and arrange for your people there to receive the guns."

"Why not drop the guns in Cuba?"

"Too difficult."

"We haven't even organized the battle. We cannot lose time smuggling guns!"

"If you can't move the guns yourselves, hire people to do it for you. You'll have money to pay them."

There it was again: that pile of *yanqui* money.

Now Rodrigo found himself cooped up in a luxury Havana apartment that the CIA used as a safe house. Because he had entered the country with a false passport, American agents were making sure that Castro's officials had not detected his entrance. Until these checks were complete, Rodrigo must remain a prisoner of the CIA.

The apartment door opened and a man came in with some groceries. This was the CIA's deputy station chief.

"You'll be dealing with our number-two in Havana," Thor had told Rodrigo in an unusual disclosure. Rodrigo found this man likeable as well as skillful. In irony and admiration both, Rodrigo nicknamed him John Paul after the American naval commander who said: "I have not yet begun to fight."

"Hey, John Paul! When do I get to start my operation?"

"We are working as fast as we can."

"How many times do I have to tell you? I was *not* detected! The longer you detain me, the more likely Lázaro will be caught when *he* starts operating."

"He's already operating," John Paul said.

"What? And you are still checking *me?*"

"Lázaro was not detected."

"How can you be so certain? What's going on here?"

"Don't throw dirt on my balls!" the American exclaimed.

Rodrigo had to laugh at this idiom thrown out by a *yanqui* who had learned to talk, walk, tell jokes and probably also do sex like a Cuban.

John Paul put down the groceries and made for the door.

"Leaving already?"

"I have to go to the underground meeting."

"Hey!" Rodrigo exclaimed. "Remember what I said? If they catch you, you get fifteen years. Why not send a subordinate?"

"I have to do this one myself."

"I was afraid you would say that. Anyway, please listen. This is *my* country, and you are here fighting for it. As such I must tell you to be careful."

"Don't concern yourself. I am here for the United States."

"That doesn't stop me from appreciating what you do – *or* from valuing your life."

At times Rodrigo had trouble believing that this valiant man and the maneuverer in Washington were on the same side, but they were. John Paul's courage and dedication also dwelt in Thor – just as Thor's deviousness made up a part of what John Paul did.

That most persistent of worries, concern for his wife and kids, came to Rodrigo's mind again.

"Another thing," he had said to Thor. "When I go in this time I have to go fully underground. I cannot take care of my family; and since *your* decisions are the ones putting *my* life at risk, I need extra help from you."

"What do you need?"

"My father is presently working as a hotel food-server. I would like him to have a job more in keeping with the life he has led."

"We have a bureau in Miami where we collect information from all over the Americas. He can go on staff there as an analyst."

"No trouble putting him there?"

"I can do it next week, if you want."

"I *do* want. Also, my wife should receive support equal to an agent's salary. If anything happens to me, you should give my family the same help you give to your own agents' families in that situation."

"I agree to all of that."

"Okay, we proceed."

Could Rodrigo trust these promises? Concerning his father he was on solid ground, since Thor had promised immediate delivery. The matter of his wife and kids was more doubtful. He could not ensure compliance from the grave. *My only recourse is not to get myself killed,* he decided.

* * *

Rodrigo awoke to the sound of someone entering the safe house. He jumped out of bed, snatched up his .32 and took aim.

"John Paul! What are you doing here at two in the morning?"

"I came to tell you about the meeting!" The American was beyond himself with excitement.

"Okay," Rodrigo said with weariness. "How was it?"

"It was stupendous! The underground is really getting strong!"

"That's the impression Castro is trying to give us," Rodrigo answered coolly.

"Why would he have us think *that?"*

"He wants us to feel over-confident. It is not enough for him to build up his forces. He needs us to lower our guard."

"You are much too pessimistic!" the CIA man objected.

"And you the optimist! But then, you are acting like a Cuban."

"Very funny! But you are wrong. The country is turning around. Castro's days are numbered!"

"Of course they are. We just don't know what the numbers are."

John Paul left with a tight *yanqui* grin quite different from the broad Cuban laugh he did so well.

Should Rodrigo have talked so bluntly? He might be damaging his prospects. If the Americans understood how weak they were in Cuba, they might quit the fight. Rodrigo and his friends needed the Americans to keep up their interest, because they themselves could not wage this battle without American help; and, unlike the Americans, they did not have the luxury of quitting. Their blades had to stay sharp – an image that called to mind his friend Antonio Moreno, whose angular, attentive face he had lately seen behind the

Thunderbird's wheel.

"Smuggle guns into Cuba?" Antonio had said as they cruised Miami Beach with the top down. "*¡No jodas, chico!* You know I don't mix in politics!"

"It's because you *aren't* in politics that I trust you."

"What the hell! All I want is to practice law! I have a job in a good firm. Soon I will pass the Florida bar exam. What do I want with undercover work?"

"You will be doing a favor to the people of Cuba, and you will have the honor of working with the U.S. government."

"Some honor, having the U.S. government do to me what it does to half the world! When do they deliver the guns?"

"As soon as we have the men."

"Wonderful," Antonio had said. "Rather than send guns to protect your men, they tell you to gather men who will protect their guns."

"They gave me no choice."

"Tell me. What are *you* getting out of this? Money? A job?"

On hearing no answer, Antonio had told his friend: "You are a fool. You should have asked for a hundred thousand dollars *and* a job. Well, let's see. My bosses are good patriots. If I take part in this thing and word gets out, they will not be upset. Is there money in it?"

"And how."

"*Está bien, entonces*. I will do it because you are an idealistic fool as well as my friend, *and* because I can make money. I must warn you, however. I have never done anything like this. All I can promise is that I will try to do it right."

"That's enough for me! One more thing, and this is personal."

"Go ahead."

"I need to settle my wife in Miami but I can't be with her. Can you help her buy a house and watch over her?"

"Taking care of the guns I will make my business. Looking after your family will be my pleasure."

* * *

Before sunrise, as Rodrigo was getting up, John Paul reappeared in the safe house.

"You can begin your operations this morning," the CIA man said.

"Good! I need some things from you."

"What?"

"New disguises. The ones I have are ruined from humidity."

"Okay."

"Also, can you get me a .45-caliber weapon?"

"No problem. How about money? Do you have enough?"

"I left the States with plenty. When I need more I will tell you. And I keep records of my expenses."

"No need."

"I insist," Rodrigo answered.

"Thor doesn't want expense records," John Paul said flatly.

That statement put Rodrigo into a fury. With records he could show himself as a frugal and responsible partner, keeping his burden of debt to a minimum. With unrecorded money changing hands, the CIA could and would stake a claim to his soul.

"John Paul, you are going to get records from me whether you want them or not. You want to know why?"

"Not really."

"Then let me tell you anyway. I don't want you and Thor to imagine that I use your money to see prostitutes. The thought of it might depress you."

John Paul made for the door, grinning tightly.

X.

SERENITY

"Doctor! Is that you?" the Moor exclaimed.

"Yes, it's me. As you see, my vacation has done wonders."

Meeting on a busy sidewalk, the Moor was in his militia uniform while Rodrigo, in a light-colored moustache and a wig, had also put newspaper in his shoes to alter his walk – perhaps the most convincing of disguises.

"How are our friends over there?" the Moor asked.

"Fine. Lázaro was with me."

"I know."

"How is Peleón?" Rodrigo asked.

"Same as ever. He wants to see you."

"What's up?"

"Your wife has been trying to find you."

"My wife!"

"She's worried about you."

"But I sent messages every couple of days!"

"Who knows about women? Probably she felt something was

wrong and began calling your friends. She found Benjamín in Miami."

"*Moro*, I have to see her. Please arrange it."

* * *

One thing Rodrigo would not change about himself was a penchant for dressiness. Eighteen months into Castro's revolution, Havana was still elegant. The green guerrilla costume and peasant short sleeve had not yet driven into exile the pressed linen suit or the full *guayabera*. Even in this revolutionary atmosphere, a conspirator only gained in safety by looking like a banker. With his choice linens and subtly patterned neckpieces against plain white shirts, Rodrigo was quite in place on the streets of a city that looked as handsome as a set for a black-and-white film.

As he was fixing his tie at seven one morning, Rodrigo answered a knock at the apartment door.

"Good morning Doctor. My name is Carlos. I think you are expecting me. I am here to work as your chauffeur. For some years I have been a bus driver. I know how traffic works all over Havana. Just tell me where you want to be and at what time. I will put you there to the minute."

The CIA had offered a driver, but Rodrigo preferred to use this man who was a friend of the Moor. Carlos wore the misleadingly impassive expression of a *barrio*-dweller. His cool, clear eyes would impress anyone who paused to look at them.

"Carlos, thank you for coming. Today I need to ride to the Almendares."

They drove to the Almendares River, which marked a line between the old city and Havana's newer, more elegant neighborhoods. In places the narrow stream had yachts and pleasure-boats at anchor.

Carlos pointed to a worker thumbing for a ride. "Is that the man?"

"Yes!"

The car stopped and the man got in.

"Lázaro!"

"*¡Viejo!*"

The comrades embraced.

"Carlos, just drive around. *¡Hermano!* Tell me. How are you enjoying life as a yacht-hand?"

"It's beautiful. So peaceful! Especially at night. A few minutes from the hubbub of the city, a man can sleep under the stars. Except ..."

"Except what?" Rodrigo jumped.

"Some noises from a building across the river."

"The fisherman's cooperative?"

"They must be holding meetings at night. It's odd. I never see anyone go in, but what a racket! It sounds like Fidel himself screeching to the masses."

"Has anybody spoken to you more than once?"

"Just the owner of the yacht, a dental surgeon. He doesn't know anything about politics. Believe me, I'm invisible," Lázaro said.

"How is it with your force?"

"Fine. How about the guns?"

"Nothing until you put the men there."

"*¡Coño!* We have two hundred men!"

"Lázaro, excuse me, but I'm wary of high estimates. Are you sure of your number?"

"*Fíjate.* No one is going overboard in this. We organized the militia in groups of ten. One from every group reports to me about the others. Would you like to see names and addresses?"

"It's okay. I had to ask. What are you doing about infiltrators?"

"Charo is looking after that. Very little gets past her."

"Yes. Women are the softer sex. They are also the tougher sex. I would not want to be an infiltrator in front of Charo."

"I watch her interview recruits. The way she looks at those men, she hardly has to say a word. Some of them just don't come back. Charo says we haven't been infiltrated. I believe her."

"Let's hope she's right." Rodrigo paused. "I must ask a favor of you."

"It's done," Lázaro said.

"That's a comrade! All right, let me tell you what you agreed to. I need ten or fifteen of your best men for a stakeout in the city. Should be men without wives or steady women. We can't afford gossip."

"You'll have the men."

"It's a dangerous assignment," Rodrigo cautioned.

"The men will be there."

"Thank you, Lázaro."

"All right. Now I have a message for you. We are setting up drop zones. The Americans want you to work with the MRR."

"What is this!" Rodrigo burst out. "Our friends told me to find routes for weapons! I have a man in Miami working on it!"

"Tell him to stop. We have new orders."

"Let me confirm them."

"Already confirmed," Lázaro said with military crispness. "You will meet with Francisco. He is setting up drop zones near the new camp."

"No chance! I won't work with Francisco!"

"But he is the head of the MRR!"

"I don't care! I will not use his drop zones! The MRR is chock-full of infiltrators! Castro knows their every move! The Americans don't want to believe this. They *do* know my opinion, which is why I am getting this message from you instead of directly from them."

"My friend, I am sorry," Lázaro said. "When you have orders you can do only one thing."

"I know," Rodrigo answered. "Patience and saliva."

"Saliva?"

"It's what the elephant uses to put himself inside the ant."

"What a fix that would be!" Lázaro exclaimed.

"Especially for the ant," Rodrigo said.

* * *

"*Señora,* please excuse me. I will be back in an hour."

The Moor had escorted Rodrigo's wife to an apartment in the fashionable district of El Vedado, and now he went quickly away. Elena knocked, and her husband answered.

"It's you! Thank God! That man told me he was taking me to see a friend of yours. I was hoping it would be you! That wig is awful! And the moustache! Is it real?"

"Please don't touch it!"

They were laughing. Her clothes were off and he was in and out of her as fast the Minute Waltz. The encounter was deeply satisfying to both of them.

"*Mi amor,* what is going on?" she said seriously. "You tell me you are looking for a job in the States. Then a strange man takes me from our home, I find you in a wig, and you greet me like a woman in a two-hour hotel!"

"I am sorry for the confusion. The needs of the country are more important than my personal needs. Cuba needs to be rid of this ruler. That's what I'm working on."

"What about our family?"

"Listen, *mi amor,*" he said. "I do not make a move without thinking of you and the children. This situation was not of my making; but as long as it goes on, you will be safer in Miami."

"So now we must leave the country!" She was crying.

"With luck you will be back soon. You know Miami. It's a Cuban city, and it's away from the war."

"War! I hate this talk of war! And if there *is* a war, why do *you* have to fight in it?"

"Look at it this way. We are living in a house with grizzly bears all around. If we don't do anything, one day soon they will invade the house. You ask me to stay inside with you and the kids, but doesn't it make sense for me to go out and try to chase the bears away?"

"I would not want you to go out if that put you in greater danger. I would want you to take care of yourself," she told him tenderly.

"Thank you for that, but I'm already outside and the bears have seen me. You and the kids have to move." He paused to make room for her tears, then said: "When you get to Miami you'll be receiving an income."

She recovered herself and asked: "Are you working for the *americanos?*"

"Yes and no, but it's more of a 'yes.' Please do not speak of this to anyone. I mean *anyone.* It could put all of us in danger. Okay?"

"I would never do anything to hurt you!" she gently exclaimed.

"When you get to Miami, call my friend Antonio Moreno. These are his telephone numbers. He is waiting for you."

"Where will *you* go? Who will take care of *you?"*

"I have to keep moving. When you get to Miami I can visit you. Try not to worry. My friends are very good at what they do."

"Please be careful!" she said.

She took him again, more slowly this time.

Promptly at the end of their hour the Moor appeared to escort her home. As he watched them go, Rodrigo felt the poignancy that often touched him through Elena. The woman loved him fully. How sad for her!

Rodrigo could hardly look at Elena or see her in his mind's eye without feeling the pain of her situation; and because he knew his part in it he was overcome with guilt, an emotion that was one of his cornerstones. Having caused his brother's suicide, and seeing his wife lose her moorings because of a fight he had chosen, he was bound to take issue with himself; and so he did, profusely. Withal, he could not help noticing that his regret over Elena's troubles also gave him a feeling of serenity.

Serenity? How come? Was it the song of the happy warrior? Actually it was something more, the next piece of his journey, a terrain he had only started to glimpse: a conviction that the approaching fight was his way to make up for past injuries – injuries he himself had caused.

Central to Rodrigo's idea of himself was the notion of a just warrior: one who suffers without complaint, and who never fails to regret the harm he brings to others. How could Rodrigo pay back for the injuries he had given? Through a seven years' war he had killed other men. He had taken fathers from their children, husbands from their women. And to what end? A tyrant had fled, and an even more fearsome one was in his place.

Rodrigo, after thinking he had finished one war, then vowed to fight another. To seal the bargain with himself, he compelled a brother's suicide. Now he was putting on a second seal by forcing Elena and the kids to fend for themselves. The pact of the happy warrior was complete. Rodrigo had nowhere to go but the battle, for only there could he redeem the sense of self he had given up. This ineluctable duty raised his battle-spirits far above those of most others who face the miseries of war. What most find unbearable, Rodrigo held as a virtue, even a joy. The battle was his marathon of the spirit. As he ran, he felt buoyed up; and without knowing quite why, he was frankly serene.

* * *

The piece of the battle nearest Rodrigo's heart was also the most inner and guarded.

He and the Moor were walking on the seaward side of the Hotel Nacional. That monumental structure, the most famous hostelry on the island, also housed the ghosts of civil strife. In its rooms twenty-seven years ago, Sargeant Batista and his fellows had broken the power of Machado's officer corps in a famous gun battle. Today, grey and wintry, the hotel faced the sea in a stately attitude as whitecap waves broke up on the rocky shore.

"The Nacional offers many chances but also many dangers," the

Moor said. "Fidel comes here to talk to foreigners and make publicity for himself, but it is a hard place for shooting. Too many people are around, and the escapes are poor."

"How about getting something into his food or drink?"

"We checked on that. It seems that some others already had the idea. They were not careful. Castro's people got wind of a plot and packed the hotel staff with agents."

"We might have to give that one up. What about the Potín?"

"Seems to be one of Fidel's favorite restaurants. We can rent two apartments that would give our men good shooting on the Potín's entrances. The getaways are excellent: Linea and Paseo, both busy avenues. Do you have shooters?"

"I can get them from Lázaro."

"How soon can they go into the apartments?"

"As soon as we have telescopic rifles."

"When do the weapons come?"

"The Americans have promised to drop weapons when Lázaro and his men reach the camp."

"Too many conditions," the Moor said. "Can't you get guns for this operation?"

"I don't want the Americans to hear about it."

"Of course! If they know we killed him, they kill us."

"We have to do this one ourselves. We have the people. We have a plan. A few minutes after the shooting Peleón blows up police headquarters. We make other strikes around the city. That keeps Fidel's people disorganized. We hide the shooters in safe houses and lie low until the search is over. All we need are those guns!"

"By the time Lázaro's force is armed we might have lost our chance at the Potín!" the Moor said, crestfallen.

"We must find others. An uncertain chance is worse than none at all."

"We should get a woman to kill him," the Moor blurted out.

"*Moro,* that is a fantastic idea. How did you come to it?"

"I don't know. *It* came to *me.*"

"You have spoken like Zarathustra. Pure wisdom!"

"Pardon me, Doctor. Who is that?"

"An old Persian I used to know. All right then. Let's get to it!"

* * *

"Tell me, Margot. How is business?" Rodrigo asked.

Rodrigo and his procuress were meeting at a café in Old Havana. If any woman in Cuba could trap Fidel, Margot would know her.

"Business is beautiful!" Margot said. "Whenever you have movement in public affairs, my people work like bread-bakers. What about you? Can I give you a case or two?"

"Me? No! I'm extremely busy right now. I just wanted to see how you were doing."

"I'm doing fine!"

"Morality laws aren't a problem?" Rodrigo asked.

The wily madame lowered her voice. "I *was* worried by the shutting of the two-hour hotels, but it seems the new laws only apply to the masses. The people in charge have not stopped enjoying themselves. A few of my customers are real big shots."

"Careful!" Rodrigo said. "They might try to rehabilitate you."

"*They* are the ones who should be careful, because I am the one rehabilitating *them*."

"Really? How so?"

"Those people are windbags! Their arrogance makes them stupid. They think no one has ever seen people such as themselves. It's curious. My old customers used to come in business suits and act rich. The new ones come in fatigues and act like Fidel. I tell you, not one of these warriors could run a peanut stand! And they need me, because there are some businesses that even revolutions cannot do without."

"How amusing!" he said rather loudly. "We should meet more often."

"Whenever you like, old friend," she answered.

"One more thing," he said quietly. "Don't tell anyone you saw me."

"*Fíjate.* Even the cats and dogs know you are against this government. I will not make trouble for you *or* myself."

"Take care, old friend."

* * *

"Doctor, I have news of your mother-in-law," the Moor said.

"Is she dead?" Rodrigo asked. "No, that can't be!"

The two of them were in militia uniforms, walking through the old city.

"*La doctora* called your father. She complained to him that you have abandoned her daughter to fight against Castro. The lady fears you will divorce. She said, better for her daughter to be a widow than a divorcée. Your father called Benjamín and asked him to get word to you." The Moor paused and said ominously: "Doctor, this is not good."

"I know, *Moro,* but let's not jump to conclusions. The woman is not stupid. Probably the call to my father was the only one she made. Let me look into it. Do you have other news of my family?"

"Your wife and children are in Miami."

"Good!"

Elena had done just as Rodrigo had told her. He was glad of it, immensely glad, and he respected her for it. Still, he felt emptied by the news that his kids were no longer nearby. In his underground life, the idea that he might catch a glimpse of them going on errands or traveling in a car with their mother had filled him with spirit. At this news he felt another piece of his old self go away, and he was sad to be so alone.

"Doctor, can I help?"

The Moor's voice broke this feeling. Here was a companion who, come what may, would stick by the promise: "Till death do us part."

* * *

"Carlos, I need you to deliver a note for me," Rodrigo told his driver as they crossed Havana. "The man is a surgeon. Call his clinic and request an immediate consultation. Say that you are calling at the suggestion of *Doctora* del Monaco. That is the man's wife. When you go there, say that you do not want to discuss your problem with anyone except the doctor. As soon as you are alone with him, give him this note."

* * *

"The present message is addressed to *la señora.* Her son-in-law requests a meeting with her at the following place and time. She is to inform no one of this meeting, to come by herself, and to be punctual."

In an examination room of his luxurious clinic, Elena's father looked at the note and quickly stuffed it in a pocket.

"Dress down to your undershorts and lie on the table," the doctor told Carlos.

"What for?"

"I need to examine you!" the doctor exclaimed.

Carlos did as the doctor directed.

Every few minutes a ravishing nurse in peach-colored fatigues looked into the room and said: "Is everything all right, Doctor?"

After he had gone through the motions of carefully checking his patient, the doctor said loudly: "I do not believe surgery is advisable at this time. First I want to try medication. Take this prescription to your chemist. Call me in three weeks if you are still in pain."

When Rodrigo got the prescription he opened it and read: "Your message has been received."

* * *

An elegant middle-aged lady entered an apartment building in the El Vedado district and began climbing the stairs. A fair-haired man with tortoise-shell eyeglasses came up the stairs right behind her.

Once inside the apartment *la doctora* told Rodrigo: "I recognized you immediately, but almost no one else would have."

"I asked for this meeting," he said, "because I want you to know I am concerned about my family and am doing my best to protect them."

"Elena has bought a house in Miami," *la doctora* said. She was cordial, cool and hard. "My husband and I are also making arrangements to leave but we are having difficulties with money."

"How so?" Rodrigo was surprised.

"The old one-for-one with the dollar is gone because of uncertainty over Castro and Cuba's economy. In Miami our money now has little value."

"How much do you need?"

"Five thousand dollars."

"If you give me five thousand pesos, I will try to change them at the old rate."

"Here," she said and took the cash from her purse, obviously ready to do business.

"Now, *Doctora*, I must ask something of you."

"And that is?"

"I must ask you to avoid speaking about me and my present work."

"Why? Do you think you are above criticism?"

"No, and it is not my place to ask that you think well of me."

"What *are* you asking? Perhaps you will be good enough to tell me."

"Please!" Rodrigo entreated. "Let us resolve this matter without hard feelings."

"*You* speak about feelings?" the lady exclaimed. "How do you think I feel to come to a meeting and find guns pointed at me?"

"Am I pointing a gun?"

"No, but your people outside were. Do you think I failed to notice them as I came into the building?"

"I apologize," he said. "It is a routine precaution to guard against capture." In truth he had feared *la doctora* might bring police.

"What kind of man are you? You promised to protect my daughter and instead you desert her!"

"I am sorry for whatever suffering I have caused. The country is living through a hard time which I hope will be over soon – for your sake, for the sake of my family, and for everyone who has left Cuba."

"That situation is not your main concern. Your wife and children are."

"Let us at least agree on one thing," Rodrigo said. "I cannot be any good to my family if I am in prison. The more you speak about your son-in-law who is working against the government, the worse your daughter's situation becomes. You are an intelligent woman. You know Castro's agents are listening everywhere, and that means Washington and Miami as well as Cuba. If only for the sake of my wife and kids, please avoid speaking about me!"

"Very well. For my daughter and grandchildren I will bite my tongue, but hear me well. If any further suffering comes to them because of this, take heed of yourself, because I will destroy you!"

XI.

AT SEA

As he went into MRR's clandestine gathering, Rodrigo found a set of men he didn't know, whose faces were yet familiar. Where had he seen them before?

In a few moments, he understood it wasn't the faces he recognized. It was the facial *expressions* of an earlier time: the beginnings of the war against Cuba's most recent overlord but one. These were the faces of people who have just realized that a tyrant is holding sway, and they feel with all a young man's ardor that they must push the tyrant out.

To the field of battle and to the maze of espionage, these men came as novices. They had not known the disillusion of finding out that one's comrade is a spy feeding himself with blood-money, wasting his fellows for a meal in a fancy restaurant or a few hours in a nightclub. They had not known the agony of looking into the face of a comrade whose arrest is imminent and who cannot be warned, because a warning will cause a breach of information that unravels many lives.

The faces in the meeting-room were empty, too, of the gratitude one feels at having encountered danger and for whatever reason – courage, cleverness, or plain good luck – survived it. The sense of raw dedication in these men was overpowering. Any of them would have said, as Rodrigo had said to Benjamín: Put me in the place of maximum danger. And where, for these men, was the Benjamín who would wisely and tenderly say that putting oneself in danger does not always make others more secure?

These fledglings had no elders. They were not getting help from men who once had been youngsters ready to jump into the pit, and who had lived to learn the difference between courage and foolhardiness. Castro's revolution had driven their elders away. So it was that the young patriots, instead, were taking their orders from the CIA – foreign strategists who were quite ready to be gallant with Cuban lives.

"I am Tomás Guillén, a physician. *Mucho gusto*."

"Rodrigo. The same."

"I will take you to Francisco."

"Very good. Let's go."

They went out of the building. The other man showed Rodrigo to a car almost in front of the house.

"Tell me, Dr. Guillén. When you come to a private meeting, do you always bring your car this close to the meeting-place?"

"We have no security problems. Please don't worry."

A few minutes after they had gotten on the road, Dr. Guillén said: "I think someone is following us."

Rodrigo was simmering. "Make a few turns and we'll see."

After three or four turns Dr. Guillén said: "They are still with us."

"Listen," Rodrigo said with a snap. "We need a building with two entrances. We get out of the car, enter by one door and leave by the other."

"Calixto García Hospital!" the other man said.

"Good! We can lose them there. Step on it!"

They raced to the hospital and parked in the lot. The pursuing car stopped a short distance away. Rodrigo strode into the hospital's main entrance, with Dr. Guillén on his heels.

"You keep ahead," Rodrigo directed. "I'll go this way."

As Dr. Guillén went forward, Rodrigo ducked into a corner, peeled off his wig and moustache, removed his sport-coat and rolled up his sleeves. He turned back to the main entrance and left by the same door he had entered not thirty seconds before. The agents hurried past him without seeing who he was. Outside he grabbed a taxi and returned to the safe house.

* * *

"*Fíjese,* John Paul. This confirms what I have been telling you and Thor. All the MRR sections have infiltrators!"

Rodrigo and the CIA man were walking across the immense Plaza Cívica, dressed up as *guajiros* on a pilgrimage to Cuba's heart of destiny.

"It was bad luck," John Paul said. "They've learned their lesson. They'll be more careful next time."

"No! That's a misconception. We were *not* unlucky. We were *extremely* lucky. At this moment we should be in jail. Only by a fluke did we escape. That kind of luck sets a bad example. It makes people careless. Lázaro has two hundred men. Soon they will be in the mountains without guns and ripe for ambush. We need a commitment from you *now.*"

"Two hundred men for sure?"

"I can give you names and addresses, but I shouldn't have to. It's a clean force, no infiltrators – just good men who are waiting to fight."

"Put the men there and we will drop the guns."

"How quickly can you do the drop?"

"Immediately."

"What does that mean?"

"Twenty-four hours, maybe less."

"Is that a promise?"

"I said it. You heard it."

* * *

The setting sun and rising moon faced each other across a big indigo sky that stretched over the Almendares River.

"All ready, Lázaro?" Rodrigo asked.

"We have set up our lines of communication and supply. The men are already on their way to the Escambray. My car leaves in a few hours. At dawn tomorrow I meet my guide, and we go to the camp."

The comrades embraced.

"Listen," Rodrigo said, full of emotion. "If anything happens to you and I reach power, I will take care of your family. If something happens to me and you reach power, you take care of my family."

"Stop that talk! Neither one of you will have to do that!"

It was the commanding voice of Lázaro's wife, Charo. Each time Rodrigo saw her, he was surprised at her stature. She stood under five feet, but physique meant nothing with such a person. As always, Rodrigo found himself looking up to her.

* * *

To all appearances they were just another pair of well-dressed men riding through Havana on a balmy December night.

"Whew! Whenever I am not moving dynamite, I forget how heavy it is," Rodrigo said.

"It has a heavy job," Peleón answered. "It lifts whole buildings off the ground and makes them fly! Well, tonight at least the air is cool."

"Yes. Otherwise we would be soaking from sweat."

"And we would not be the only ones to sweat, either."

"How do you mean?"

"Have you ever seen dynamite in warm weather?"

"I don't think so."

"If you had, you would remember. During the fight against Batista I had dynamite hidden in my apartment – under the bed, in fact."

"How come? You wanted to give your wife a really big bang?"

"Very funny! I was moving the boxes when I saw beads of moisture on the dynamite sticks. At the time I didn't know the cause. I was afraid the stuff would go off by itself. I took a fan and blew air on it until the moisture went away."

"*¡Caramba!*" Rodrigo shouted. Both men were in an uproar.

"Excuse me, Doctor."

"What is it, Carlos?"

"Someone is directing us to stop."

Rodrigo looked to his right. A man was motioning the car to pull over. His air of authority marked him as a plainclothes policeman.

Keeping up his good spirits, Rodrigo leaned forward and said with a laugh, as if he were making another joke: "Get us out of here!"

The car spurted ahead.

A police car came up quickly behind them, machine-guns blasting from two windows. Rodrigo and Peleón returned fire with pistols. The police car jumped a curb and smashed into a tree.

"Cruise for a few minutes and park it," Rodrigo said.

Carlos drove for a mile or two through light traffic and stopped at a normal curb-spot. Everyone got out.

"None of us comes back to this car," Rodrigo said. "And we make changes in our physical appearance. Carlos, please remove your moustache as soon as you get home."

"My wife will think a stranger is getting into bed with her," the driver said. "But who knows? That might prove an advantage."

* * *

"Well, John Paul, that's the story. Can you find us a car?"

Rodrigo and his CIA contact were strolling along the Malecón. It was another grey day, big sea-waves pounding the rocky shore.

"It's hard for us to give you one, but we know a man who can. Let me talk to him first. I am sure you will get your car."

"That will be fantastic."

"It looks as if security is onto your operation," John Paul said.

"I don't think so. Those were ordinary policemen. It was a routine check. We couldn't let them stop us but I'm sure they didn't know who we were. A simple case of bad luck."

"The man riding with you was Peleón Fernández, correct?"

Rodrigo recoiled. "Why do you mention an operative by name?"

"The action you are planning with him should not take place prematurely. You don't yet have the forces in place to make it work."

"Of course we don't! Do you want to know why I know that?"

"Why?"

"Because if the forces were there, we would already have attacked!"

* * *

"Why do you think the American gave you that advice?" the Moor asked.

"That was no advice. It was a warning: We know who your people are. We know what you are planning. We know everything you do. You cannot even think without us overhearing you."

Rodrigo was talking with his comrade at a department-store bathroom that accommodated a pair of men at a toilet stall and an adjoining urinal. The bathroom was recessed from the store by an anteroom and two lockable doors. Anyone else, in order to get at them, would have to break down both doors or be hiding in the toilet-tank.

"What about our plans for the attempt?" the Moor asked. "Do you think the Americans are following that?"

"I have kept it to myself. I have not even told Lázaro."

"I have told only one of my people," the Moor said. "If the Americans know my agent, I give up my *cojones*."

"Careful! Those are sacred. And let's not underestimate the Americans. Anything from Lázaro?"

"I'm jumpy there," the Moor answered.

"How come?"

"Castro is beefing up his army in the Escambray. People in the hills are raiding government outposts. Officials are getting scared. They've put a news blackout on the whole business but in the last few days I've been hearing about army movements. They're supposed to be pretty massive. I'm afraid Lázaro might have walked into a trap."

"When was he to contact you?"

"Two days ago."

"There might be a simple explanation," Rodrigo said. "We have done everything in our power to make things right. Let's expect positive news."

"Doctor, I'm not very good when it comes to expecting."

"Neither am I, *Moro*. Neither am I."

They parted with an unusual heaviness.

* * *

Rodrigo got a message from John Paul, telling him to visit the man who could provide a car.

"Welcome. Please call me Ernesto."

"I am Rodrigo. *Mucho gusto.*"

They were in an apartment on an upper floor of the "Focsa" building, a new high-rise that had quickly become one of the swankiest addresses in town. The man offered Rodrigo a seat in a large, elegantly furnished room with a splendid view of Havana and its harbor.

Ernesto was a Spanish kind of Cuban, outgoing and opaque at

the same time. He was in his mid-forties, trim and poised.

"Our friends have told me about your need," Ernesto said. "I think I have just the vehicle for you. Here are the keys. The man downstairs will show you the car. Please keep it for as long as you like."

"Thank you very much, Don Ernesto. Your car will get the maximum of care, and I will return it as quickly as I can."

"Be at ease. Do you have time for a drink?"

"Certainly."

"I am curious about you and your group – what your ideas are, and exactly what you are trying to do."

This was sticky territory. Ernesto looked like someone who might be pining for Batista.

"Do you have a particular question for me?" Rodrigo asked.

"I do. Where do your people stand on the issue of land reform?"

"Castro's popularity rests in large part on the land reform. I think any future government would have to take account of that fact."

"Tell me," Ernesto said. "What kind of legal basis do you think the government has?"

"I am a lawyer. I would say the government's legal basis is open to question."

"In that case, doesn't it make sense for a successor government to reinstate land ownership as it existed on December 31, 1958?"

"It might make legal sense. I am not sure it makes political sense."

"I think it makes sense from every angle, and I know many people who share my views."

"You and your associates may be looking at these issues from the perspective of business or economics," Rodrigo answered. "My colleagues and I look at them as political matters. The important thing is what your people and mine have in common. We all share the same desire for new leadership. And I hope our groups will learn much from each other."

"Good luck with the car," Ernesto said. "And please call on me again if I can be helpful."

* * *

"... Then the man said we should restore the land situation to the status of December 31, 1958."

"A *batistiano* and a fool," the Moor said strongly.

"Anyone is a fool who disagrees with Fidel!"

A passing clown had put in that remark. Rodrigo and his comrade were walking across a circus grounds. *El Moro* fixed the clown with a look, and the painted man shied away.

"What a disgrace!" Rodrigo said. "Even here we cannot escape that!"

"Please go on, Doctor. I am sorry for the interruption."

"This is the kind of Cuban with whom the Americans develop relations!" Rodrigo said. "I tell you, they are *comiendo mierda!*"

"So you lost out on the car?"

"No! I got it! A burgundy Oldsmobile."

"I'm sorry for you, that you must now have an obligation to such a man."

"He didn't really give the car to me. He gave it to the Americans. They have the obligation to him, and I to them."

The Moor gave a grunt of distaste.

* * *

Rodrigo filled up with dread on receiving another summons to the department-store bathroom.

"Lázaro?" he asked as the Moor joined him.

"Yes."

"Are you sure?"

"The story is all over the prison. It's one of their biggest captures yet. Castro's people are practically singing ballads about it."

"What did you hear?"

"When Lázaro reached the camp, the army had just overrun it

and had taken or scattered the men. The Americans made a thirteen-parachute drop which the army captured. Lázaro and the guide went looking for men who might have escaped. Finding no one, they walked toward Cienfuegos. While they were crossing a cooperative farm, the militia saw them and opened fire. They got away, but police picked them up in Cumanayagua."

Rodrigo put his face in his hands. "I was hoping you might be mistaken, but all these details!"

"At first the police didn't know who they were. At the station, someone came in and said: Hey! Do you know who you have there?"

"*¡Me cago en diez cabrón!*" Rodrigo was almost in tears.

"They lost no time putting him on trial," the Moor said. "Apparently the judge and prosecutor talked so much political nonsense that Lázaro fell asleep – in the middle of his own trial! He must have been exhausted."

"No!" Rodrigo exclaimed. "In the face of death you cannot be exhausted. You can, however, be extremely cool." He paused. "What about Charo?"

"She is making arrangements to leave the country."

"Good. It's the time to get her kids out. Castro's people have no reason to hold her, and every reason to let her go. Widows make trouble."

"Especially that one!" the Moor said with pride.

Someone knocked at the outer bathroom door.

"Occupied!" Rodrigo shouted.

The Moor pulled his gun.

"Forget it, *Moro*. It's only a customer in trouble."

"What now?" the Moor asked.

"We start over. We re-think everything. Lázaro's force was the centerpiece of our operation. We need a new plan. I cannot work this out in Havana. I have to go back to Washington."

"How will you leave the country?"

"I will manage."

"Let me know if I can help."

"*Cuídate, Moro*. We may not be seeing each other for a long time."

* * *

"Rodrigo! This is a surprise. When I invited you to call on me, I didn't think it would be so soon."

"At times, Don Ernesto, that is how the Fates weave their threads."

It was against intuition that Rodrigo had gone back to the Focsa building, and to this man who plainly bristled at seeing him.

"What is your situation?" Ernesto said.

"We have had a change of plans. I am returning your car. Thank you again for its use. I trust you will find it in good order."

"Did it serve?"

"Extremely well – but I will not be needing it any longer. I must make another request of you."

The other man said nothing and looked even more perturbed. Rodrigo's urgent need pushed him forward.

"I must travel to the States by private means. Can you help me make the trip?"

"Rodrigo, I am in an awkward position with you. The fact is, I am not certain who you are."

"I don't understand."

"In spite of the fact that you came with highest recommendations, I decided after our last meeting to verify that you are who you claim to be. And it seems you may not be who you say you are."

"Really? What have you discovered?"

"I have looked into your political associations. Several of your close friends have been officials in this government. I have reason to think you may be a government agent."

"That statement has no foundation!" Rodrigo said, losing patience.

"Mind you, Rodrigo, I have only said 'reason to think you may be.' If I were certain, I would not even bother to accuse you. I would kill you at once!"

"And do you understand, Don Ernesto, that if I were a government agent you would just have doomed yourself with those words? Please! Let us not speak carelessly about killing and dying. We already have more than enough of the real thing! *Fíjese, señor.* You can be sure our mutual friends checked me many different ways before taking me into their operation. Why don't we put my request on hold until you get an explanation from them."

Ernesto kept an impassive expression and simply said: "All right."

Rodrigo departed from the man's home as from an insane asylum.

* * *

"I'll have a talk with Ernesto," John Paul said. "He's really a very good fellow, and has given us a lot of help."

The CIA man had come to the safe house at Rodrigo's request.

"I cannot speak about how he has performed in your other operations. I can only observe his conduct in this one," Rodrigo answered. "Anyway, how did he learn my identity? It seems you trust that man far too much. Perhaps you and your colleagues assume that people who are successful in business will also be skillful at politics. In my experience, that idea does not hold up."

"I don't appreciate your tone, Rodrigo."

"All right – no need to say more. Let's work on getting me out of the country."

"What about using the passport we gave you? It should still be within the time limits of your visa."

"No way! Going through passport control is too dangerous! You of all people, who held me captive while you checked my entry, should know better! Ernesto is not my dream comrade but for this job he will do perfectly. Does he have a yacht or a plane?"

"Both."

"A plane is quicker but a yacht is safer. I will make a plan and give you the details. Please convey to Ernesto that he must follow my instructions to the letter. I assure you, his part of it will be a great deal easier than mine."

"Okay."

"One more thing. Here are five thousand pesos. I need to exchange them one for one."

"How come?" the CIA man said.

"*You* are the one who said not to bother with expense reports, and this is not even an expense. It's an exchange."

"Actually it's a gift."

"True," Rodrigo said, "but someone else is getting it. For me it's the solution to an unexpected problem, nothing more or less."

* * *

January 1961. Before six on a wintry morning, the beach at Santa María del Mar was exquisite. The sand was deserted. The wind blew hard and the sea was choppy. A deep grey light framed the rugged seascape, one that had warmed Rodrigo's insides ever since boyhood.

On this morning the beauty was laden with peril. Now that America and Cuba had come to the point of war, Castro's naval and shore patrols had blanketed the area. To try leaving from here was utter folly – and for that very reason it appealed to Rodrigo, who believed that at times the best way to elude a giant was to go under its nose. The patrols would be looking for people in dinghies or small boats. They would not be looking for swimmers because no one would be foolhardy enough to try a swimming escape across the white-capped winter sea.

Rodrigo had given strict instructions for Ernesto: "You are to meet me two thousand meters due north of the beach. Do not wait for more than a couple of minutes. If you have to move on, do not backtrack." To which he had added his favorite suggestion for undercover work: "A woman is your best decoy. Bring one with you. The younger and more beautiful she is, the better. Best of all is a young, beautiful, pregnant woman." The idea of that last sentence – and with it the love he felt for women and children – spurred Rodrigo as he tightened his flippers, jumped into the water and swam ahead.

Progress was hard. Rodrigo had to keep checking his orientation and to duck whenever a patrol came near. The heavy waters and constant submersions held him back dangerously. As the minute for his rendezvous approached he saw Ernesto's yacht moving parallel to the shore, straight in front of him but still far away. His limbs grew heavy with fatigue. He was swallowing water. He wouldn't meet the yacht, and even if he could keep free of the patrols he probably wouldn't make it back to shore either.

How many ways can a man screw up? My comrade destroyed – my children gone from home – their mother abandoned – her *mother crying for my head – and my brother, always my brother, to whom I have given eternal life as the ghost of my remorse. All of them – the monsters I created – are pulling me under. I will hit bottom and when I come back up my flesh will feed the seagulls.*

Feeding seagulls. Last time in Miami – with the kids – I took them to a pier. We bought some breadcrumbs – which they threw at the gulls. A flock of gulls came down. The birds hit into each other like drunkards, crazy for food. The kids howled with laughter. One of the birds bit Yrene's hand, broke the skin, drew blood. Her older brother cried. She screamed: You bird, you aren't going to make me cry! She so courageous – and he so tender, caring for her.

No! I do not accept this. I do not agree to die. It's not me. It's my kids. I will not leave them to fend for themselves!

Rodrigo's energy surged. He swam toward the yacht, pulling ferociously, impelled by his own exhaustion, driving toward a tremendous nothingness.

Next thing he knew, Ernesto was pulling him on deck.

"You disobeyed my instructions," Rodrigo gasped. "You turned back to shore."

"Are you unhappy?" Ernesto asked.

"Not at all."

"Want a cognac?"

"No!"

Rodrigo saw a lady scrutinizing him. She was young, beautiful, and ready to shed a baby.

"Is that your wife?" he asked Ernesto.

"No, just a friend," the other man said.

"I see we understand each other."

"I think we do," Ernesto said modestly. "Now, try to get some sleep."

Slowly Rodrigo took the stairs below deck and stretched out on a bunk. When he awoke, the yacht was at anchor in Key West.

XII.

A WHORE FOR THE CIA

The day after exfiltrating Cuba, Rodrigo sat in a guest room of the Madison Hotel, wolfing down his lunch and inhaling the perfumes of Thor's double martini.

"Apart from what happened to Lázaro, what's your assessment of the whole situation?" the CIA man asked.

"As of now I would say we are heading for defeat," the Cuban replied.

"Let's not lose perspective, Rodrigo."

"I haven't. Even now my people have plenty of morale for the fight. *But* – Lázaro's fate should be a sign to us all. If we are not more careful, we will go to the slaughter."

"The force we are preparing will certainly be able to defeat Castro," Thor said across the top of his drink.

"How many men do you have training in Central America?"

"Close to a thousand."

"And you expect such a force to overthrow Castro's government?"

"Let's just say we have learned how to accomplish a great deal with rather little."

"I see. After your intelligence victories in Iran and Guatemala, you think Castro will go the same way. I don't agree. Cuba will be a much harder case than those others."

"We don't make assumptions, and we are well aware of the difficulties. We do have other components of this operation that I am not at liberty to discuss."

"Can you at least give me the flavor?"

"Flavor! What do you mean?"

"I mean that pie in the sky. What flavor is it? Apple? Blueberry? Cherry?"

"This is *no* pie in the sky!"

"To *me* it is, if I cannot put solid ingredients into my thinking."

"All right," Thor said with energy. "Let's talk about something solid: the help we'll be getting from yourself and others inside Cuba."

"I agree the underground can play an important role – but right now we are in poor form. The different groups are not working together. Most of their leaders are ignorant and optimistic at the same time. That's a dangerous combination. Most have never been in a fight like this. They do not imagine what it will take to overthrow Castro. They are depending on your government to solve that problem for them. Instead of giving attention to the hard tasks, they are jockeying for positions in a post-Castro régime. Excuse me for saying so, but your agents in Cuba are only feeding this tendency. Many underground leaders believe the U.S. is backing them personally. They think they are driving to the Presidential Palace, while more probably they are heading for the execution wall."

"Don't equate those others to Lázaro!" Thor blurted.

"I do *not* equate them to Lázaro! Why do you mention it?"

"Lázaro died because he was not careful," Thor said archly.

"I have been very candid with you about our security problems. Why criticize a man who has just lost his life?"

"Just before Lázaro went into the Escambray we overheard him in a *bar*, talking about his relationship with us!" The CIA man spoke with a surprising bitterness.

Rodrigo collected his thoughts. "Of course Lázaro should not have talked about you – but why question the place he chose? A bar is where people go to let off steam. Where do *you* go to let off steam?"

"I meet with foreign agents in hotels. And when I meet them, I drink!" Thor spoke with an equally sudden and surprising humor.

"Listen, Thor. If you and your colleagues had to free America from a tyrant, and your only choice was to work for the secret police of Japan or Germany, what would you do?" Rodrigo asked.

"I think I would work with them," Thor answered.

"Of course you would! And in your off hours you would be sitting at the bar with Lázaro."

"But I would be *drinking,* not *talking*. Excuse me for saying so, Rodrigo, but it seems to me that very few of your countrymen can keep their mouths closed."

"What have I been telling you and John Paul for months? You denounce the indiscretions of my late comrade, yet you are lenient with MRR! Why?"

Thor contracted his brow quite sternly. "I am debriefing you, Rodrigo. You are not questioning me."

"All right then, I will use a declarative sentence. You are favoring those Cubans who tell you what you want to hear."

"No! We favor those Cubans who can get the job done."

"With respect, MRR will not be the group that beats Castro – not so long as Castro's agents receive engraved invitations to MRR's clandestine meetings!"

"As a matter of fact, we would rather not have to count on the underground at all," Thor said with menace. "If you call our activities pie-in-the-sky, perhaps I should call the underground's efforts a will-o'-the-wisp."

"That is unfair! I agree that if the invasion comes any time soon, we cannot help you in a meaningful way; but if you give us a chance to do what we are good at doing, perhaps we can serve you better than you imagine."

"And how can you do that?"

"By creating chaos. A few well-placed attacks would make people see that Castro cannot protect them. Indeed, a number of people in the government are already unhappy with Castro. Our disruptions would give those people a reason to act."

"How numerous are they?" Thor asked.

"Not very – but they are there, and waiting for a pretext. When we make our disruptions, they might move; and at *that instant* you invade!"

"Our plan is rather similar," Thor said. "We begin by sending in a small force. Castro moves to crush it. At that point a number of things can happen. Listen carefully, because now I am leveling with you. The worst outcome is that our invasion fails outright. Even that outcome works for us, because this government will not tolerate a defeat. If a first invasion fails, the United States will send a larger force. We know very well that a small invasion can't win by itself; but if we strike with surprise and give the soldiers adequate cover, they *can* reach the Escambray and secure a territory. As soon as they raise a flag we get a call for help, and we send it. So whether the first invasion survives or fails, another one follows."

This was a kind of candor that Rodrigo had no right or reason to expect. For whatever reason – or maybe the effect of the martini – Thor had let loose with something far more than official-speak. It felt like the living truth.

In Thor's account, the CIA was playing an influence game. Agency leaders understood that their covert methods – the ones that had brought them glory in Iran and Guatemala – wouldn't work in Cuba. Any operation that finished Castro must be large and visible, while the CIA had to stay covert; otherwise it would lose its own reason for being. At the same time, the CIA wanted to lead the operation and keep its place in the forefront of *yanqui* policy. The game here was for the CIA to put its foot in the door, starting a play that others would finish. Who would those others be?

"Will the follow-on force will be multilateral?" Rodrigo asked.

"Maybe," Thor answered.

"When a diplomat says 'maybe' he means 'no.' Thor, if you are going to listen to me on any single point, let it be this. Leaving other Latin nations out of this would be a big mistake! I know multilateral efforts are difficult; but at this very moment the Latin governments, even the ones normally hostile to Uncle Sam, are ready to work with you – because they are extremely fearful of Castro's friends in Moscow. If other Latin countries go in with you, then you have diplomatic cover as well as military strength – while if you try to do this yourselves, you are courting political *and* military failure."

"We are *not* going to fail. Our battlefront in the Escambray is already operational. We are supplying a four-hundred-man guerrilla unit there. Several different groups adding up to about a thousand men are active. We need you and your group to help them. Go back to Cuba, get your force together, and we'll send you what you need."

"You are still withholding weapons until we organize men. The weapons must go in first. Anything else is a waste of time *and lives*."

"No!" Thor objected. "This time you fly in with a group of your own officers. Those men can set up drops and help you organize a force. We already have men training for this mission. Go to the base in Guatemala. Meet with the men and see which ones you want. Can you parachute from a plane?"

"I have never done it, but I have no hesitations."

"I didn't think you would," Thor said with a smile.

"My hesitations concern the plan in general," Rodrigo said, smiling back. "I have a lot of experience at this. If you send me in without weapons I will expend myself organizing drops; and until I have guns I cannot recruit men. Another thing: If Castro's people have not already found me out, they will soon – a month or two at most. Maybe I can stretch that by moving in and out of Havana; but without weapons my hands and feet are tied."

"Even if we agreed that putting weapons there first was the right thing to do, we don't have time for it. The invasion force has to move soon. We may not be talking of months but weeks. We have to train you for the jump, get you to the camp, set you up with your men, and fly you in on a night with a waning moon."

"May I speak candidly?" Rodrigo asked.

"I think you already have!" Thor exclaimed.

"Then I will be more candid still. You are responsible to many people, and those people are obviously expecting you to give them something soon. That's a hard position, and I'm sympathetic; but I cannot rush my operation to keep pace with whatever is pressing on you. My people and I cannot think, as you do, that a second wave will succeed if a first wave does not. Your reasoning is that of a great nation. Our situation is like that of almost everyone else in the animal kingdom. We cannot count on second chances; and my animal sense is that we do not yet have in place what we need to win."

"What will you do if we stop working together?" Thor asked.

In that unexpected question Rodrigo perceived a threat to remove him from the operation, and it shook him to the bones.

"I don't know," Rodrigo answered as nonchalantly as he could. "I might remain in this country for seven days or for seven years."

Thor took that answer in stride. "Look Rodrigo, we've covered a lot of ground and you could use a rest. Take some days for yourself. We'll pick this up next week."

* * *

Rodrigo guessed that Nathalie would be waiting for his call after the interview with Thor. He was not wrong; and when she came through his hotel door he just took off her clothes and drank her up.

It was Nathalie who opened the business portion of their meeting.

"I must say your country has been keeping me rather busy of late!"

"How so?" Rodrigo asked lightly.

"Haven't you followed the news?" she said. "The Americans are developing some big plans for Cuba!"

Her post-coital cigarette smoke mingled with Nathalie's own essences. Cuban women were more pristine; but these novel fragrances were arousing in their way.

"Ah. You mean the secret Cuban exile force that the CIA is preparing for an invasion. A curious American phenomenon, these secrets which tens of millions of people share!"

"So what do you think?"

"About what?"

"About Cuba, of course!"

"I think the Americans will stay out of it."

"Why do you say that?"

"Because Castro is very strong, and the U.S. government will not involve itself in a venture that is bound to fail."

"But you would like the Americans to show their strength in Cuba, wouldn't you?" she asked, quite clearly dogging him for a reaction.

"I don't know," Rodrigo said. "If the Americans invade, we are back to an old pattern of the U.S. rushing in to solve Cuba's problems. In those situations the Americans do not give charity, and Cuba winds up paying a heavy mortgage to Uncle Sam."

"So you resent the United States."

"Quite the contrary. I respect and admire the United States."

"But you want the United States out of Cuba."

"I no more want the United States out of Cuba than I want Cuba out of the United States. We are part of each other. Severing our tie would be like cutting off an arm or a foot. It's true we have not found an ideal balance in our relationship. Then again, neither have most families. It doesn't cancel the fact that they are families."

"Can Castro deal with an invasion force?" Nathalie asked.

"Maybe Castro *wants* an invasion," Rodrigo said.

"You don't mean that!" she exclaimed.

"Why not? What unifies a country better? And what would be better for Fidel than to face the U.S. in battle *and win?* Every time the Americans threaten Cuba, they put the Cuban people in Fidel's pocket. If he actually repelled an invasion, he could stay in power for a century."

"Do you imagine Castro has thought of that?"

"You may be sure he has."

"But then the Americans must know it too."

"They have a handicap."

"And that is?"

"Their own power. Success has spoiled them. Fidel is tougher and smarter. He knows that at any moment he can lose everything. That knowledge gives him a major part of his strength."

"Fidel is a personality," she said. "Don't you think?"

"Every woman loves Don Juan," Rodrigo answered with scorn.

"Well, not even Don Juan's charms can avail against a force of twenty-five thousand men," Nathalie said matter-of-factly.

"Where did you get that number?"

"I am a journalist. I do not reveal my sources."

"I don't care what your sources tell you. The number of Cubans ready to fight does not come close to that."

"I am not talking about Cubans. I mean Americans."

"But it can't be!" Rodrigo blurted, quite surprised and emotional.

"Why not?"

"Because it can't! The Americans might send advisors or gunboats or planes. They might help coordinate troops from other Latin countries, which would be a very smart play because Cubans would accept other Latins on their soil, even if they didn't like it. But *American* troops, and in such numbers? No! The Cuban people would hate the U.S. government as they never hated Batista! We could not allow that! Cuban men would never sit in Miami while blond boys from Wisconsin died in a Cuban war!"

"Well there you are!" Nathalie said, triumphant. "You people who have sprung from the fragrant soil of Spain, the birthplace of the *caballero*, cannot bear the idea of *yanqui* soldiers helping you in your own country!"

The word *yanqui* on this Frenchwoman's lips provoked him. He took Nathalie's elbows, pushed them apart, fell on her chest, thrust into her for a number of minutes and could not climax.

"*Pourquoi tu viens pas?*" she asked when he had slowed down.

"It's my semen," he said.

"What about it?"

"It must have gone back to Spain!"

* * *

"*Lo difícil no es llegar. Lo difícil es mantenerse.*"

Rodrigo's father was staring out into the warm white air of Miami Beach. From his parents' apartment you couldn't see the ocean but you could feel its breezes.

Even on a Saturday morning the old man was darkly elegant in a sport-coat and tie. Something about him was motionless: the inertia of a villager who sits in the Andalusian sun day after day. How different was this man from the one Rodrigo had known all his life. That man had been electric with motion, hardly landing at one place before he went to another. His habitual dictum, about how easy it was to get somewhere and how hard to stay, had a twisted new meaning in this half-life that the old man now led. Here he had nothing to do but stay put, and that was more difficult than ever.

"Why don't you call Benjamín?" *el viejo* said. "He is waiting to see you."

"My time here is short, and my family takes all of it. Besides, it's awkward. Benjamín would ask me about things I cannot discuss, and I would not want to be evasive with him. So I prefer not to meet."

"Too bad. He knows a lot, and he wants to help you."

"I hope you are being careful in what you are doing!" *la vieja*, making coffee, exclaimed from the kitchen counter.

La vieja was spry and youthful. Unlike her husband, who had lost his focus in life, she had seen her focus intensify. Her focus was the old man. His increasing despondency required ever greater exertions on her part. She was doing a woman's critical, irreplaceable work, the thing that made her strong and feminine.

"Careful as I can!" her son said with a smile. "And now it's time for me to go."

"Tell Elena we would love to see the children," *el viejo* said.

As he drove across one of the bay bridges to his next rendezvous in the burgeoning Cuban city, Rodrigo thought about *el viejo's* request. Since their arrival in Miami the old ones had not visited Rodrigo's children. *La doctora,* in a rage over Elena's unhappiness, had plainly directed her daughter not to invite Rodrigo's parents. Normally Rodrigo could resolve things, but these times and his place in them had banished all sense of normalcy. So the rift widened. If Rodrigo fell in battle, it might happen that some day his kids and parents would walk by each other on the street without recognition.

How strained Rodrigo's marriage had become! Only a year ago Elena had looked up to him as to a god. These days she treated him with the last vestige of courtesy. In bed she received him with such a lack of enthusiasm that Rodrigo was on the verge, if not at the actual point, of declining to touch her. And when he held her he found himself thinking of Nathalie.

Why Nathalie? Nathalie is unreal, an illusion – but that's love. Love is an illusion, a dream for romantics. Men are romantics. They fall with their eyes, they fall for illusions. No woman would have written 'Ode on a Grecian Urn' because women do not fall with their eyes. Women wait and think and listen and when they fall, they fall with their ears. Women are not romantics. They are the practical members of the species. They want reliable men who will take care of her kids and not run away. Women use us for their purposes, while we use them for our dreams. My poor wife cannot love me because I am no use to her, and reason is on her side. Do I love Nathalie? It makes no sense for me to love Nathalie but that's irrelevant. I love her anyway. Does Nathalie love me? Probably not, but that doesn't matter either. When the sexes encounter each other, it is the man who says "I love" while the woman says "He loves."

* * *

On entering the restaurant – a cool, shaded refuge with tiles and fountains in the Spanish vein – Rodrigo was taken aback to find his friend Antonio Moreno eyeing him grimly from across the room.

"I am sorry," Antonio said as soon as Rodrigo sat down. "I have difficult news for you."

"Whatever it is, it's my situation and not yours. Please tell me."

"It appears your wife has been meeting someone."

Rodrigo got hold of himself. "What have you discovered?"

"At first I worried some *batistiano* might do you a bad turn by bothering your wife; so I got a man to pass by the house from time to time and make sure no one was watching her. One evening my man saw something peculiar. Your wife was going out with her two maids, and all three were dressed for a social occasion."

"That is strange."

"The man followed them to a nightclub and took a photo. As you see, your wife is sitting at a table without her wedding band."

"I do see."

"It is not my habit to go poking into people's lives, but in view of this I felt a reasonable step would be to watch her mail."

"And?"

"We found this." Antonio produced a sheet of paper.

Rodrigo took the hand-written sheet and murmured: " 'My dearest one, The last weeks with you have been the happiest of my life. I have loved your playing, I have loved your kisses, and now I want us to be together in body and soul. Soon I will offer my life for Cuba. I am, as your husband and my friend used to call me, a fair-haired *yanqui* from Connecticut, but it may be my destiny to die for the country we all love so much. Before I go into battle, let us share a time that will make up for what you have lost, and for what I may lose forever. Your loving William.' "

"So you know the man," Antonio said.

"Indeed I do. He is an American patriot."

"That note is demented!" Antonio exclaimed.

"Well, at least he kept it shorter than the Gettysburg Address."

"I am sorry, my friend. It's life."

"Perhaps it's espionage, too."

"Are you serious?"

"I don't doubt the man wants her, but he is also an agent."

"For certain?"

"Yes. Now I must find out who or what else might be part of this. I will look into it in Washington, and I will not make a move until I have *all* the facts. Just tell me, and please don't worry about giving offense. Has anything happened?"

"Not that we can see. Anyway, the offense would be in *not* telling you."

"Moreno, you are the best friend a man can have. Let's drink to it!"

* * *

Wednesday evening, January 18, 1961. The day after tomorrow John F. Kennedy would be President. Under their weight of snow, even the curbstones of Washington seemed to be whispering about it.

In the elegant lobby of the Madison Hotel people sat sipping their drinks, talking in pairs or small groups. They gave out an air of not wanting others to overhear. They also shot glances to see who might be noticing them.

Among these denizens Rodrigo was the invisible one. The man, if anyone had noticed, would have seemed to come from another time and place: the dreamy, melancholic world of idealists who are strangers in modern society.

An exotically lovely woman came trotting into the large room. She was dressed in a mink stole and full-length black gown topped by a single strand of pearls. Rodrigo stepped quickly toward her.

"I've just met Kennedy!" Nathalie said in a burst of energy, and with Scotch on her breath. More than one head in the lobby turned.

She probably fucked him, Rodrigo thought as he whisked her toward the elevator.

"How did it happen?" he said in her ear.

"He arrived from Florida and had a pre-Inaugural meeting with a small group of reporters. Someone got me an invitation."

"Who else was there?"

"A few of the grey eminences."

And you, the CIA girl, in party dress. "Did you hear anything about Cuba?" he asked while opening his door.

"I'm not sure what to make of it. On the one hand, he is all for getting Castro out. On the other hand, he thinks victory is impossible without the open involvement of the United States, which he definitely does not want."

"What about the force of 25,000?"

"It's there, and ready for action. The question is whether he will use it."

"Will he?"

"I just told you he doesn't want to!" Nathalie said almost defensively.

"Wanting is not the same as doing. *Will* he do it?"

"I don't know. He is full of doubts, or perhaps he lacks assurance."

"Maybe it's something better: cool-headedness. If you can't do a thing well, don't do it at all."

"How would *you* do it?" she said with a laugh, changing the subject. "Is *your* invasion force up to the job?"

Hardly a man resists that change of subject. "Why don't you turn around and find out?" he answered.

Nathalie put her hands on a nearby sofa-arm. Rodrigo pulled her gown up above her hips. As he had guessed, she was wearing nothing underneath. Without touching his suit-jacket he unzipped his pants and thrust inside her. Suddenly the world appeared in a vast, exalted perspective. As for Nathalie, she let go the other stimuli of her evening and dissolved in convulsions as Rodrigo pressed his attack.

"Wait! Don't come!" she exclaimed.

"Why not?"

"I'm unprotected!"

He pulled out of her with a huge backward thrust as she moaned excitedly. Sitting down on the sofa, he said: "Finish me!"

With a sleight-of-hand she did, catching his fluid in a handkerchief that she had brought like a magician from out of nowhere.

"Can I take your wrap?" he asked. The mink was still dangling from her shoulders.

"Why don't you just zip up and we'll have a drink downstairs."

* * *

"What else have you heard about Cuba?" he asked when they had taken seats in the bar.

"A curious thing. Agents in Havana are telling the CIA that if an operation takes place anytime soon, it will end in disaster."

"American agents?" Rodrigo asked in a casual tone.

"No. Cubans."

"Really! Cubans are usually optimists."

"Not this time," Nathalie said.

"Are people paying attention?" Rodrigo asked.

"They are."

"Good. Perhaps it means there will be no acting in haste."

"When do you leave Washington?" Nathalie asked.

"Soon."

"I'm curious about the situation in Havana. I am speaking to one of my papers about sending me there."

"Careful! It might not be safe."

"But those are the best kinds of situations for journalists! And perhaps our paths will cross."

"That would be difficult."

"Of course! Mrs. Don José might have to kill me, or you, or somebody."

"Let's leave her alone. She is in Miami. Besides, in this situation *I* am Don José and *you* are Carmen."

"Oh my! Then I had better go."

"I thought you liked danger."

"I prefer my life!"

She stood up, tossed the mink over her shoulder and strode to the hotel exit. Rodrigo caught up to her in the bitter cold outside the revolving door.

"You have nothing to fear from Don José, because you have already slain him!" he declared.

As the attendant opened a taxi door for her, she threw her arms around Rodrigo and kissed him before the envious onlookers.

* * *

Rodrigo went pacing on the frigid streets of Washington. The cold and snow didn't bother him. In truth he enjoyed them; and he needed to walk off the residue from his pair of encounters with Nathalie. It was not the sex that had touched him as much as the stories she told. One image, in particular, would not leave his head: the image of all those Americans waiting to fight on Cuban soil.

Clearly the President-to-be viewed an intervention in Cuba with reluctance. That might be bad news for the Cuban underground, or it might be good. If it meant a lack of resolve, it was bad. If it meant a resolve to "act well or not at all," it could be a salvation in disguise. Merely aborting the mission, leaving Cuba to Castro and the Soviets, would be an offense to the Cuban people. Worse by far however would be the failed attempt, a U.S.-backed operation that Castro defeated. Such an event would disgrace the U.S., would give a twisted new shape to global politics, and would put Castro on a throne.

In this set of possibilities the "wild card" was that story of 25,000 *yanqui* soldiers. If the Americans landed their own soldiers in Cuba, Castro was as good as gone. It would also mean reviving the unhappy two-step of Cuban-American history: step one, Americans "protecting" Cuba; step two, Americans dominating Cuba with the consent of Cubans who were glad to take *yanqui* money and accept *yanqui* influence.

In the present circumstance, Rodrigo thought, the greater good was getting rid of Castro. *If the devil offers a means of doing that,* he told himself, *I will take the offer and live with the devil afterward.* And if the Americans were sending their own forces – as unattractive a prospect as it was in so many senses – Rodrigo must jump in with them. The more he thought of it, the more he let go his reservations and gave himself up to the powerful current bearing him, feet first, into that sea of troubles where the happy warrior must go.

Could he trust this information about the 25,000 men?

Nathalie, as Rodrigo well knew, was Thor's mouthpiece. Perhaps, in telling Rodrigo about the invasion force, Nathalie was divulging what the "official" CIA man must not. Or perhaps it was Nathalie herself who had given the story to Thor. After all, Nathalie was now in contact with official levels that went far higher than Thor. Indeed, she seemed to be in close contact with the highest level of all.

The CIA, determined to take the lead on Cuba, had put Nathalie at the side of the President-elect to deliver the agency's story in a way no official briefer could. In time her crucial task would be to convince Kennedy, once the CIA operation was under way, that he must back it up with more force. Now however Nathalie was herself a "wild card" beyond the CIA's control.

Nathalie is a whore for the CIA, Rodrigo thought. *As with most women in that line of work, the men who deal with her will underestimate her. I can't make that mistake. Whatever game she plays, it's going to be a very strong one; and I must consider it well.*

* * *

At Inauguration minus twenty-four hours, Rodrigo was again with his principal American contact in the Madison Hotel.

"Thor, it seems our situation requires that I tell you about a matter in my personal life. May I do so?"

"Of course."

"I hope this doesn't embarrass you, but it looks as if my wife is receiving attentions from a man who is part of your operation in Cuba."

"Really!" Thor said with interest. "What do you know?"

"The man's name is Whitmore. You may read for yourself. Here."

Thor took the letter and glanced it over. "Let me see what I can find out. May I keep this?"

"As you like."

"Let's go to the subject of guns," Thor said hastily. "We've thought about your request. What we can do is drop the guns with you and your team."

Rodrigo paused for a few moments. "That can work as long as your people pack the guns to withstand moisture."

"If the container sits in a swamp for a month, the guns will still be fine."

"Good," Rodrigo said. "This looks like progress."

"Do you have any other questions?" Thor asked.

"One more thing. While staying here, I have gotten to know a woman journalist who has extensive contacts. As far as she knows, I am an attorney looking for work. She has been picking my brains about Cuba. From her questions I gather she is a specialist in intelligence matters."

"Is the woman's name Nathalie?"

"I imagined you would know her. Anyway – she has told me a plan exists to put an army of 25,000, including U.S. troops, into Cuba. This sounds very much like the 'forces in reserve' you mentioned last week. Since your government is being careful with this information, I cannot imagine why such a story should be traveling in the street."

"Rodrigo, this is Washington!" Thor said with a mixture of exasperation and humor. "In this town, secrets are *supposed* to travel on the street!"

"Can you comment on the story itself?"

"I'm afraid I can't."

"Well then, can you can give me a hint or two?"

"What would you say if I told you that one of our contingency plans includes the use of thirty PT boats within the invasion force?"

"Before I made any comment at all, I would ask if your contingency plan actually does include such a proviso."

"And I would answer that it does," Thor said.

"In that case I would say: Holy cow! Thirty PT boats would have to mean that the force includes tens of thousands of men, with naval and air cover."

The CIA man looked at his watch. "I'm sorry I have to leave you. The Inauguration seems to have tripled my work for the week! So are we agreed on your mission?"

Are you going back into Cuba? With a major American force at the ready, this question answered itself; and Rodrigo felt the swift current of destiny roaring between his ears.

"We are agreed," Rodrigo affirmed.

XIII.

THE JUMP

"Hey! My balls are like ice!" Vladimiro said.

"Mine too!" Alejandro put in.

"It's the high altitude," Rodrigo explained. He had been noting this piquant effect ever since the two-engine C-47 had begun its climb over central Guatemala on its way to Cuba. Indeed, his testicles were as cold as anyone's; but his job was to lead and not complain.

"*¡A singar!* Why didn't they warn us about this at the camp?" Alejandro, a former lieutenant in the Rebel Army, asked.

"What about the case officer?" Vladimiro, the radio operator, put in. "Didn't he know?"

"Surely the answer is yes," Rodrigo said in the tone of a friendly schoolmaster. "By climate and by disposition the Americans are well acquainted with this problem. At their home latitudes it gets so cold that sometimes the male organ just goes to sleep."

"You mean, hibernates?" Vladimiro asked.

"No. The American organ sleeps. The *Soviet* organ hibernates.

Didn't your father tell that to you when he explained the facts of life?"

Vladimiro was the son of Cuban Communists who had named him after the father of the U.S.S.R. For a while Vladimiro had been a member of the Cuban Socialist Youth, but he had drifted away from those early loyalties.

"What would you like to accomplish in Cuba?" Rodrigo had asked Vladimiro in their first interview.

"I would like to put Castro and his friends on trial as counter-revolutionaries," Vladimiro had answered.

"Welcome to this mission!" Rodrigo had said without further ado.

Over the Caribbean the night was clear, the sea vaguely lit by a slender moon. Their jump onto Cuban soil was two hours away. Rodrigo thought back to his parachute training near Washington, a simple affair. The important part was that Thor had shown up for it.

Why should this official have left his busy agenda to watch an exercise? That day the CIA man had been almost *too* personable. The parachute instructor had begun by lecturing Rodrigo on various ways he might injure himself.

"Forget it!" Thor broke in and snapped at the instructor. "This man is an expert at judo. He has taken thousands of falls. He is going to jump very well!"

Rodrigo didn't know how to read this behavior. The CIA man was projecting a broad confidence in the mission. Rodrigo had seen however that men at war show their feelings in paradoxical ways.

An indirect guide to Thor's feelings came from "Max," the CIA case officer at the Guatemala training camp. When Rodrigo had picked the two men he wanted for the mission, Max told him: "You will be the last to jump from the plane."

"No!" Rodrigo objected. "I am leading those men, and they must see me go into action. I will jump first."

"Fair enough," Max answered, "but they will go out of the plane in any case."

To Rodrigo that had seemed notable. Why talk about pushing men from a plane? These men were not recruits but volunteers. Did CIA people think that Cubans chicken out? Perhaps the Americans were confusing style with substance. Cuban soldiers, in mortal situations, went overboard with jocularity – not with clipped smiles or gallant attitudes, as one might see in black-and-white movies of Americans at war, but with belly-laughs and jokes in the midst of bullets and bombs. The Cuban battle-stand was just too lighthearted for serious Anglo-Saxons to make sense of it. So it happened that the very measure of a Cuban's pride, the raucous humor with which he disdained his own fear, marked him as unreliable in *yanqui* eyes – and what a pity that was!

A short time later Max told Rodrigo: "In case they capture you, we need a code."

"Why?"

"Because they are going to make you talk."

"Listen," Rodrigo said flatly. "If I am captured I am not going to talk."

"That's not usually the way it works."

So now they were pushing *him* out of the plane! Max's statement was as close to a *yanqui* panic-attack as Rodrigo had heard. Thor himself would not have said it but his reticence would have been simple good manners. In this exchange Max was a delivery-boy. Thor was the one who did the worrying. Clearly he worried Rodrigo would break in captivity.

Some days before the launch, Max had come and told Rodrigo: "We have a third man for your mission. He is ready to be your assistant. Take him and use him for whatever you want."

Rodrigo looked at the name and looked again. It was Bill Whitmore.

Again Max was the carrier of a message whose source and meaning were clear. Thor was telling Rodrigo: The life of the man who tried to cuckold you is in your hands. You may kill him when you wish.

The offer gave Rodrigo a sense of elation. A second reflex however told him not to accept right away.

"Please give me some time to think it over," he answered Max.

"Okay," Max said, "but if you're taking him he needs time to prepare."

Why was Thor making a gift of this kind? Bill was no expendable Cuban. Why should Bill's people give up a man who had been their neighbor, had gone to their schools and churches, had been a member of their social clubs and was now a member of their secret society? Even more, why should they give up this piece of themselves to a Cuban?

Bill's play for Elena had clearly not been part of a CIA program. It had been a wayward act that signaled a loss of self-control. If Bill's fellows merely "put him out to pasture" he might find other ways to embarrass the agency and harm the country. That concern alone would have sufficed for Bill's people to scrap their fellow-feelings and "go Sicilian."

Rodrigo was to be the enforcer. Why? It struck Rodrigo that Thor, by giving the removal job to the offended party, had acted in keeping with old-style honor codes. The whole thing went with a delectable irony that Rodrigo hugely relished.

Still, the more he thought about it the more it didn't cohere. Max's statement that Bill "needs time to prepare" had left Rodrigo with a queasy feeling he couldn't identify. It was something old and familiar, a reflex from far in his past.

From where, exactly?

In high school Rodrigo had seen how girls avoided pushing even a shade too quickly in a boy's direction. For *boys* to push was fine and natural. After all: *The man says, I love. The woman says, he loves.*

Girls had to do their part more carefully. The young women at the Instituto del Vedado were quite equal to this task. Smart and well bred, they knew how to coax a boy's attention without raising his defenses. Hardly a boy could withstand their gentle, well-played assaults. At moments, however, an extra word or gesture – even a thing as slight as quickened breath – would tell a boy he was falling prey; and when he saw it the boy took off like a startled bird.

With that remark about giving Bill time to prepare, Max had overplayed his hand as no clever girl would have done; and Rodrigo saw Thor setting a trap for him.

This trap was the one gangsters used on new recruits. In a crime syndicate, when your bosses picked you out as partner material, they gave you an inspirational talk about joining the family. Then they gave you your first important job, which was to kill someone. As soon as you killed for those people, they had you. You would do anything they asked; you would never turn on them; and they would keep that hold on you forever.

The CIA bosses were no different. They wanted to be sure of their family members. Bill was a family member who had gone perilously outside the fold. The family had to get rid of him. Rodrigo was a recruit, promising but independent – far too independent for their taste. How then break the back of his attitude? By getting him to kill. And how move him to that ugly deed? By using the "happy warrior" principle – rouse his anger, invoke his wounded honor, stir up his inmost grief.

It was a beautiful play, and it should have worked with any man – but Rodrigo was not any man.

I am a warrior, he reflected. *My business is war. This thing with Bill is not war. It's a mess – a mess for his people, not for me, to clean up. If I fall, I fall as a soldier. I do not fall into some yanqui garbage can.*

"Thank you for the suggestion of the third man," Rodrigo told Max, "but I think the mission will go better if I take just the two I have."

Having to deal with this matter of Bill brought to Rodrigo's mind the unhappiness between himself and his wife.

He had no heart for chastising her over the flirtation. He had put her through too much, and did not want to add more. Never would he mention it to her; but other things he must not omit to say.

If he died in battle, she should remarry quickly. If he went to jail, an outcome far more painful to consider, she should divorce him. Before leaving Guatemala he had posted a letter to her, saying so.

"I see all too well that I have not been the husband you wanted," he had written. "For that I am deeply sorry. I hope you understand that I *have* loved you, while being as good a man as I have known how to be. As for our children, whom I have loved more than anything in this world, I know you will raise them well; and I only hope that as they grow up they do not come to think too badly of me."

Reflecting back on all of it from a height of many thousand feet, Rodrigo grew quite sad.

"We're descending!" one of the men shouted.

The plane was in a nose dive, hurrying through Castro's radar.

"Three minutes to the Escambray!" the Cuban pilot shouted from the cockpit. "Prepare to scan for ground signal!"

They leveled off at a low altitude and searched for the fire signal that would tell them, "Come ahead." Even in close-to-total blackness they could make out tree lines covering the hills and could feel the empty terrain below them.

Where was the fire? They scanned anxiously, for if they missed their signal they must return to Guatemala, set up another drop, and do the whole flight again.

"On target!" the pilot shouted. "Signal at eleven o'clock!"

Rodrigo yanked open the bay door. The fire was clearly visible.

"Prepare to jump!" he snapped. The men were on their feet behind him.

"Go! Go! Go!" the fresh-faced pilot called out commandingly, and with a cat-like movement Rodrigo pushed off into the night.

* * *

As he fell, Rodrigo looked up and saw the plane scurry across the heavens. Where were the other parachutes? *Max was right. The men aren't jumping.* As he thought it, two more parachutes burst open and then a third: the container of weapons and ammunition.

Rodrigo came down into lush hip-deep grass that cushioned his landing. A breeze caught his canopy and began to pull him along. He yanked his chute in, bundled it, took off his helmet and made an animal's call. The other men answered and converged.

"Everyone fine?" Rodrigo calmly asked. He was exhilarated from the jump but held that feeling down, the better to keep on his toes.

"*¡Estupendo!*" they said with excitement.

"Good job! Now I must find our hosts. Don't move until you hear my signal."

"Go on!" they told him.

Rodrigo drew his Colt .45. He had lost his bearings in the jump, so he moved in a wide circle to give himself the best chance of meeting his contacts. If they had seen the falling parachutes, they would join the men and he would find them when he circled back.

In the distance he saw a blur that took shape as a pair of men and three horses. Rodrigo gripped his weapon.

"Ernesto?" he said. This was the same man who had carried him to Florida.

"Ernesto sent us. I am Gregorio," one of the men answered, giving Rodrigo a match and a toothpick.

Rodrigo put away his gun and made the sound for his comrades to come ahead.

"Did you see where the weapons container fell?" Rodrigo asked.

"Yes. Let's go and load it," Gregorio replied.

In a few minutes they had packed the container and parachutes on the horses.

"I assume you have a hiding-place for these things," Rodrigo said.

"Of course," Gregorio replied. "Now, come. We are going to show you where you will sleep."

After a short walk they reached a sugar-cane field. Gregorio, pushing through the stalks, led them to a clearing just large enough for three men to lie side by side.

"Rest well," Gregorio said. "In the morning we will bring food."

Gingerly they arranged themselves on the floor of the clearing, put their pistols in reach and quickly fell asleep.

"Wake up, Doctor!" one of the men was saying.

Rodrigo was already awake. "I hear the noises," he said. "Those are field animals, probably even hungrier than we are."

"How can you tell?"

"I know the sounds. Don't worry; but don't hesitate to wake me if you have doubts."

They all kept waking up, skittish as rats.

Breakfast appeared promptly at daybreak, and they ravaged the food.

"When do we see Ernesto?" Rodrigo asked.

"Tomorrow," Gregorio said. "He is still busy arranging your travel to Havana. Use the day to rest up. It's going to get quite hot. You will want to go to the brook, that way."

Gregorio was right again. By mid-morning the heat in the cane-field had gotten so intense that Rodrigo and his comrades had fled to the brook.

As they talked about strategies, the younger men surprised Rodrigo with their detailed knowledge of irregular warfare. Vladimiro had an up-to-the-minute knowledge of Cuban affairs. Alejandro, a strait-laced military man, was a lot like Lázaro. He too, during the last war, had excelled in the crucial campaign of Las Villas.

"Alejandro, your job is a difficult one," Rodrigo told him. "With the loss of Lázaro we have to depend on Ernesto and his people. It's not a situation I like because Ernesto has had no experience in war, and his judgments might be off-base."

"At least Gregorio and the others are efficient," Alejandro put in.

"Yes, but it's a businesslike efficiency rather than an aptitude for warfare."

"I see what you mean."

"Between now and the battle a thousand tasks will arise that they will not even recognize as such. Your job is to make sure they see those tasks and carry them out."

"I understand," Alejandro replied.

"And whatever else you do, keep an eye on those weapons!"

"Count on it, sir!"

At dusk Ernesto came with his men and gave Rodrigo a big *abrazo*. He was full of that Spanish front-and-forwardness which makes a grand impression before dissolving into a lack of specificity.

"I am driving you to Havana tonight," he said, pointing to a jeep.

"Where are the weapons?" Rodrigo asked.

"We have them in a safe place," Ernesto said. "Please don't worry."

As they embarked on the long ride to the capital, Rodrigo thought: *Why do people tell you not to worry? They do it to mark the moment at which you should start worrying.*

XIV.

¡VENCEREMOS!

Havana had braced for war. The avenues teemed with young men and women in olive-green trousers and blue militia shirts. Almost all carried arms. A fair number had submachine guns across their chests.

"Where did these weapons come from?" Rodrigo said, bedazzled. It hurt his heart that he had spent months begging the Americans for a single munitions container while Castro had all this.

"They are part of a shipment from Czechoslovakia," Vladimiro said. "Everyone calls the machine guns *checas*."

"Ha!" Rodrigo let out a huge guffaw and lowered his voice. "The Americans think they are going to conquer *this* with a thousand men? No! The battle must wait until Fidel's people get too confident and let down their guard."

"It wouldn't be a bad idea to find out what Fidel's people are thinking," Vladimiro mused.

"Not a bad idea at all!" Rodrigo exclaimed; and for the first time he experienced, with a twinge of nostalgia, the fact of younger people coming up in the ranks behind him.

* * *

The imposing statue of Spain's ancient King Carlos the Third, gazing down the popular avenue of that name, did seem – if you looked at the face from a certain angle – to frown on the idea of a new monarch in Cuba whose glory surpassed even his own.

At the base of the statue Rodrigo took a bulky shopping bag from that most reliable and steady of comrades, the Moor.

"Everything I requested?" Rodrigo asked.

"A T-23, a T-25, a *metralleta checa* and militia uniforms."

"Good."

"Doctor, when can we get the weapons in the Escambray?"

"Whenever we want," Rodrigo said. "Do we have a target?"

"I think so."

"Not a moment too soon! When can we be certain?"

"Give me a little more time. Then you come into it."

"What do you hear from Peleón?"

"I'm concerned about him," the Moor said.

"How?"

"His emotions have gotten control of him. He takes too many chances."

"I have never found a way to calm him down," Rodrigo confessed.

"Let me try," the Moor said. "You have plenty to do."

"Thanks, *Moro.* I know you will manage it."

* * *

"Hey!" Vladimiro whispered to Rodrigo. "Don't look now but those three coming in the door are editors of *Mella.* They are important guys. For sure they have contact with the top leaders!"

Rodrigo and his younger colleague, dressed as militiamen, were sitting quietly in the back corner of a coffee bar. Vladimiro had brought them there to eavesdrop on cadres of the Rebel Youth – successor group to the Socialist Youth of which Vladimiro had once been a member. It was quite late at night when the cadres came in – extraordinarily self-possessed youngsters lit up by the excitement of their jobs and by the burning matters of the moment. Ignoring the *barista,* who was a piece of furniture to them, and apparently taking no notice of the militia uniforms in the back, they talked quite freely.

"Get off it, Velázquez! The invasion is coming. It's an established fact! And even if it were not, we must play it up in order to strengthen the militant feelings of our readers." The speaker was a neat young man with a wispy beard and an easy smile.

"Listen, Bartolo, I don't care for that kind of journalism," Velázquez answered. He was wiry and intense, the picture of a cadre and without personal hygiene, his clothes like a vagabond's. "I prefer to be logical, and logic tells me the United States will never invade. The revolution is much too popular even for the Americans to take on, and they must know it. Probably they are just making threats."

"Alejandro, I am sorry to disagree but in this case you are dead wrong." A bespectacled man in clothes as natty as a tourist's was addressing Velázquez. "The Americans *must* invade, no matter what else they think or see, because they cannot accept a socialist order in a country which they have treated for more than a century as a private preserve!"

"Hey, Gálvez!" Bartolo drawled at the bespectacled man. "When are you ever going to graduate from that university of yours? I am amazed at how you academic socialists continue to debate fine points when our task is already decided! We are to speak to the masses and warn them of an invasion. If you propose anything else, you will only call attention to yourselves."

"Cut it, Bartolo!" Gálvez snapped. "That's out of line! *I* am in charge of *Mella.* That means *I* tell *you* what to do, not the other way around! There is no substitute for understanding the situation we are in. The only way to understand it is through sincere, open discussion among comrades. If my comrade Alejandro Velázquez and I invite you to talk with us, we do so in a spirit of letting you develop your viewpoints, not of enabling you to suppress ours!"

"Wow! He's angry. It's a real division in the ranks: ideology versus opportunism," Vladimiro whispered.

"Yes!" Rodrigo said. "Fascinating!"

"The revolution is already under attack!" Gálvez was talking still more heatedly. *"Fíjate,* Alejandro. What do you have to say about the constant sabotage in Havana? We have explosions in the city almost every night. This terrorism could be the very thing that brings the invasion on!"

"No chance!" Velázquez answered with a sneer. "Terrorism shows the weakness of our enemies, not their strength. The Americans and their mercenary friends have nothing to count on in Cuba. Random bombings only expose that fact."

"Most people do *not* see the bombings as you do," Gálvez replied firmly. "And even those bombs are not the biggest problem we face. Look at the fighting in the Escambray. Our publication calls it a 'bandit's war' but we all know it's a lot more than that. During the liberation it is certainly true that some soldiers claiming to be on our side did abuse people in that region, killed their cows, took their women, whatever. Now those people are presenting the bill to us, and we are having to pay it. All this can only encourage the Americans."

"Hey!" Vladimiro whispered. "We are making an impact!"

"You bet we are!" Rodrigo said.

"Almost everything the Americans drop into the Escambray, we capture," Velázquez was saying. "Whenever people see parachutes they run to tell the police or militia." Turning to Gálvez, he added: "Félix, don't lose heart! Remember what Redbeard told us. The revolution is so strong that even our problems give us the advantage."

"What the hell does *that* mean?" Bartolo asked.

"Drop this, Alejandro!" Gálvez directed.

"Redbeard is *Comandante* Piñiero, the head of counterintelligence!" Vladimiro whispered.

"I know!" Rodrigo said. He reserved a special loathing for Piñiero, who had been the judge in the trial of the Batista air-force officers.

Velázquez had lowered his voice. "It means we can infiltrate enemy groups with spies who say they are defecting from the revolution."

"It is time to move to another subject!" Gálvez insisted.

"There's always the literacy campaign!" Velázquez joked.

"Gálvez!" Bartolo said. "Where is that editorial you promised about Nikita's policy in the Congo?"

"Let's go back to the office," Gálvez said.

The cadres got up and left.

"*Muchísimas gracias, caballeros,*" Vladimiro said after them.

* * *

"Rodrigo! This militia uniform you sent me is pinching all over the place!"

"Sorry, John Paul. These uniforms are our best cover for meetings in the center of Havana. Why not have your people make up some of them?"

"We might expose ourselves trying to find materials. With embassy relations cancelled, there is ice under our feet."

"Point taken," Rodrigo said. "Anyway, I'm glad you asked for this meeting because I was about to contact you. "

"How come?"

"We are listening in on Castro's officials. It's not a steady source, and the people we overhear are below the topmost levels, but they say quite enough to let us follow how the leaders are thinking."

"Have you heard anything good?"

"Castro's counterintelligence chief has told cadres that his spies have succeeded in infiltrating the opposition. This clearly confirms what I have been telling you for some time."

"Yes, that is interesting," the CIA man said. "I will report it."

"*Report* it? Why not *use* it?"

"I'm not sure how to. Anyway, we're dealing with other problems."

"Like what?"

"Castro's government is planning to issue a bogus announcement that an invasion has taken place. It will say that forces have attacked Cuba's southern shore. The purpose is to trick the underground into premature actions and create a pretext for mass arrests. If you hear an announcement of this kind, you should lie low and do nothing."

"John Paul, there is something I don't understand."

"What?"

"I don't see why the government would make false statements that cause people to fear for their lives. People will get mad if they see officials creating panic for no reason. And regarding the invasion, I am under the impression that the plan *is* to strike at the southern shore – isn't it?"

"I wouldn't know."

"Look, John Paul, we don't have much time so let's drop the masks, okay? You know as well as I do that the plan is for the invaders to get a foothold in the Escambray. They can't very well do that without striking at the southern shore, can they?"

"Probably they will strike at the southern shore."

"Thank you! So this bogus announcement contains a scenario that might be the truth?"

"It could be."

"Then what is going on here? If an invasion really does come and the underground follows your instruction to lie low, then we will be doing *exactly* what Castro wants us to do! This may be a counterintelligence maneuver by Castro's people. Do you mind if I check the story with my own sources?"

"Check anything you like, but whatever you find out, be sure to do as I tell you."

At that the CIA man turned on his heel and vanished into the mass of uniforms.

Rodrigo told himself: *Even at ten before midnight, the Americans have no idea how Fidel plays. They play checkers with him, while he plays chess with them.*

* * *

"I am sorry, Doctor. Peleón is under arrest."

Looking at the Moor, who strolled along the busy avenue in his perfectly sized militia uniform, Rodrigo had a premonition he didn't want to heave into words.

"What happened?"

"Last time I saw him, he told me he was going to a meeting of the section chiefs."

"What?" Rodrigo interjected. "All those people together in one place?"

"I didn't like it either but he wouldn't listen. The next thing I heard was from Peleón's driver. He saw Peleón and some others leave the meeting with plainclothesmen. Peleón, before he got in the police car, looked at the driver and did this."

The big man pinched his own throat.

"Yes," Rodrigo said with a catch in the voice. "He is done for."

"What now?"

"We regroup. We lay plans for more attacks. And we need our guns."

"How do we bring them?"

"Truck-drivers from Camagüey will carry them on their next trip. *Moro,* we have to move! The Americans are chasing their tails. The underground is in a mess. Getting Fidel is our only chance. We have to put him in our trap!"

"Agreed," the Moor said solemnly.

* * *

"Ernesto, my people are ready to take the weapons from your farm. Transport to Havana will occur in the next few days."

Rodrigo had summoned his contact to a central café.

"There's a problem," Ernesto said. "The weapons are no good."

"What?"

"A heavy rain soaked the ground where we buried them. The guns have rusted. They are unusable."

"All of them?"

"All."

"With respect, Ernesto, the people who packed those guns told me that even if the container fell into water the contents would stay dry. And if the guns *did* get wet, they should have dried out. Did you personally see the weapons?"

"I do not take accusations!" Ernesto screamed, red in the ears. "If you do not believe my story, then come and check the guns for yourself!"

"Ernesto, we have no need for that kind of talk," Rodrigo said, but the other man was already striding away.

* * *

"That man has stolen your weapons," the Moor said in an undertone. "We should remove him."

"No!" Rodrigo answered. "I agree he lied, but he lied because he's in a panic."

The two were in militia dress, walking in the colonnade near the Presidential Palace.

"What do you mean?" the Moor asked.

"I mean that people like Ernesto are not used to political troubles. He has never known anything like the tension we are now facing. He must be terrified. He fears that if anyone moves the guns off his farm, the police will catch him and he will go to jail. He needs a bit of time to cool down. In a few days he'll give us the guns."

"I don't agree," the Moor said. "I think he took the guns and sold them. The man is a danger to us."

"Let's give him the benefit of the doubt. I know he can be foolish, but he is also the man who pulled me out of the sea." Rodrigo paused. "Now let's go to the main matter. How is your lead?"

"Very solid. It's time for you to see my man yourself."

"When?"

"Tomorrow. Come back here just before noon. You have a suit the color of pistachio, right?"

"Right."

"Wear that one with a Panama hat. Someone will meet you."

* * *

Havana, near the Presidential Palace. Saturday, April 1, 1961.

"You seem to be looking for something. May I be of assistance?" Rodrigo said to a pair of enormous young women who clearly were not locals.

"Thank you, sir! Can you tell us the way to the Malecón?"

"With pleasure! and excuse my curiosity. May I inquire where you are from?"

"We are from Germany."

"Excellent! You know, before today I thought the Valkyries were part of myth."

As the big girls laughed, Rodrigo caught hold of himself. *Here you are before the most important meeting of your life, and you are flirting!*

Quickly he gave them instructions for the Malecón and moved off. As he did, a woman of astonishing beauty, dressed in the style of a film heroine, brushed by him.

If we were playing in a movie, he thought, *that woman would turn back to me and say: Excuse me, sir. Are you looking for someone?*

Just as he thought it, the woman turned around and said: "Excuse me, sir. Are you looking for someone?"

"As a matter of fact, I am," Rodrigo answered as if it were the most natural thing in the world.

"Will you kindly accompany me?"

"With pleasure."

She beckoned him to the curbside, and to a handsome Checker with darkened windows. The driver was holding open the passenger door. Rodrigo followed the woman in and found someone else.

"Hello, Margot," he said as if expecting to see her.

"Hello Núñez. Do you have some extra minutes? I have to drop Norma at the Hilton. Excuse me! I mean the Havana Libre."

"Of course," Rodrigo said.

He should have known. It only made sense that he and the Moor would use the same "man," since no one was tougher or savvier than Margot. He also saw the sense of the dress-up meeting. Even with Castro's new order all around them, hardly a soul in Havana would look twice at a dandy getting into a car with a whore.

"All right, let's talk business," Margot said after the beauty had left the car. "I have your man for you."

"You mean...?"

"Yes. Himself."

"How?"

"He meets a number of women through me."

"I don't understand. He can have any woman in Cuba."

"He doesn't *want* any woman in Cuba. Of course they all want *him,* and I'm sure he knows how to humor them – but what he really cares for is information, influence, power. He prefers women from America and Europe who can help him in that. His people know I can find those women, so we have an arrangement."

"Why are you talking to me?"

"I like you, and I like your associate. When I met him I had the idea you two might be a pair."

"That honors me! But my question is: Why give the man up?"

"I don't like what the country is becoming. That leads me to follow my own interests. I think I can do very well with you."

"Good! Self-interest is a motive I trust."

"Be clear, Núñez. I'm not acting out of charity. If you succeed in this, I expect a piece of your success – a nice piece."

"You will not be sorry."

"And I know that if you say it, you will keep your word."

"All right, then. How do we do it?"

As she drew a breath, Rodrigo prepared to take the secret that would let him overthrow history.

* * *

"Along the Almendares River is a small building that houses the offices of a fisherman's cooperative," Margot said.

Rodrigo knew. It was near where Lázaro had worked as a yacht-hand. He quickly recalled the conversation in which Lázaro had told him of strange noises coming from the place at night. *You would think Fidel himself was screeching to the masses....*

"Yes, I've seen the place!" Rodrigo answered. "Does he use it for assignations?"

"Not always," Margot said. "Sometimes he visits with the cooperative officials. At other times he has a private encounter. Either way his escort is no more than twenty or thirty men. You can take a position on the opposite bank of the river, in one of the fisherman's shacks."

"I know the shacks you mean!"

"You can rent any of them for some days of use. From there it's a fifty-meter distance with nothing in your way. Often his men don't bother to check across the river."

"So we have a chance they will overlook us."

"An excellent chance."

"We will be ready to deal with them in any case."

"At worst you will escape."

"And the getaway is perfect!"

"As clear as can be."

"It sounds like a job for me and one other man."

"That's probably right," Margot agreed.

"Want to do it with me?"

"Look, Núñez. You fight your way and I fight mine!"

"Just kidding, old friend. With you on our side we cannot fail!"

* * *

Margot was as expert in plotting as she was in procuring. When he went back to look over the place, Rodrigo saw that the fisherman's shacks did indeed give easy shooting into the cooperative. The short distance made telescopic sights unnecessary. Rodrigo and one other marksman could do the work with plain rifles. They need only lie in wait until the target appeared. If they dressed as fishermen and rented a shack, no one would notice them. At night they could sleep in the shack with one or the other on lookout. And the getaway was clean.

Looking over the scene, Rodrigo kept hearing a thought that echoed in his ears like the sound of waves in a sea shell. "We are going to win!" his insides kept murmuring, and he filled up with an unbearable joy.

XV.

THE TRAP

Calm down. Don't lose yourself by paying too much attention. The only thing that concerns you is the sound of horsehair snapping.

As he sat in the fisherman's shack waiting for Fidel, Rodrigo worked hard to keep his thoughts from overwhelming him.

Every so often, in the manner of someone who avoids scratching an itch, he moved his mind away from the disturbing news Alejandro had brought. Ernesto's statement about rusted guns was far more mischievous than the fear-based lie Rodrigo had imagined.

As the Moor correctly guessed, Ernesto had seized the chance to unload the guns for a pile of money. Alejandro had witnessed the sale from a hiding-place.

Rodrigo was enraged. Not only had Ernesto taken his guns. The man was in a position to betray clandestine operations as well as the people in them. At any other moment Rodrigo would have killed the man. Now, however, putting a bullet in Ernesto's head would take him away from putting one in Castro's.

At times the itch, Rodrigo's impulse to ruminate, was overwhelming. He could only withstand it by reflecting on something else. He chose the tale of the sword and horsehair.

For the final exam at a Japanese fencing school, every student had to lie under a sword that hung by a strand of horsehair twenty meters above. The student could not move until the hair had broken. Then he had a second or two to jump away from a falling sword.

This exam took place in an epoch that predated industrial uniformity. The strand holding the sword could be a thirty-minute hair, a three-hour hair or a three-day hair. Since no one could predict when a given hair would snap, one's escape had to be an improvisation of the most skillful kind.

Many a student in the exam watched the hair and sword to look for signs of wavering. After some hours this exertion wore out the mental faculties. When the hair did break, that delicate sound was easy to miss by one whose senses were dull from exhaustion; and the student perished.

Other students figured out that they must refrain from looking at the sword and instead go into a state of deep relaxation. That way the senses remained supple and receptive, so that when the breaking hair made its "ping" the instincts registered it and quickly took the body out of the way.

If I allow myself to think about this business of Ernesto or anything else, I am going to become like those students who tried to think their way through the exam. When I start to go down that road I must picture a horsehair and then I must picture nothing at all, only a faint blur beyond the eye-lids....

Voices piped up on the other side of the water. Rodrigo saw many men bustling around with an air of importance. Their movements recalled the presidential guards he had seen as a boy.

"Alejandro!"

The other man jumped up like a student in the fencing exam.

"Look," Rodrigo said. "They are preparing a room."

Across the river men moved between a group of vehicles and the building like a trail of ants, carrying boxes and other items. They were not working in a usual sense, not even like a presidential guard. They filled the role of indentured men but they were not humble; quite the contrary. They went with speed and panache, full of themselves and happy to do what they were doing. In their excessive willingness they became less than full men, laboring in the service of one who had the mysterious power to diminish them and make them glad of it at the same time. They might have been servants to the King of Spain; and how much more compelling was this new leader whose footmen seemed to be dressed in fineries, even while being clothed in army fatigues! It was the men's very subservience – their sense of the master's importance – which made the spectacle so resplendent. Alejandro watched with the wide-eyed astonishment of a boy; and so in spite of himself did Rodrigo.

"There he is!" Alejandro exclaimed.

"Stand by!" Rodrigo snapped.

Fidel had emerged from one of the vehicles and was moving in the center of a close bodyguard. Several of his escort were bearded, like himself, and also quite tall, though none came up to Castro's extraordinary height. The men in the shack raised weapons and followed the entourage with their gun-barrels.

"Not until we have him clean," Rodrigo said.

Even Castro was not tall enough, with those heads bobbing around him, to present a target.

Inside the building a kind of revelry got under way. Fidel never quit. Even in this remote place, with only his guards for company, he was working an audience. He paced the room, coming into view for fractions of seconds before the window-frame cut him off. If his form was elusive, his voice was anything but. The distinctive timbre that no Cuban could fail to recognize – high-pitched, hectoring, strangely feminine – went stampeding across the gentle currents of night.

Fidel was holding forth on the subject of food. Some of his words were inaudible but most of them resounded all over the area. He was lamenting the high cost of certain beans and grains and began quoting prices from memory.

The leader fell silent, then abruptly demanded: "Who knows the per pound price of lentils in the international market?"

Apparently he had suffered a memory slip, extremely rare for him.

In a moment Fidel was again orating. "If you compare with black and red beans you will find ..."

Most of that sentence disappeared into a breeze.

"The dietary preferences of the Cuban people are erroneous! We have inherited from Spain the feeding habits of a cold climate, while what we need here are lots of greens, lots of fruit, lots of fish ...."

"What is this?" Alejandro blurted.

"Fidel is feeding the people," Rodrigo answered.

"All right," Alejandro allowed.

"No! The people should feed themselves. He's a cheat."

"Rice, for instance," Fidel pronounced, "has all the nutritional value in the husk, and we take it off to eat the grain. It would be good for us to save the money we spend on imported rice and buy corn flour, which is much cheaper and has more nutritional value."

"A cheat, how?" Alejandro asked.

"He eats in Spanish restaurants."

"How do you know?"

"We tailed him for a year. Stand by!"

Men were streaming outside to take up security positions at the perimeter, while someone in a grey hooded outfit was moving quickly to the door.

"It's the woman," Rodrigo said.

From inside the room the leader's voice grew quite a bit softer, with many words muffled. In place of boldness, Rodrigo heard the voice of a shy young man talking to a woman he wants. Both were out of sight in the rear of the room, Fidel asking questions. That too was unusual.

"You are certain they are coming?" the leader asked.

"Certain," she said.

"No doubts?"

"None."

"How are they thinking?"

"They are confident they can defeat you with a small force."

This was the invasion! And this woman was a spy.

"When do they come?" Fidel asked.

"Very soon. You will get a warning."

"What kind?"

"Probably a bombing raid."

"Are they really that stupid?" Rodrigo said to himself just as the same words left Fidel's mouth.

"The *yanquis* think it will be easy," the lady said.

The sound of the word "*yanquis*" jarred Rodrigo.

"Maybe they will change their minds," Fidel said.

That's it! Rodrigo thought. *He's worrying the yanquis will* not *come!*

"They will come, only in small numbers," the lady said. "And when they do, you will destroy them."

"No! Not I alone! It is the people of Cuba who will destroy them!"

Fidel and the woman were moving toward the window.

"Prepare to fire!" Rodrigo said.

They came into plain view. The woman still had not removed her hood. She stood with her hands propped on the window-frame and Fidel stood behind her, moving turbulently. They were having sex, and their motions made him an uncertain target.

"*¡Coño!* Alejandro said. "They don't keep still!"

"Why would they? Just wait till he finishes. Then we'll get him clean."

The woman had no words, only moans, as the leader flailed about. His movements were not sexual, they were declamatory. He was giving one of his speeches.

"The *yanquis* are puny. They have their armies. We have the people. What army is mightier ... than the people? Armies do not win wars. People ... win wars. No army liberated Cuba. No man liberated Cuba ... not even I. Cuba. It was the people ... the armed people!"

"He never shuts his trap!" Rodrigo muttered.

"Yes! Let the *yanquis* invade!" Fidel hollered. "The people will destroy them! They think we are weak. They think they can destroy us. We have told them ... your mercenaries can conquer Cuba! They believe it! The mercenaries will come ... and the people ... will crush them. The world will see ... everyone will know ... how mighty we are!"

The leader's movements had greatly sped up. He was in the chute toward climax, that delectable stream which no man great or small can resist. He pulled off the woman's hood so at the moment of his joy he could caress her hair.

Rodrigo froze. The woman was Nathalie.

"Fire low!" Rodrigo ordered. "Draw the woman off! No hitting her!"

Alejandro, a soldier, obeyed.

Their barrage hit the window-sill. It did not separate the lovers, as Rodrigo had hoped; for Fidel grasped and held her in front of him like a shield, instinctively protecting his sovereign life. In a split-second he had drawn his weapon and pulled himself as well as Nathalie back from the window-frame.

Some of Castro's men ran into the building, while others formed a crouching line at the river's edge.

"Take out the guards!" Rodrigo snapped.

He and Alejandro fired machine guns into the line of men at the river. Those men had no protection, and it was a devastating assault. Five or six of the guards fell. The others retreated back toward the structure, firing as they went. Two or three more went down.

"Let's beat it!" Rodrigo shouted.

They jumped into the car and Rodrigo peeled out. As they sped away, Castro's men got off some shots and Alejandro answered. Rodrigo could feel bullets whizzing by the back of his neck.

"What happened?" Alejandro asked when they were away.

"Fuck it! Fuck it! Fuck it!" Rodrigo said, worked up and furious.

"Who *is* that woman?"

"A spy!" Rodrigo was nearly moaning. "She works for the Americans. I met her in Washington. And now we have met her in Havana!"

"A double?"

"At least. Maybe a triple. But no doubt who her master is."

"Castro."

"Of course! And they have set a trap for the Americans."

"How?" Alejandro asked.

As Rodrigo sputtered out his words, he kicked up the car to a terrifying speed.

"They have convinced the Americans that Castro's régime is ready to crumble! The Americans believe they can win with a small invasion. If that invasion comes, it will fail. This is a terrible trap. We must prevent the Americans from falling in!"

"All right, then. We do it!"

"It won't be easy." He paused. "Tonight we could have settled the whole thing, and I was weak!"

"Failing to kill is no weakness," Alejandro said bravely.

"It is if it means cutting off your own arms!" Rodrigo cried with a desperate energy. "Fuck it! Fuck it! We should have killed them all!"

XVI.

FINDING FIDEL

Havana, early Saturday, April 15, 1961.

"Get up! Something is happening!" Rodrigo heard Delia, his hostess, exclaim.

Massive explosions were rocking the apartment house and everything around it.

"Where can this be coming from?" Delia asked.

"It must be the invasion!" Rodrigo jumped to his feet. "But how can it be starting without our knowledge? The invasion and our actions were supposed to go off together!"

"Maybe the invasion is so big it doesn't need any help."

"No it's not!" Rodrigo said, beside himself. "How could the Americans do this without telling us? With those planes they have told Castro to hurry up and make his arrests! Right now the police are looking for us, and we cannot protect ourselves!"

* * *

Rodrigo's comrade Vladimiro felt himself in the middle of a downpour. He had no idea from where the rains had come, or exactly where he was.

A door opened abruptly and slammed into a wall.

"Wake up!" someone shouted. "They are bombing Havana!"

Vladimiro rubbed his eyes and crawled out of the hammock in which he had fallen asleep after a busy day and night at the *Mella* offices. Before him stood the bespectacled figure of Félix Gálvez, the "responsible person" of Cuba's Rebel Youth journal. After that first eavesdropping session, Vladimiro had approached Gálvez and asked for the privilege of doing chores at the magazine. Gálvez had remembered Vladimiro from the old Socialist Youth and given him a job.

"This is it, Félix!" another young man shouted from the hallway.

"You said it, buddy! Come on, Vladimiro. We are out of here! The Marines are probably in the streets! Take this."

It was a pistol. Félix's voice was rippling with terror and joy.

They ran down to the street and jumped into a Ford convertible. Félix took the wheel and sped off toward Carlos III Avenue.

"Hey!" Vladimiro said. "Where did you get this beautiful machine?"

"My father gave it to me," Félix answered rather sheepishly.

The explosions had stopped. Instead of the bombed and cratered city they'd expected to find, everything looked normal.

"Where are we going?" Vladimiro said.

"To IRO. They can tell us what's going on."

The offices of the "Integrated Revolutionary Organizations," Cuba's command center, were oddly empty in the aftermath of the bombs. They ran into Joaquín Ordoqui, a senior Communist leader and member of the IRO Central Committee. He was wearing the usual olive-green uniform as well as a visibly foul mood.

"They have bombed army headquarters! And also the airports of San Antonio and Santiago de Cuba," Ordoqui snarled.

Félix said: "So the explosions..."

"...were not bombs, but ammo dumps exploding," Ordoqui put in.

"Nothing else? No landings?"

"No landings."

"Maybe this is not a war after all," Félix said with disappointment.

"Or maybe the Americans are preparing something big," Vladimiro offered.

"The *revolution* is big!" Ordoqui snapped. "Imperialism is a pile of shit!"

"Do you think the invasion will come?" Félix asked the older man.

"How the hell should I know? I have not yet been able to speak with Kennedy!"

"What should we do?"

"Stay alert," Ordoqui said and strode off like a gorilla.

"You have to be patient with these elders," Félix observed drolly as they went down to the car.

"Yeah," Vladimiro said. After gaining entry to this key installation with a high-ranking cadre like Félix, he was crestfallen at having seen and heard nothing of importance.

Vladimiro and Félix made their way back to the *Mella* offices on avenues now teeming with army trucks, patrol cars and militia squads. Horns and sirens blared. Announcements kept spreading the alarm, repeating the latest news and warning that further attacks were imminent. Everybody seemed to have a gun.

"I wonder what's going to happen," Vladimiro mused, his senses clouding over with dread.

"One thing I can tell you for sure," Félix said like a man inspired.

"What's that?"

"The Americans have lost Cuba no matter what they do. If they invade they lose it, and if they do not invade they also lose it."

* * *

Rodrigo approached the guardhouse of La Cabaña prison in ragged clothes, with tousled hair and a soiled face. For good measure he had sprayed himself with urine. He thought his best pose would be as a lunatic, for on this most terrifying of nights only soldiers and madmen would be outdoors.

The Moor appeared and hurried Rodrigo into a side-room.

"*Moro*, I am sorry to come. I had to see you, and I could find no one to carry a message."

"Don't worry, Doctor. Everyone here is fixated. They will only think one of my strange friends needs help."

"Have you heard from your people?"

"I managed to talk to some of them before everything went crazy. No one had word of the attack."

"So our friends just kept this a secret," Rodrigo said, still not quite believing it.

"What do you suppose they were thinking?" the Moor asked. "Are you in contact with them?"

"For two days I've been calling on shortwave. No one answers."

"What can we do?"

"By the time the invasion force hits the beaches, we could all be in jail. I see only two ways out for us. One, they send a force that is huge. This is all but impossible. Two ... "

" ... someone dies."

"Which should already have happened." Rodrigo had managed to brief his comrade on the missed attempt.

"Don't be hard on yourself," the big man said. "I have never brought myself to harm a woman."

"Thank you for that, *Moro*." Rodrigo felt his burden grow instantly lighter as this champion among killers bestowed absolution on him.

* * *

Seven Cubans died in the island-wide bombings. Fidel decreed a ceremony in honor of the dead and commanded that everyone attend.

Heeding the call, hundreds of thousands of people converged on the enormous Plaza Cívica the following day, Sunday, April 16. A number of Fidel's top youth cadres gathered at the office of Joel Iglesias, director of Cuba's Rebel Youth, to watch the ceremony on TV.

Iglesias, an amiable nineteen-year-old *guajiro* who moved about with a limp from his war injuries, welcomed the members of this group with cigars. Vladimiro, whom Félix had brought along, quickly noticed a difference among the cadres. In one corner Félix, Alejandro Velázquez and others immersed themselves in talk of issues. Another group, including Federico Bartolo, enjoyed their cigars and the high spirits of the moment. On middle ground was Iglesias, whom everyone seemed to like.

As Fidel began speaking, the exceptionally warm feelings between the masses and himself came quickly to the fore. His rhetoric was a magic carpet that raised Cubans far above the struggles of daily life. Félix and his friends, however, were hard to impress.

Before the crowds, Fidel had invoked the United States and was exclaiming: "What they do not forgive us..."

"He'll say something insipid: 'we are on the side of the humble,' " Alejandro Velázquez predicted.

"Hey!" Bartolo snapped. "Why don't you people hold it down!"

Fidel's voice was about to burst the TV tube. He screamed: "What they do not forgive us is that we have made a socialist revolution under their noses!"

The Youth cadres turned to each other electrified. At the rally, pandemonium broke loose as thousands of people raised rifles. Before this image the cadres leapt up and, dropping their hostilities, embraced each other wildly.

"He's done it! Really done it!" Velázquez exclaimed.

"Declared Cuba a socialist country!" Bartolo marveled.

"And at just the right moment!" Félix pronounced. "When it

comes to timing in politics, this man has the genius of Lenin!"

"Of course!" Bartolo said. "Anyone who is against socialism will look like a coward in the midst of a war."

"Something else!" Félix exclaimed. "Cuba has come into the big leagues of history! At last we have a leader to put with the great ones: Roosevelt, Churchill, Stalin, de Gaulle. And in the annals of socialism, no one has ever done anything to equal this!"

"You mean Fidel is as great as Lenin and Mao?" Joel Iglesias asked.

"Greater, my boy, far greater!" Félix said beatifically. "Those guys made revolutions in Russia and China, but Fidel has made a revolution against the greatest capitalist country that ever existed. He has made a revolution *inside the United States!"*

"Imagine! Cuba in the vanguard!" Joel was almost singing.

"And all counterrevolutionaries to jail!" Bartolo said with a valedictory air.

* * *

The general order from Fidel was: Arrest anyone suspected of counterrevolutionary sympathies. In short: Arrest anyone. Cuba's populace hurried to enforce the measure. Street by street, house by house, people arrested other people. As prisons quickly overflowed, police used other kinds of buildings to confine many more.

"We are really in the shits," Vladimiro said.

"Don't worry just yet," Rodrigo said with his strange humor. "Worse is coming."

"How can that be?" the younger man asked. The two had crouched in a doorway like vagabonds.

"When the battle breaks out again, we have to be there."

"What are your orders?" Vladimiro asked like a soldier.

"Thank you," Rodrigo said. "That's the way I like it. When the invasion starts, your cadres will be running to the front. Find us a way to go with them. They can take us exactly where we need to be."

"What's the mission?"

"To find Fidel and kill him."

"Wonderful," Vladimiro said grimly.

"I knew you would like it," Rodrigo answered.

* * *

After midnight, Monday, April 17. The word ran in every channel: Invasion! Mercenary landings on Girón and Larga beaches in the Bay of Pigs!

The Bay of Pigs? Why the Bay of Pigs? Rodrigo pondered as he sat at the corner of Infanta and San Lázaro Streets near the Gentleman of Paris. Havana's most famous vagabond was apparently the one man in Cuba whom Castro's police would not dare to touch, and Rodrigo felt safe next to him.

The Bay of Pigs is eighty miles from the Escambray. Can the invaders fight their way past eighty miles of Castro's forces? No. From the Bay of Pigs they cannot reach the Escambray. Why didn't they land near Cienfuegos? That would have placed them a few miles from the objective. What is going on here? Is this a case of the Americans not wanting to show their faces? Did they think that if they put the force down in a remote place, they could have an invasion with nobody noticing? Who can say? Maybe the people who planned this, when they go home at night, sneak up on their wives and take some sex without the ladies finding out.

* * *

At Rebel Youth headquarters, ablaze with excitement, cadres were hurtling over each other to get to the battle.

"Hold your places! We need every one of you in Havana," Joel Iglesias announced to a general groan. "Only Félix goes to the front."

"Why *him?*" someone asked.

"He is combat correspondent for *Mella,*" Joel said matter-of-factly.

Félix told Vladimiro to fetch a safe-conduct document from the IRO offices.

"May I accompany you on the trip?" Vladimiro asked Félix.

"How are you with a jeep?"

"Great! I have done a lot of terrain driving."

"In the combat zone I will have to go by jeep. You can be my driver."

"One more thing," Vladimiro said, trying to contain his nervousness.

"What is it?"

"I have a friend who wants to fight. He is in the *Directorio.* He took part in the assault on the Presidential Palace. He's a good man, even if he's not a socialist," Vladimiro added like a partisan.

"Forget that, Vladimiro. At this moment we are all Cubans, and we need every gun firing. Tell your friend to come."

* * *

On the road to the invasion beaches they were the lone civilian vehicle in a giant swarm of army caravans. Militiamen directing traffic looked hard at Félix's convertible, but when they saw his written orders they gave him quick passage.

The town of Jovellanos was an improbable scene of mass arrests. On almost every street, buses, trucks, autos and ox-carts were moving people to confinement centers.

Félix's car pulled up to the local Rebel Youth headquarters.

"Vladimiro, come inside with me," Félix said. "Núñez, you stay with the car. This is Rebel Youth business only."

Though Félix had said it cordially enough, Rodrigo feared the other man had noticed his grief at the arrests and at the victory shaping up for Castro's government.

After the meeting they went to sleep in a hotel, then left for the front before dawn.

Aguada de Pasajeros, the town nearest the invasion beaches, had become a giant military camp. Everything swayed to the constant rumble of heavy trucks.

"Park it," Félix told Vladimiro. "I have to find out what's going on and get us a jeep. You two stay here."

Rodrigo and Vladimiro shared a spell of quiet apprehension. They felt like juicy targets in the open convertible as great numbers of enemy soldiers went buzzing around them.

Félix was back with a jeep far sooner than they had dared hope.

"Fidel has set up headquarters at the Australia sugar mill but the way there is impassable, so we go to San Blás and the combat zone. Vladimiro, take the wheel!"

The road to San Blás was a rocky dirt path over desolate swampland. *Marabú* shrubs extended across the horizon. Vladimiro had to go slowly to avoid damage from rocks, and soon the fiery midday sun was cooking them.

At San Blás a militia contingent was assembling for a march into the battle. As Félix got out of the jeep, a thin young *guajiro* approached.

"Pijirigua!" Félix cried out with jubilation. "I knew this guy in the Socialist Youth," he explained to his companions. "What are you doing here?"

"Serving in the militia under *Comandante* Drake!"

Félix glanced ahead and saw a Rebel Army major in a green beret, a short man covered with dirt, talking with militia officers.

"That's Duque, isn't it?" Félix asked.

"Yes."

Félix went to meet the major and Rodrigo followed.

When Duque saw Félix he blurted out: "These militia soldiers are superb! I didn't think political people could fight but I have never seen better."

"Political people were fighting this war long before soldiers came into it," Félix said staunchly. "You know, a lot of guns are coming up toward the swamps."

"I am waiting for them," Duque said. "When they get here we

will pound the enemy into dust!"

The militia troops formed ranks and began to move.

"What are you going to do?" Pijirigua called to Félix.

"Go with you!" Félix answered. He turned to Rodrigo and said like an officer: "Núñez, you are with me. Vladimiro, wait here."

Pijirigua joined Duque at the head of the troops. Félix grabbed a Checa submachine gun and fell into the ranks. Rodrigo walked behind him. The soldiers went forward in two columns, one on either side of the road to be able to take cover quickly.

The column in front of Rodrigo snaked around something. It was a corpse in the invaders' uniform. The dead man lay on his side, so covered with dust his features were barely visible. The men just kept moving; their boots made a dull tramp on the road.

Machine-gun fire burst out.

Everyone dove for cover. Félix rolled to his back, flipped off the safety of his Checa, rolled back to his belly and fired into the *marabú* shrubs as the others did. Rodrigo aimed his pistol above the bushes.

No one answered these salvos.

"Cease fire!" A bearded militia captain had come along. "Get up, you queers! No enemy in sight! Form ranks! We keep marching!"

Félix shot the captain a look of scorn as he and the others obeyed.

A jeep spreading clouds of dust scooted up to their position.

"Where is Aragonés?" the driver asked.

"Ahead," the captain said.

On hearing the name of that key official – director of the Integrated Revolutionary Organizations – Félix strode to the jeep driver and asked: "How is Aragonés ahead of us? I thought these troops were the most forward ones."

"Aragonés is in the advance party," the man answered.

Félix put his papers into the driver's hand. "If you are going to Aragonés I have to see him."

The driver looked at Félix's papers and said: "Get in."

"This man comes too." Félix motioned Rodrigo into the jeep.

They drove to a large clearing with a tank in the middle. A soldier on the turret was leaning against a 12.7mm machine gun. Aragonés stood next to the tank, field glasses hanging from his neck.

"What are you doing here?" Aragonés asked Félix. "Where is Joel? And who is this gentleman?"

"Joel is in Havana. This is Núñez from the *Directorio.* What's happening here? We just saw Duque near San Blás. The mercenaries ambushed us on the road."

"They are still around but we have them in a box," Aragonés answered. He pointed to a pair of large magazines on the ground and told the two of them: "Put those on the tank."

They hoisted the heavy magazines. No less heavy to Rodrigo was the idea that those rounds would soon cause grief to his fellow fighters.

Darkness was falling. "I can take you to San Blás," Aragonés told Félix. "Fidel is in the Australia. You should be there but you look tired. Get some sleep and start early."

Their jeep started off at high speed and passed by Drake's column without stopping.

In San Blás, Aragonés took them to the spot where they had left Vladimiro. He was waiting for them right there. Félix greeted him warmly. As the three men walked to a house where they would sleep, Félix told Vladimiro about the ambush. Rodrigo was happy to see that the Rebel Youth leader had grown fond of his comrade.

When they reached their beds Rodrigo told himself: *Tomorrow I kill Castro no matter who dies*. He thought of the sword hanging by a hair and dropped off.

"Let's go!" Félix was exclaiming. Only a minute or two seemed to have elapsed but it was early morning Wednesday, April 19.

"Where to, *caballero?*" Vladimiro said to Félix as he went to start up the jeep.

"To Aguada, and the Australia."

"Australia" meant Fidel. Rodrigo braced himself.

Back across the swamp they went on that rocky dirt road. The trip felt longer than before but at least it was cooler, the sun not yet up.

Aguada was humming with activity. Vladimiro drove to the makeshift command center. Félix jumped out and Rodrigo followed.

"You stay here!" Félix snapped at Rodrigo, who froze.

By now Rodrigo was certain Félix disliked him. That by itself was not hard to swallow. The hard part was Félix's evident disdain for all those who were Not One of Us.

The sun was rising when Félix returned to the jeep.

"Fidel is no longer in the Australia," he said.

"Where is he?" Rodrigo asked.

"No one knows for sure."

"But he commands the army!" Rodrigo exclaimed.

"Yes," Félix reflected strangely. "He is also Fidel. At times his closest comrades lose days looking for him – and they lose time for nothing because the very idea of finding Fidel is a misconception. One doesn't find Fidel. Fidel finds *you.*" Félix paused. "The front has moved forward. The mercenaries have their backs to the beach. It will be over soon. We should be there."

They passed back through San Blás and toward Playa Girón under broiling sunlight.

A minute or two beyond the village they saw a field full of militiamen. The soldiers were picking up various items that the invaders had left behind. Pijirigua came over with some empty cans and dark tablets that looked like soap.

"These are K-rations. I learned that during training," the country lad said with pride.

"Hey!" one of the men exclaimed. "A Colt .45!"

"Don't touch that!" an officer shouted. "It might be a booby-trap!"

"Let's move on," Félix said. "We are not combatants. We have no right to take trophies."

It's a decent thing to say, Rodrigo thought. *He's a man of some principle.*

Pijirigua scampered onto their moving jeep. Félix welcomed him.

As they came close to Playa Girón, Pijirigua said: "Look at that!"

Two men dressed in the camouflage uniforms of the invaders were walking toward the road with their hands in the air. Behind them were the raised rifles of militia soldiers. One prisoner was tall and thin, the other short and sturdy with a crewcut. At the sight of these captives Rodrigo felt sick in his heart.

"The Americans left us in the lurch! This has been hell!" the man with a crewcut said.

Of course, Rodrigo thought. *The skies have been completely peaceful. That means the Americans gave no air cover; and without air cover the invasion has died on the beaches.*

"How dare you speak that way? How dare you? How *dare* you!" Félix, quite out of himself with hostility, was yelling at the crewcut prisoner.

Rodrigo pulled Félix aside and asked: "What is the problem?"

"That man is using the language of a Cuban city-dweller!" Félix whispered ferociously.

"What else would he use? It's his language."

"A mercenary has no right to talk like a Cuban!" Félix insisted.

"But he *is* Cuban."

"People who betray their country give up their country. A man who works for the CIA has no rights as a Cuban!"

"I see," Rodrigo said, containing his own explosive anger.

The prisoners were severely dehydrated; each man had disfiguring cracks on the lips. Pijirigua threw them a water bottle and they drank desperately.

"Thanks," the tall man said after a minute or two. "It's a strong sun here. I'm from La Víbora. Where're you from?"

"This is not a polite conversation!" Félix yelled. He turned to the militiamen and asked: "Should we take these two off your hands?"

Félix was apparently ready to execute the prisoners. Rodrigo put a hand on his pistol, ready to shoot Félix if he made a move to do so.

"No need," one of the soldiers answered Félix. "The militia are holding large groups of mercenaries. We can just add these in."

"Let's keep going toward the beach," Félix told Vladimiro.

As the jeep moved out Rodrigo asked Félix: "Where *are* you from anyway?"

"Why repeat the question?" Félix countered.

"Why avoid it?"

"I do *not* avoid it. As a matter of principle I do not speak about myself."

"Why not?"

"A man's private life doesn't matter. What matters is the revolution. And right now the *only* thing that matters, in case you haven't noticed, is this goddamn war!"

"Human life matters. Would you annihilate those men?"

"Of course! We are at war!"

"All the more reason not to kill wantonly."

"*I* am defending the revolution. *You* are not!"

"Please stop the jeep," Rodrigo said to Vladimiro.

"Keep driving!" Félix ordered and pointed his Checa at Rodrigo. "You are under arrest!"

"On what charge?"

"Suspicion of counterrevolutionary sympathies!"

"Go to hell!" Rodrigo screamed and slapped the barrel of the Checa downward. The gun began firing as if of its own volition. Vladimiro hit the brakes. Rodrigo leapt from the vehicle and ran for cover. Félix pulled the gun back up and aimed, but Vladimiro took off so abruptly that the cadre lost aim and very nearly fell out of the jeep.

XVII.

A PLACE TO SLEEP

Havana, early morning, Sunday, April 23, 1961.

"Doctor! I almost did not recognize you. You have really perfected your vagabond disguise."

"No disguise, *Moro*. I have been on the road for five days."

"When did you arrive?"

"An hour ago."

"Have you had food and rest?"

"Along the road. You know, *Moro,* the people of Cuba are generous. Not even socialism can take that away."

"I guess you have been following the news."

"Actually the news has been following me," Rodrigo said. "No one except the bugs and mice can escape it."

"The Americans beaten! Who could have imagined those people losing a war?"

"Only a nation with the power and intelligence of the United States could have produced a fiasco of this magnitude."

"What do we do?" the Moor asked.

"Ha! That was Lenin's question! Well, here's what I think. Castro's people are hugely overconfident. When people are overconfident they get sloppy. This might actually be the perfect time for an attempt."

"I agree, but first let's find out where our people are."

"I will be looking for them today. And you know, *Moro*, I am still an optimist. Maybe this setback, *even* this setback, will be a benefit if it shows us how to get it right next time."

"I don't know if you really mean that, Doctor. Maybe you just said it to cheer me up. Anyway, thank you. Do you have a place to sleep?"

Rodrigo laughed. "Even an optimist needs a bed! Well, I have one. My ladies in El Vedado are lodging me."

"Be careful! They are still making arrests."

* * *

After a morning and afternoon on the street, Rodrigo was resting in a bedroom at Delia's place. This partisan of the anti-Castro resistance, a widow, lived with her mother.

On a bookshelf near the bed Rodrigo had found a volume of García Lorca and was relishing phrases as delectable to him as pomegranate seeds:

Verde que te quiero verde.
Bajo la luna gitana,
Las cosas la están mirando
Y ella no puede mirarlas.

Rodrigo heard raised voices in the living room. It sounded like an argument. He left his book and walked down the hall.

"What's wrong, Delia?"

"It's the police!" she exclaimed.

Rodrigo saw a submachine gun pointing at him.

My weapon. Where is my weapon? Fuck it! I left my weapon in the bedroom!

"Who is this?" a lieutenant asked the women as he waved his gun at Rodrigo. At the officer's side was a civilian – surely an informant.

"This man is a guest in our house," Delia said nervously.

"We know that conspirators have met here!" the lieutenant snapped. "Are you hiding this man from us?"

They don't know who I am. They didn't come for me. They are here by accident.

"The lady spoke correctly," Rodrigo said. "I am a friend who happens to be visiting."

"What is your occupation?"

"Freelance journalist."

"Did you need this for your reporting?" Another agent was holding up Rodrigo's pistol.

"Who in Cuba does *not* have a weapon?" Rodrigo answered. "I have been carrying it for my own protection."

And if I had not broken my own rule by leaving that weapon behind as a courtesy to the ladies, I would be firing it now.

"It will not help your case if you talk shit to us!" the lieutenant said.

"I think my reply was reasonable," Rodrigo answered.

"Listen, young man." Delia's mother was addressing the lieutenant. "I know you have a job to do, but you do not do it well by using that kind of language before people who are in their own homes!"

"*You* listen," the lieutenant snapped back. "Harboring an enemy of the state is a serious offense!"

"I am not frightened by threats," the lady answered. "I have lived enough. But this man is in the bloom of his life and I *do* care about what happens to him."

God bless you, old woman. Ché Guevara is not more heroic than you are.

The agents did not make an arrest. They simply stayed in the apartment, holding Rodrigo, his hostesses and their own informant like prisoners.

Why keep us here? Maybe they are fishing. They think other conspirators will show up and they want to make a catch.

Hours elapsed, and still the agents did not move from the apartment.

Perhaps they are waiting for nightfall. Secret police, like raccoons, like to hide their doings in darkness. No, I should not compare these agents to raccoons. It would insult the animals.

In mid-evening the agents escorted Rodrigo to their car and drove him to State Security headquarters. At Security they showed Rodrigo to a bench in the receiving area.

Minutes, quarter-hours, hours ticked by. No one approached him. He watched the comings and goings of plainclothes agents, many of whom proclaimed themselves as homosexuals through their effeminate manner of walking and talking.

These men do not hide who they are, and that's to the good. Why shouldn't queers have a decent place in society? Under Batista society treated them like animals. Now they are overjoyed to work for Fidel, who pretends to honor them. Actually Fidel despises them even more than Batista did; and when their utility to him is done he will persecute them with the ferociousness of Torquemada. These queers cannot anticipate that because, for now, Fidel has rescued them from their loneliness; and in that rescue they are paying the terrible price that all lonely people pay. They are giving their hearts in exchange for counterfeit kindnesses.

Just before midnight police took Rodrigo to a tiny office. Three men sat behind a table that filled up almost the entire space. The prisoner sat in a chair next to a red-haired *comandante*. At once Rodrigo understood he was dealing with Manuel Piñiero, Castro's counterintelligence chief, whom everyone called Redbeard.

The arresting officer was there along with another man Rodrigo didn't recognize. All lights in the room were off except for a lamp on the desk which, when Rodrigo sat down, glared into his face from four or five inches away.

"You are Mariano José Núñez Hidalgo," Redbeard said.

"I am," Rodrigo answered.

"Attorney by profession, though you now claim to be a journalist."

"Freelance for *The Washington Star*. I have credentials."

"Of course you do," Redbeard answered. "So would any CIA agent."

He doesn't know anything about me. He's bluffing.

"I do not see how I can be of help to you gentlemen," Rodrigo said.

"You can help us because you are in politics," Redbeard said. "I know you were politically active during the revolutionary struggle."

"As a matter of fact," Rodrigo said, "I consider myself one of the founders of the Cuban Revolution."

"How is that?" Redbeard said skeptically.

"In my student days, along with a newspaperman who was a friend of my father's, I started a group called Journalists United for Liberty."

"That was not revolutionary," Redbeard said. "It was individualist. Many people with political ambitions did similar things at the time. None of it had to do with the revolutionary struggle."

Yes, and what a wonderful revolutionary you are. As judge in the trial of the Batista airmen you threw out a jury's verdict and allowed Fidel to sentence innocent men. In exchange for which you got your promotion to counterintelligence chief. A fine career for a man of principle.

"With all due respect," Rodrigo said, "those people whom you call individualists fought a very dangerous war against Batista in the cities. The urban fighters, unlike the guerrillas, were alone or in very small groups and under constant attack by Batista's forces. The casualties in the cities were maybe fifty times greater than in the Sierra Maestra."

"That is counterrevolutionary talk," Redbeard said ominously.

"I don't agree!" Rodrigo said as he began inching the lamp away from his face and toward the wall. "The people I'm speaking about are revolutionaries! We favor many of the laws that the government has put into effect. We want to be supportive. It's fair to say however that few of us anticipated our fight would lead to a socialist régime."

"Do you not perceive that this government has the overwhelming support of the people?"

"I regard Fidel as an immensely capable leader," Rodrigo said. "If instead of socialism he had embraced some other doctrine, the people would have gone along. Which do *you* think the Cubans love more – socialism or Fidel?"

"They love both! But you yourself are not in sympathy with socialism, are you," Redbeard said.

"I am a patriot. I am in sympathy with anything that advances the country."

"Do you think socialism will advance the country?"

"Perhaps it will. I hope so."

"Doctor Núñez," Redbeard said evenly, "my assessment of you is that you are educated, intelligent, courageous, and quite untrustworthy."

"With respect, sir, I think you can trust me as well as you can trust anyone."

"This interview is over," Redbeard said.

At a sign from the counterintelligence chief a policeman entered and took Rodrigo from the room. The officer led him into another, somewhat larger room that had become a holding cell. About twenty men were on the floor, asleep.

Rodrigo found a piece of floor, lay down and closed his eyes.

Do you have a place to sleep? Who asked me that? The Moor. Long ago, it seems. Can it have been just this morning? We were on the street, in the open air.

At least I'm alive. So what if they don't trust me? They have tens of thousands, hundreds of thousands locked up. So many suspects and so little time. Perhaps they will have no time for Doctor Núñez. If only they do not find out Rodrigo!

XVIII.

THE DOGS ARE TALKING

La Cabaña fortress-prison, early May 1961.

"*¡Moro!* This is not a way I wanted to meet you!" Rodrigo laughed.

"*Sí doctor*. And this is not a disguise I wanted to see you in!"

Rodrigo wore the khaki uniform of a political prisoner. The Moor had sent a younger guard to fetch Rodrigo and bring him to an interrogation room.

"Seriously," Rodrigo said, "what if someone catches you with a prisoner? It might not be safe for you."

"Forget it," the Moor said. "Prison guards are not cadres. We don't ask questions or tell on each other. How are you managing?"

"Not too badly. I pass the time listening to stories. A jail is a house built on stories, wouldn't you say?"

"I would."

"Well, I'm hearing them by the hundreds. Mostly they concern the mass arrests. I've heard about people cooped up in stadiums or theaters; a number dying from heart attacks; women giving birth in the middle of crowds; whole families living under heavy rains."

"Horrible!" the Moor exclaimed.

What do *you* hear?" Rodrigo asked.

"Rumors, lots of rumors: anti-government groups forming up in the mountains; conspiracies in the army and militia ..."

"Hey! I've heard that stuff too! I thought it was a case of prison talk, but if you also are hearing it..."

"Castro's people are spreading rumors again."

"Of course!" Rodrigo exclaimed. "They are still using their counterintelligence. It makes sense. They are not yet out of danger. The Americans are still big, and madder than ever. Fidel's people are afraid that the Bay of Pigs might be their Little Big Horn—"

"Excuse me, Doctor. Is that where the Indians massacred the blond *yanqui* general?"

"George Armstrong Custer. And everyone knows what the *yanquis* did to the Indians after that!"

"Everyone says a second invasion is coming," the Moor added. "Militia units are marching at all hours. The government is keeping up the war fever." He paused. "Have they interrogated you?"

"One meeting with Redbeard, almost cordial. Worse will be coming."

"Doctor, watch out for yourself. They are shooting prisoners with or without trial. Men are doing anything to save their lives. They are giving up their mothers for the chance to go into rehabilitation."

"Hey! That reminds me. Have you seen a man called Juan Pérez?"

"No! Who is he?"

"I met him in one of the converted residences. Day and night prisoners were telling stories about women – women they have loved, and women in their families. One man said: 'I have a daughter, and she is the biggest whore in Cuba!' That was Juan Pérez. Everyone stopped talking and listened to him."

"I bet they did! What did he say?"

"He said: 'From what you men are telling, you fuck everywhere. You fuck your wives and you fuck many other women, but your wives and sisters and mothers and daughters are all saints. If all those women are saints, I have to ask myself: Where do you do your extra fucking? You know what I think? You must all be fucking my daughter!' "

They laughed.

"I have to take you back to your *galera* now," the Moor said. "We cannot speak often, but I will watch out for you – I mean, as long as..."

"I understand. Till death do us part."

* * *

"We have a record of your leaving Cuba last summer, but nothing since then. How did you get back into the country? What have you been doing for the last ten months?"

Hardly an hour after transfer from La Cabaña back to a crowded cell at State Security, Rodrigo was facing a single questioner who sat in an office behind a large desk.

"I have been working in the United States. At present I am a freelance journalist with credentials from *The Washington Star*. I am also trying to sell my articles to CBS television and *The New York Times*. I did not want the government to interfere with my income, so I decided to enter the country without showing a passport."

"Have you received your money?"

"No."

"I see. And how did you enter the country?"

"As crew on a freighter from Central America."

"That story is not believable!" the officer said with annoyance.

"People at *The Washington Star* can confirm it. Let me give you their names. You can check for yourself."

The officer held up a ballpoint pen and said sharply: "If you tell me this pen is gold and ask me to check it, I will not have to check it because I can see the pen is not gold!"

Rodrigo said nothing. He had a sinking feeling inside.

"Do you know what dooms you?" the officer added. "It is that you think in terms of legal processes, evidence, proof, juries and so on. At your trial none of that will count. The only thing that will count is the opinion of State Security. Cooperate with us, and we might take a favorable view of your case."

"I tell you I am a freelance journalist!"

The officer called for a guard.

* * *

Rodrigo settled into the life of State Security Cell Number Three and waited for them to pull him in for more questioning. They didn't; and he found that strange, unnerving.

In Cell Three and in a number of rooms like it, Cuba's most eminent suspects – with some of Redbeard's agents mixed in among them – awaited interrogation. The rather airless room housed fifty men in three-tiered bunks. They shared a single shower in the center of the room with a hole in the floor under it. Despite the lack of luxury, the room was in some sense a prestige location. All the men in Cell Three were there because State Security wanted to empty them of their important secrets. Otherwise they would not be at Security, where space was tight.

As the days and weeks went by, and no one made a move to question him, Rodrigo asked himself tens of times, then hundreds and thousands of times: *Who do they think I am? What do they think I know?*

* * *

La Cabaña fortress, July 1961.

"What do you have to say for yourself, *Moro?* It seems to be getting hot, and I am not just referring to the weather."

"What kind of time did they give you at Security?"

"They gave me time. Security is not the place I would choose to spend a summer holiday. Anyway, it wasn't so bad. I am pleased to see you again."

"Me too! Did they interrogate you?"

"Questioned me just once, very lightly."

"Why did they hold you there all that time?"

"I was hoping you could give me a clue on that."

"I can't. The more I see and hear, the less I understand. Things around this place have gone haywire."

"How so?"

"Well, for one thing we now have Spaniards working as prison guards. Did you see any of them at Security?"

"I am not sure. Who are they?"

"Spanish Communists who went to Russia after the Civil War. The Soviets have sent them here, and now we have them as bosses."

"What a nightmare! *Gallegos* who trained under Stalin, guarding us! No, *Moro,* I have not met any of them and I would not want to. Their sweat would kill an elephant!"

"Well, at least you are not an elephant. You're a man."

"So it appears, and as a man I thought I had seen everything. But the Spaniards back here! And think how they have done it!"

"How do you mean?" the Moor asked.

"I mean, they have returned to Cuba by becoming Soviets!"

* * *

After another transfer to Security, Rodrigo quickly understood why he was there.

As he laid out his few belongings on a vacant bunk bed, a fellow prisoner drew to within inches of Rodrigo's face and boomed out: "Do you know who I am?"

"No, I do not," Rodrigo answered, even though he recognized the man perfectly well.

"Then let me tell you," the man said, swaggering. "My name is Manuel Serrano. I am the boss in this place. Nothing here happens without my permission. Understand?"

As a few men in the background snickered, Rodrigo repeated, "No, I do not," and left the man hanging.

"You will do as I say!" Serrano kept up. "I have influence in here! When this business is over, I am going to be a captain!"

"Well, now that you mention it, I do appreciate your telling me," Rodrigo answered. Serrano, missing the irony, strode off satisfied.

If Rodrigo had been meeting this man for the first time, he would have thought him a fool. Anyone in that cell who actually had authority would never have announced it. As it happened, Serrano was the informer who had brought Security agents to Delia's apartment and caused Rodrigo's arrest.

Serrano was one of those many political captives who had turned state's evidence in a desperate effort to avoid the firing squad. He had convinced himself that by informing he would not merely save his life but get a promotion, too. Rodrigo, as certain as a mathematician who knows the rules of algebra, understood that Serrano would never make captain. This was just the type of man that Castro's officers loved to use up and then destroy. Serrano was a loser who didn't yet see he had lost.

Clearly, the authorities had put Serrano and Rodrigo together in Cell Three to see if a relationship existed between them. Any talk with the man would sink Rodrigo deeper into trouble. This was a quagmire he must step around. He must have nothing to do with Serrano, nothing at all. He must not denounce the man as a snitch, for that would get the man's attention and would make Rodrigo look like someone turning on an ex-comrade. Rodrigo could only ignore Serrano and hope the other man ignored him, too.

That seemed unlikely; but as the hours passed, Serrano made no further moves or gestures in his direction. Indeed, Serrano gave no sign of knowing him at all. How come? Had the man informed on so many people that he had lost track of individuals? Or was his inner turmoil clouding his physical perceptions? Whatever the reason, it was an amazing piece of luck.

On this slippery slope, however, even a lucky turn sent a man sliding further down. After four days of watching Rodrigo escape recognition, Security agents were apparently all the more eager to bag him. Hardly had Rodrigo settled back into the routine of Cell Three than they yanked him from it again.

A trio of guards led Rodrigo out of the building to a car park and opened the back of a small van. The midday summer sun was ferociously hot.

"Inside!" one of the guards directed.

Rodrigo looked in and saw no windows, seats or padding of any kind.

"Where would you like me to sit?" Rodrigo asked.

"Anywhere you can," another said impatiently.

Rodrigo got in and reclined on bare metal as the door slammed behind him.

Minutes elapsed. The van did not move. In minutes more the airless metal compartment was an oven. Rodrigo peeled off his clothes as he began to sweat profusely.

After some two hours a soldier opened the door and asked: "Warm?"

Rodrigo breathed in and smiled. "A bit on the warm side, yes."

The soldier slammed the door in a pique.

The van started to move. Rodrigo could hear a car in front and another behind. All went in high gear, attacking the curves like racers. In the metal compartment with nothing to hold onto, Rodrigo worked like a judo wrestler to keep the tumbles from killing him.

In something like an hour they had slowed down. The van stopped. The compartment door opened. Rodrigo emerged naked, carrying his clothes and shoes. When he focussed he saw he was at the rear entrance of a large house.

A gang of tough men surrounded him and made threatening gestures. One of them threw a towel over his head; others guided him up some stairs. When the towel came off, Rodrigo was in a room that State Security had re-designed for its purposes. Boards were tightly nailed across windows and closets. The room was bare, with no place to lie down or rest one's head except the floor. The door had a one-way peephole. In place of the light fixture on the ceiling was a large bulb with a metal frame.

Guards took Rodrigo's clothes and shoes away, leaving him only his drawers. In the broiling room, even they were too much to bear. He used them for a pillow. When his eyes began to burn, he hung the drawers over the bulb.

"Take those drawers away from the light!" a guard shouted through the peephole.

"But the bulb is hurting my eyes!" Rodrigo said, playing naïve.

"That's why we put it there!" the guard yelled back.

Day became night and then day again; or so Rodrigo supposed, because the earth's passage between light and dark was invisible to him. All he saw was the bulb, and pretty soon he was seeing spots.

One way to tell time was to observe when he wanted to sleep, but sleep was irregular because at all hours the guards made terrible stamping noises with their boots and went around the corridors yelling at no one in particular: "On your feet!"

Another way to tell time was from the food. Milk with coffee and a piece of bread meant breakfast. Lunch and supper consisted of rice and beans, at times with a little meat. A plastic milk container, cut in half, served as a water cup. Rodrigo's jailers knew to a measure how much food and water a man needed to survive in a hothouse. That was precisely the ration the prisoner got. After a couple of days Rodrigo was thinning out from dehydration.

To go to the bathroom he had to call for the guards. A pair of soldiers came into his room while another stood outside with a rifle. They took him down the hall to a closet with a hole in the floor. They permitted no bathing or shaving. For lack of soap and water, an irritation on his scalp developed into a massive itch.

Rodrigo spent his days and nights in a constant practice of yoga and meditation, his only means to keep fit and retain the sense of self that his captors were working to destroy.

"Bring down the yogi!" someone shouted.

From the blurred focus of a sitting meditation, Rodrigo saw the door open and two pairs of boots come into the room, with another pair outside. This was the drill for the bathroom; only, he had not requested the bathroom.

"On your feet!" one of the guards snapped.

Rodrigo drew himself up to standing posture, making the guards wait a good long time. He pressed into these men with his gaze and found a pair of apprehensive youngsters. They seemed to be lost in a forest, looking at a mean old tree that might any second come alive and thrash them with its limbs.

Ha! Rodrigo thought. *I have my balance, and you lack yours.*

One of the soldiers put a towel on his head, and they guided him downstairs.

When the towel came off Rodrigo saw he was in a room with a small liquor bar. The cooler air of this room felt like rose-petals on his skin; and the light was gentle to his eyes. Glass doors faced a terrace and back yard. Two men in "civvies" were looking at him.

"We work with State Security and are here to question you. Please take a chair," one of them said.

Rodrigo sat on a bar stool, the first piece of furniture he had enjoyed in many days.

The man in charge was tall, slender and light-skinned. The other was shorter, stockier, and dark. Rodrigo made up names for them. The lead questioner became Porfirio, the other man José.

"We need to know when and how you arrived on your last trip to Cuba, and what you have been doing since then," Porfirio said.

"Be sure you do not leave anything out," José added.

Rodrigo went through his story of being a freelance journalist and of landing in Cuba as a stowaway. He gave a good many of his viewpoints about Castro's embracing Communism and about the Bay of Pigs. The interrogators listened without saying a word.

When this monologue had stopped, Porfirio said: "Doctor Núñez

– or should I call you 'Rodrigo'? – you are in a very bad situation. We know who you are. We know what you have been doing. And we know that you came to Cuba not by boat but by plane *and parachute!"*

"I do not understand. My name is Núñez."

"We know you are Rodrigo," Porfirio said. "And we know you landed at *this place."*

Porfirio's finger was on the area of a map corresponding exactly to Ernesto's farm. Rodrigo kept a straight face and said nothing.

"We know what you are thinking," José said. "Who else is under arrest? Who could have talked? Let me tell you. We have arrested everyone down to the dogs, and even the dogs are talking to us."

Gentlemen, you have it wrong. There is no question here. It was not a dog who talked. It was Ernesto.

"Understand this," Porfirio said. "What we know about you is more than enough to send you to the firing squad. Your only chance to save yourself is to tell us about your activities. If you refuse to tell us, you will be executed."

"I have nothing to tell you," Rodrigo said.

"*¡Coño!* Don't talk shit to us!" Porfirio exclaimed.

"That's rude," Rodrigo countered.

The glass doors facing the terrace swung open. Another man in "civvies" entered. "You have a phone call," he told Porfirio.

The man spoke in a Spanish accent. Rodrigo cringed at the thought of those twisted men, *gallegos* trained in Russia, behind the scene.

Porfirio went outside. The *gallego* motioned José to the terrace, where the two spoke in whispers.

The inner door opened, and in came the escort of guards. They put a towel on Rodrigo's head and led him upstairs. As he entered his quarters the heat nearly took his breath away; and the light from the eternal bulb was again stinging his eyes.

Four days later the peephole snapped open. "Rodrigo!" someone said.

The mental composure he had eked out for himself kept Rodrigo from turning around at his cover-name.

The door opened, and a pair of uniforms appeared with a towel.

Porfirio and José were waiting at the bar downstairs. As before the room was cooler to him, and more gently lit. The interrogators felt familiar. Rodrigo thought back to the Moor's statement about his brother: *He is used to his interrogators, and likes to talk to them.* At once Alberto's unshaven, startled face was before him.

Porfirio began. "Listen, Rodrigo ..."

"My name is Núñez," Rodrigo snapped.

The interrogators looked at each other gravely.

"We invite you to save your life by working with us," Porfirio said. "We are not promising to set you free. You will have to stay in prison, but not for long. What we ask is very simple. We know there are still arms supplies we have not found. Let us take you to a telephone. Call your friends and tell them to leave because State Security is going there. Give us the address. Your friends escape, we take the weapons, and you keep your life."

"I know nothing about hidden weapons."

Again the interrogators looked at each other.

"What can you tell us about Benjamín?" José asked.

"Benjamín del Cordobés?"

"Yes, Benjamín del Cordobés," Porfirio said with annoyance.

"He is a friend of mine."

"We know! Has he been involved in what you are doing?"

"In my journalism? No, not at all."

Now Rodrigo's interrogators looked at him with a mixture of scorn and bewilderment.

"What can you tell us about your brother?" Porfirio said.

"That is a moot subject," Rodrigo answered in a low voice.

"Why moot?" José said.

"I believe that when a man dies, he earns the right to be left in peace."

"Not with us. Your brother was a traitor and a thief. We know you saw him in confinement, and were helping him."

"I did nothing to help my brother. In visiting him I only did a brother's duty. I regret you do not understand that. My brother was no traitor. He worked closely with Fidel and Ché, and was glad to do so. You may or may not be correct in calling him a thief. He died before those charges could be proven; but even assuming he took money, it may be that the only difference between him and others is that my brother had the misfortune to get caught."

"Those statements are unacceptable," Porfirio said angrily.

Another man entered the room and whispered something to Porfirio, who got up and left. José followed him out. A few minutes later the escort of soldiers took him back to his room.

Why am I defying these people? Am I deranged? No. I simply have a motive other than saving my life. If a man is concerned about saving his life, it doesn't matter how strong or courageous he is. That man, sooner or later, is going to talk. I am trying to keep those people from getting information. That *is what allows me not to talk.*

In a few days more the soldiers brought him for another session. Rodrigo answered questions by turning them into discussions of ideology or of recent history.

"Security expects us to make progress together," Porfirio said. "It has little use for your political opinions."

"But the fact remains," Rodrigo said. "The revolution is in danger because of its hostility toward the United States. The Americans will not tolerate a Cuba closely allied to the U.S.S.R. If the Cuban government maintains its present policy, it dooms itself."

"We will not hear more of this," Porfirio said. "By withholding your cooperation, you are marching straight to the wall. It's evident you are determined to commit suicide. Our sessions are over. If we ask to see you again, it will be for some other reason."

The interrogators got up and walked out.

Some other reason? What could it be? No, that was only their way of saying goodbye. I will never see those two again.

A few days later he was again under the towel and going downstairs. He felt himself outdoors.

I am going back to Havana for trial and execution.

When the towel came off he found himself in the liquor bar, facing Porfirio and José.

"Why don't you tell us about yourself," José said.

"Tell you about myself? In what respect?"

"Anything you like, for as long as you like," Porfirio said. "Whatever you want us to know."

That caught Rodrigo off balance. He had not expected to be here, and the interrogators' tactic was new to him.

Why refuse? Apart from the conspiracy, I have nothing to hide. Let them see my life and make of it what they can.

And then the loneliness of the last weeks, the frustration, the uncertainty, the overweening energy of fear, coursed out of him.

The words came tumbling over each other like patter from a comic opera; but this was no comedy, it was a saga that reached back through generations, each character showing in fine lines, even long-dead ones whom the narrator had not met. All of them, beloved and memorable, sprang to life under the protean mask of Rodrigo, who played everyone in his tremendous cast: the humble country grandma sweeter than a ton of sugar; the carousing uncle who looked like Santa Claus and slept with every maid in the house; a crazy aunt who told the same story over and over even when no one was in earshot; the gullible cousin who thought he could make a colt run faster by telling the horse that a mare was waiting for him; and animals too, every one of them loaded with personality: a prize-fighting cock too haughty to look you full in the eye, presenting a mere profile; the well-loved dogs and cats, the ever-intelligent pigs, the colorful spiders, the legions of ants. A boyhood of study re-emerged in the mythic figure of Achilles, to whom the gods had offered the choice of a long uneventful life or a short intense one. The student, he himself, rejected Achilles' choice and vowed to live a long intense life. He honored that resolution by entering the fight against Batista, the greatest episode of his existence – one that filled him, even now, with dread and pride....

As the massive recitative drew to a close, Porfirio said, "It would be a shame for such an existence to be cut short."

"Is there *anything* you can offer that might give us a reason to spare you?" José asked.

This question took Rodrigo by surprise. Having emptied his soul, he was in no position to answer.

"Could you let me have two or three days to think?" he asked.

Porfirio and José looked at each other. "All right," they said, and left.

In his room, Rodrigo pondered.

For those people my life or death is a matter of convenience. If it is convenient that I die, they crush me like a bug. If it is convenient that I live, they keep me alive no matter how they hate me.

How would it be convenient for them that I live?

They want to use my survival instinct for their purposes. I would be stupid to go down that road. As soon as they think they have learned what I know, they will execute me.

My way out is to use their *survival instinct for* my *purposes.*

"So what are your thoughts?" José asked when Rodrigo had been brought back to the bar.

"I do know a way we can work together," the prisoner said.

"Let's hear it."

"Very well. In these last days I have been thinking about the difficulty in which the revolution finds itself...."

"Are we being treated to another of your analyses?" José broke in.

"It's the plain and simple truth. The Cuban government has won a military and political victory; but unless the government can turn this victory to diplomatic gain, it will backfire. The Americans are determined to take revenge on Cuba. Unless an agreement is made and made quickly, they will come again, and in force. When that happens, the suffering in Cuba will be unspeakable. We still have a chance to reach an accord with the United States, and I believe I am in a position to mediate it."

"How high do your contacts go?" Porfirio asked.

"Up to the top."

The questioners fell silent.

Of course they have nothing to say to this. I have made the matter bigger than they are.

The prisoner added, like the attorney he was: "If I am instrumental in this endeavor, I do not expect you merely to drop your charges against me, whatever those are. I expect you to compensate me for my trouble."

"We will have to get back to you on this," Porfirio said.

In his room, Rodrigo turned over and over in his mind the move he had played.

My interrogators are out of the game. Not even the head of Security has power to decide on this proposal. In the one-man state, one man has authority. The thing must go to Fidel.

Suppose Fidel places me in Washington as Cuba's mediator. I will contact my American friends and they will ask me: What are you doing here, you son of a bitch? Trying to save your neck?

I will tell them: No! I am on your side. Whose side are you *on? I do not want you to negotiate. I want you to fight. I came to tell you that. And whatever you do, I will keep fighting. When our talking is done, put me back in the mountains of Cuba. Many of my comrades are dead. I want to finish what they died for, not save my neck in something else.*

Will my friends in Washington believe me? Most likely they will not. If Castro doesn't kill me, chances are the Americans will.

I am under sixty feet of water.

What does a man do under sixty feet of water? The only thing he can do. He looks around for some air.

When Rodrigo came downstairs again, he could feel tension and hostility from his interrogators even before the towel was off.

"We reject your proposal," Porfirio said. "The department has determined that you want to cheat us of yourself. We cannot allow that."

As he heard these phrases and understood the sentence of death behind them, Rodrigo felt his knees give way. This instinctive behavior disgusted him. He pulled himself up on the strength of his disgust, using every ounce of resolve to keep his body on top of his feet.

"What do you plan to tell the Revolutionary Tribunal?" José asked.

"If you gentlemen are so sure of your case against me, why should you concern yourselves about what I will say?" Rodrigo asked back.

The interrogators went away without answering, and Rodrigo went back to his room.

My defiance has gotten me nowhere. It has only made me square with myself. That will not be enough – but it has *to be enough!*

After another eight or ten days empty of human contact save for toilet trips, Rodrigo heard the peephole click open.

"You are leaving," a guard said.

"On such brief notice?" Rodrigo answered. "How can I gather up all my possessions?"

"We have your possessions here! Put these on."

The door opened. Someone handed him his clothes and shoes. After dressing he got the towel and went downstairs. When the towel came off he was at the back of a small truck like the one that had brought him from Havana. He climbed into the empty rear compartment, and in a short time the truck was moving.

* * *

After a month at the special interrogation facility, Rodrigo's old quarters at Cell Three had an almost homelike feel.

"Prisoner Núñez!" a guard's voice boomed out.

"I am Núñez," Rodrigo said, presenting himself at the cell door.

"You come with me." The guard held a machine gun, and was in a nasty mood.

As they walked down the hall, Rodrigo told himself: *You are go-*

ing to your execution. Behave! Show them nothing.

They turned into another hall, the guard scolding him all the way. Around a third corner the guard pushed him into an office. Behind some bars were his mother and her younger sister, Celia.

Rodrigo, since his capture, had not seen a mirror. Now he was viewing himself in the mirror of his mother's face. The heat and lack of water during weeks of interrogation had emaciated him. His mother gave him a horrified look. In a split second she had composed herself and resumed her habitual toughness.

"How are things with you?" she asked.

"I have kept my head high," he answered.

"Good."

"Brace yourselves," Rodrigo said. "I am going to the firing squad."

"You cannot give up hope!" *la vieja* insisted. "People everywhere are praying for you, and your *friends* are preparing to intervene."

With the guard a few feet away, Rodrigo took care not to react to this mention of the CIA.

"I want to write a message to my son and daughter," Rodrigo said to his mother and the guard at once.

"Write the message and show it to me," the guard directed as he pushed paper and a pen to the prisoner.

Rodrigo wrote: "Dear Estéban and Yrene, Take good care of each other. Your voices were always my music."

He gave the paper to his mother, who showed it to the guard.

"You may keep the message," the guard told her.

"*Vieja*, be brave," Rodrigo said. "Always care for each other."

"We know how to do that – but you will not go to the firing squad!"

XIX.

THE INQUISITION

BHAMM! A volley of rifles knocked Rodrigo and other prisoners awake. Next came a single shot, the *coup de grâce,* and the grinding of a truck engine. They were taking a corpse away.

Almost all the hundred or so men in La Cabaña prison Gallery 16 pressed themselves to the double-barred window that looked out to the execution ground. "*¡Monstruos!*" they screamed. "*¡Hijos de puta! ¡Viva Cuba libre! ¡Viva Cristo Rey!*"

"*¡Apunten!*" "*¡Fuego!*" The executioner's cry rode over this hubbub. *BHAMM!* A further single shot rang out and the truck took off with another corpse.

A few men who had not crowded at the window were reciting the rosary. Rodrigo held back from the window and he did not recite the rosary. He did not take religious remedies, and he would be seeing the execution ground soon enough. In a few hours his own trial would convene. Almost surely he would get a death sentence, and at this time tomorrow his fellow prisoners would be listening to the rifle blasts that finished him.

"Prisoner Núñez!"

Everyone turned around. The prisoners feared that one of their number was going to the wall without trial. A group formed around Rodrigo and shook his hand as he moved toward the guard.

"This way!" the guard said snappily.

It must be my turn. Well, at least I can die without a show-trial.

They walked for some minutes. The guard opened a door to an interrogation room.

"Wait here," the guard told Rodrigo and locked the door.

When the door opened again the large figure of the Moor, cloaked in a heavy sadness, was before him.

"*¡Moro!* You shouldn't be seeing me. This is extremely dangerous for you!"

"Not now. Everyone is watching..."

"Of course! They are watching the games," Rodrigo said smiling. "But what about the man who came for me? He seemed angry."

"Only because I took him away from watching. No problem with him. He is indebted to me, and loyal as a dog."

"I appreciate this, *Moro*. It is not an easy thing to say good-bye."

"Doctor, I am so sorry."

"Don't say that. I have been honored by our comradeship. Neither of us has reason for regrets. I have none."

The large man reached over to Rodrigo and folded him into his arms. Then, very quickly, the Moor was gone.

Rodrigo's return trip to Gallery 16 felt quite a lot shorter than the outgoing journey. When his cellmates greeted him he said: "The reports of my death are premature by at least a day."

* * *

"Prisoner Núñez!" It was one of the Spanish guards giving the summons.

"Right here, comrade custodian," Rodrigo answered. "I have no intention of missing my own trial. Besides, I enjoy being punctual and this could be my last chance to do it."

"You may be smiling now," the guard blustered, "but let us see how your legs tremble when you go before the firing squad!"

Rodrigo's cellmates let loose a hail of insults. "Communist bully!" "Red queer!" "Why don't you just go and drink your mother's menstrual fluid?"

"Who said that?" the guard screamed.

"You dumb cuckold! Nikita said it when he did your wife!"

"Hey!" Rodrigo called back to his fellows. "Let's not sink to that level! Please excuse my friends," he told the guard. "They do not mean to offend you. They only value my life."

The guard took Rodrigo's arm and hustled him off.

They came to an antechamber where guards were gathering prisoners for trial from all holding areas of the huge fortress. It was a hefty crowd, sixty or so men plus half a dozen women. Everyone kept quiet, surely to prevent their jailers from seeing who knew whom. Rodrigo recognized several people whose paths he had crossed in the various struggles – including Manuel Serrano, the informer he had last encountered in Security Cell Three.

A big detachment of guards led the prisoners out to a courtyard where a mob was waiting. This mob included ordinary people of all ages and types whom the authorities had collected for a "spontaneous" demonstration. They lined the whole route to the trial chamber, hurling slogans and spitting venom at the accused. As Rodrigo came into the large meeting-room, a breach appeared in the wall of people and his mother stood before him.

"You cannot give up hope!" she whispered. "Your situation might still change!"

The old lady stepped back through the mob to the side of her sister Celia. Both were smiling at Rodrigo, trying to show confidence; but they were chagrined at the massive spectacle of grief and hatred. As Rodrigo took in the old lady's words he remembered a similar line he had spoken to his brother Alberto, and his heart sank.

A crowd of hundreds had packed the trial-room: accused, family members, lawyers, prosecutors, tribunes, soldiers, journalists and diplomats, all swimming in a sea of people who had come to show the revolution's colors.

"Revolutionary Tribunal Number One is now in session!"

The speaker was Tribunal President Lieutenant Emiliano Anglada. This man, a comrade to Rodrigo in the war against Batista, had risen to become one of Castro's most eminent and dreaded jurists. Political prisoners called him "Emiliano the Wall."

The proceeding began with testimony by Security officers who gave statements against individual defendants. At times these officers answered questions from one of five tribunes or from the prosecutor, Doctor Hernán Serafín, whom prisoners had nicknamed "Pool of Blood." Rodrigo, as he listened to these testimonies, recalled some words from an officer who had questioned him: *At your trial the only thing that will count is the opinion of State Security.*

A few moments later, as if Rodrigo's very memory had summoned him, that same officer appeared before the tribunal. The prosecutor gave his name as State Security Agent Feliciano González.

Without prompting the officer said: "Prisoner Mariano José Núñez Hidalgo, lawyer and self-proclaimed journalist, is in fact the notorious terrorist leader whose code-name is Rodrigo. Under that name he has been conspiring against the revolution since Year One. In his efforts to destroy the revolutionary government he has worked as a CIA agent, has smuggled guns, has plotted terrorist attacks, and has made numerous illegal passages to and from Cuba. Last March he parachuted into Camagüey province with a cache of weapons from the CIA. Only the sale of those weapons on the black market by an opportunistic colleague prevented their use against the Revolutionary Armed Forces. Last year *Comandante* Ché Guevara ordered the arrest of Alberto Núñez, the prisoner's brother, on charges of embezzling official funds. Alberto Núñez committed suicide in prison before State Security could question him fully. In the opinion of the Department of the Interior and of State Security, the prisoner Núñez-Rodrigo has been and continues to be a serious threat to the safety of the revolution."

The thought weighing on Rodrigo was the suffering he had brought to his parents. Not even his children would suffer as much. Elena was an attractive young woman. Under *la doctora's* eye she would remarry and find for their kids the fatherly love they craved. Maybe the kids would be better off with a man who did not live at risk. Parents, though, are never better off without the children they have lovingly raised. Those mentions of Alberto must have made stab-wounds in his mother's heart, as they did in his own. To what end had he himself done a butcher's work on his own sibling? Whom had he helped or saved by that act? What use had any of it been, those years of struggle and transgression? Whose life had he bettered? Whose happiness promoted? When the shooting was over he had failed in all his objectives, he had left his family in ruins, and he had stripped his parents of their children.

After these testimonies Emiliano the Wall ordered a break for lunch. As the guards took prisoners out of the room, relatives and friends approached. Soldiers blocked the way, screaming: "You cannot go there!"

Rodrigo's mother walked right through the line of troops and got close to her son.

"How is it with you?" she asked.

"I am going to the firing squad."

"No you are not!" she exclaimed. "When they call you before the Tribunal you must not say a word."

That piece of advice fell strangely on Rodrigo's ears. Like any son he had received and discarded his mother's unsolicited views on thousands of subjects; but now he felt she had given him something quite useful. How or from where she knew it he could not say, but her advice made perfect sense. That puzzled and pleased him at the same time.

When court reconvened Emiliano the Wall summoned each of

the defendants to the tribunal and asked: "Do you declare yourself guilty or not guilty?"

A number declared not guilty and tried to dispute the charges against them. A greater number gave noncommittal answers. To many the judge only said: "Do you ratify the statements you have already made to State Security?" They answered: "I do." Those statements remained under wraps and did not come out in court.

Most active of the witnesses was the informer Serrano, who declared himself "guilty with extenuating circumstances." When the tribunal asked for an explanation Serrano spoke about other defendants, giving details of their activities. Again Serrano registered no awareness of Rodrigo and gave no evidence against him.

"Mariano José Núñez Hidalgo! You will approach the tribunal!"

Rodrigo stood before the five tribunes. His old comrade Emiliano the Wall was the one addressing him.

"How do you declare – guilty or not guilty?"

"I abstain," Rodrigo said.

"You may return to your seat," the judge proclaimed ritually, and with an undertone of consideration that Rodrigo did not miss.

The prosecutor Serafín, "Pool of Blood," rose to make his argument. He went through the defendants by name, calling for sentences that were progressively heavy: 10 or 15 years, 20 or 30. The trial-room filled up with cries from spouses, parents, relatives and friends. Emiliano the Wall slammed his gavel and ordered silence but the commotion went on, rising in pitch as the sentences got heavier.

"Manuel Serrano López: the State calls for penalty of execution before a firing squad. Carlos Vinay García: the State calls for penalty of execution before a firing squad. Mariano José Núñez Hidalgo: the State calls for penalty of execution before a firing squad...."

On hearing his name Rodrigo shot a glance at Emiliano the Wall. His old comrade was looking away from him. At that moment however the judge made a gesture of tapping his wrists together as if to say: "My hands are tied."

It was small comfort to Rodrigo but it was a comfort. Their friendship forged under fire might not suffice to save his life, but it stood for something that even loyalty to Castro could not wipe out.

The doleful sounds of people who were about to lose loved ones for years or forever had crescendoed to the ceiling. Emiliano the Wall rapped his gavel but the disorder of life pleading for life would not stop, and went on for many minutes.

When the cries had abated enough for the judge to make himself heard, he said: "Do any of the accused wish to add anything to their statements?"

At this invitation the informer Serrano approached the tribunal.

"The prosecutor has no right to ask the death penalty for me," he said, still arrogant but with a very wide tremor in the voice. "Mine is a special case."

"The prosecutor knows what he is doing," the judge said with finality; and Serrano went back to his chair a devastated man.

Emiliano the Wall declared the proceedings closed. The armed guard of soldiers and militia began leading prisoners from the court. As they did, the revolutionary mob formed for another "spontaneous" protest against the men and women whom the court had condemned.

Rodrigo saw his mother standing close behind the troops in the midst of the mob. "Good-bye, *vieja!*" he said loudly. "Say good-bye to the old man. Heads high."

"This thing is not over yet," she answered in a stentorian voice.

Outdoors, night had fallen. The trial had gone on for fourteen hours. Klieg lights illumining the courtyard showed the gracious lines of the building's architecture, a piece of old Spain. After the blackened sky had given way to dawn, after day had passed to night and day again for tens and hundreds of years to come, this old stone creature, handsome in spite of itself, would live on; and Rodrigo envied it.

As they passed through the courtyard under the looks and taunts of revolutionary partisans, the condemned encountered yet another group: a mass of screaming children, nine, ten and eleven years old, who brandished "checa" submachine guns. Soldiers orchestrated the movements of these gun-toting children, whose expressions of hatred were deeply unnerving.

In the middle of the courtyard the prisoners came to a halt near an army truck.

"The following persons will step forward: Manuel Serrano López; Carlos Vinay García; Mariano José Núñez Hidalgo; Ramón Quevedo Blanco..."

Those about to die were leaving for the execution grounds.

Under guard Rodrigo and the others stepped aboard the truck where twice their number of soldiers waited for them. Good-byes began to fly back and forth between the doomed men in the truck and the prisoners in the courtyard. These good-byes were no more than a name: "Vinay!" "Rivero!" "Núñez!" "Izaguirre!" "Quevedo!" As they cried out the names, many raised their arms with emotion; and the parting was intense for all the prisoners who, even without knowing each other, shared a kind of love through the choice they had made.

These calls provoked the crowd to a furious response. Troops gave prisoners a good many extra shoves. Cries of "Kill them all!" pierced the night-time air as the children waved their guns and screamed with ever greater ferocity.

Rodrigo surveyed the scene from his perch on the army truck, with the extra-clear vision of one who knows himself to be at the portals of death. Here were the masses pushing a few offenders to their punishment, acting with a fervor they called "revolutionary" but was really superstitious; for they were trying to appease a remote, dreaded, all-powerful God. In the night-time setting of the old Spanish courtyard set ablaze by fires of light, Rodrigo saw that the ceremony unfolding before his eyes was an *auto-da-fé*. Under the compacted meanness of modern tyranny, the Inquisition had sprung back to life in an even more sinister guise.

In ancient Spain the King and the Grand Inquisitor had been two different people. Even when Church and State were close, they were distinct; and even during the cruelest of times it had been possible for kindness to run out through the cracks between those monoliths. In that setting a legendary man called "Rodrigo" had made a breach between King and Inquisitor. Through that breach, and at the cost of Rodrigo's own life, kindness had flowed forward. Now, on the Hispanic island of Cuba and in the person of Fidel Castro, King and Inquisitor had become one. This Inquisition was airtight. Nothing touched it. People by the thousands had gone into death, into exile, into despair; and this Inquisition kept eating victims. Soon enough new generations would arise that had never known the difference between Church and State, Spirit and Society, Faith and Law. They would fall to tyranny ignorant – unable to see, much less tear down, the walls inside themselves.

Looking out from the army truck, Rodrigo saw that future now actual in the form of children hurling slogans and waving guns.

Unlike most of the Inquisition's victims, Núñez-Rodrigo would not perish for his words or for his faith. He had plotted to overthrow a government. The blood of others was on his hands. His personal downfall gave no cause for complaint. In reason he knew his death would not be unfair. To die for having fought was nothing perverse. It was natural, a part of humankind's animal heritage. The contest in which Núñez-Rodrigo had played was a struggle of kill-or-die. He saw his fate with an animal's unclouded vision. He did not lose track of himself in more layered emotions like regret or self-doubt. He simply clung to life, his thoughts quite free from any idea that things ought to have turned out better than they had.

Still, despite his animal's resolve, Núñez-Rodrigo's indignation blazed forth at the sight of those gun-toting kids – innocents who had become earnest pupils in Castro's Academy of Hate.

With his Inquisition Castro had gone beyond destroying humans. He was altering humanity – twisting children into bearers of arms and ill-will. His government was winning praise from across the world for its generosity to poor people, for its free schools and medical care; but what human purpose did it serve for millions of healthy, literate young souls to take shape or be misshapen as a single man wished?

The truck bearing the six doomed men stopped at a bridge overlooking the execution ground. A small crowd was on the bridge, waiting for the drums to roll.

"Come on, let's get out of here," one young woman said to another.

"No, wait!" her companion answered. "It's going to start any minute!"

From the truck Rodrigo boomed out: "*Señoritas*, don't leave! We'll give you a good show!"

The women lowered their heads as the truck went forward.

Very well then, old fellow. Soon you will see whether the human soul really does transmigrate.

You know what your trouble is, Núñez? You have always been too much the optimist.

XX.

COURAGE

"I have brought harm to my fellow men. I have strayed from the sight of God. I do not want to die in disgrace. *Caballeros,* I am at your feet. Forgive me!"

The informer Serrano had been weeping ever since the *auto-da-fé.* As the condemned men awaited their turn in a cluster of "chapels" or one-man cells, he kept begging for absolution.

A very young guard appeared in the narrow corridor between the cells. "Quevedo Blanco!" he demanded.

The ex-Rebel Army captain stood up. Before going with the guard he looked at Serrano.

"Let God forgive you," Quevedo said gallantly. "I have already done so."

Serrano bawled even louder.

"What is he doing?" Carlos Vinay muttered.

"He is more afraid of God than of Fidel," Rodrigo said.

"It's the ultimate heresy," Vinay answered.

"*¡Apunten!*" "*¡Fuego!*" A barrage rang out, followed by the *coup* *de grâce*, and Quevedo was gone.

The guard was again in the passageway. "Serrano López!"

The weeping informer stood on wobbly legs. Rodrigo thought of his brother at their last visit.

"Hey man, don't worry," the guard said. "At the wall things are over quickly."

The other men felt disgust at this comment.

Serrano looked at the guard and said: "It's what's on the other side of the wall that worries me."

In that moment the unthinkable became true: the informer had gained his dignity.

"¡Apunten!" "¡Fuego!" BHAMM! Serrano was gone.

The guard was back, looking straight at Rodrigo. "You next, old man."

Rodrigo stood up. "Aren't you going to say my name, too?"

"Núñez Hidalgo! All right, you old stinker. Are you satisfied?"

"Well done! I hope you still have some courage left in you for *my* execution."

"You son of a turd! In a minute you'll get what's coming to you!"

"Perhaps, but you will not be the one who gives it."

The guard grabbed him roughly and pushed him down a corridor, then out to the execution ground.

The commander placed Rodrigo in front of the wall.

"Blindfold?"

"No, thank you."

Rodrigo looked toward the bridge to find the women he had seen earlier. They were still there. He gazed intently at them.

"¡Apunten!"

Good. I die with the feeling of those women inside.

"¡Descanso!"

Rest?

"Mariano José Núñez Hidalgo! The Commander-in-Chief of the Revolutionary Armed Forces has been pleased to commute your sentence of death to thirty years' imprisonment."

Thirty years. More than my age. It's a life. A new life. I have come back for another life.

He felt like a field of freshly cut grass.

The commander took Rodrigo by the arm and handed him to the guard.

"So they let you stay on this side of the wall," the guard said decently.

"I don't know where I am," Rodrigo answered. "My eyes are still opening."

XXI.

TIME FLIES

From Rodrigo's memoir, composed in 1983 – Year 25 of the Cuban Revolution:

Time in prison moves very slowly. The important thing is to make sure it does move; for when it no longer moves, you die.

During the weeks and months after the mock execution, time did not move for me but that was only natural. I had been reborn. My senses were groping through life as if for the first time, and the passage of days and weeks was as unremarkable to me as it is to a child. Inevitably I regained my senses and became a man again. I was in a huge circular cage, crowded with other men for whom time was standing still. These men knew their children were growing, they could feel their wives longing for them, while they themselves, who suffocated from lack of love, were going nowhere; and I came to understand the old Chinese saying that the man who goes nowhere is drifting toward oblivion.

About myself I had a simple question: Why was I here? Who or what had concerted to save me? On that point I saw nothing clear.

I was simply glad to be alive. A life in prison – even a lifetime in prison – was better than no life at all.

For a while my fellow prisoners and I were able to distract ourselves with the threat of war hovering over America and Cuba. A war could give us our freedom if Castro perished. A genuine peace could do the same if it included a release for us.

Most prisoners hoped for war, including a thousand men from the invasion force who were now captives. Those men were wild with anger and impatience. Every time we heard airplane noise in the circulars they bolted up and screamed: "Here comes our air support!" It was an embittered reference to the planes the Americans had failed to send to the invasion. Nothing would have made those men happier than to hear American bombs falling.

As it happened, we were living with bombs of another kind. Before our eyes Castro's men had set dynamite charges in all four circulars at the enormous complex for political prisoners on the Isle of Pines.

The message was clear. If the Americans invaded Cuba, Castro would stage a *Götterdämmerung* which would blow us to bits. Over a period of months, through painstaking secret labor, we found and pulled the wires from all the dynamite charges. Of course this was not the end of our worries, for we could hardly guess at what other surprises Castro – a man with the brains of a chess-master, the soul of a gangster and the devices of absolute power – might have in store for us.

One of the odd felicities of our prison life was that we were able to inform ourselves quite well about events on the outside. And having an unusual perspective on Fidel's régime, along with plenty of time to think and discuss, we could interpret these events in a way other people did not.

In March 1962 Fidel announced rationing. He presented it as a temporary measure against what he called the American blockade of Cuba. As I write twenty-one years later, that same temporary measure is still in force. Even then we found it perplexing. Castro had been swimming in money. He had begun with the vast wealth of Cuba's old régimes. He had taken nearly all the property of Cuba's business class. He had stripped billions from the Americans. He was getting loans from the Soviets. He had a prodigiously capable people and one of the most naturally rich lands on earth. To all of that he added his own economic policies, and what was the result? After a mere three years in power the wealthiest liberation régime of modern times had to institute the ration book.

Soon after the notice of rationing, Castro and his media began to issue statements critical of the Cuban Communist Party. They alleged the Communist leaders to be power-hungry sectarians who had seized control of the country's governing bodies and had spread inefficiency. They launched a campaign and cut off the Communist Party's head, removing hundreds of its leaders from public life.

Castro's evident goal was to scapegoat the Communists for Cuba's troubles. He succeeded beyond his wildest dreams. After the purge, almost everyone liked him better. The non-Communists found him more "trustworthy." The Communists whom he had left standing accepted him not just as absolute ruler of Cuba but as the *de facto* leader of their party. And something that looked anomalous but was only natural: the purge enhanced him in the eyes of Soviet leaders, who knew better than anyone that "Communism" was just another word for the monolithic régime Fidel was building.

All this time Castro was busy as a beaver protecting himself against the one force in the world that could still bring him down. He knew the Americans were furious over the Bay of Pigs, and intent on revenge. Castro also understood from events in Europe, where the Soviets were winning great victories against the U.S., that Nikita – as we called the Soviet Premier – was preparing to trump JFK. Why not make it a Cuban-Soviet joint venture? From such an enterprise the Soviets could gain a dominant footing in the Americas, while Cuba would get all the firepower it needed to hold off the U.S. That was how Castro and the Soviets came together to produce that epic drama-farce, the Missiles of October.

In Cuba the interesting part of it was to see how people behaved under a cloud of death. Through those days that seemed to go on for lifetimes, we prisoners felt as if we had rejoined the world; or perhaps the world had joined us, for the threat of death had made prisoners of us all.

The way people faced into that calamity was an expression of how they had lived their lives. Our prisoners were gallant and humorous. They talked about how, as the end of the world came near, so many women must be appalled at the fact that they were still virgins. Chances for men had never been greater; all over Cuba women would be chasing men down, while here we were in prison sitting on our hands!

The prison guards, true to form, outdid themselves in hatred. "If your friends put us under the mushroom," they yelled at us, "you pieces of shit will be the first to die!"

Our answer was easy. We just told them that if we were dead, then Castro would be dead too. That reminded them of something they knew and didn't like remembering. Castro's régime was the only excuse they had for their banal and sordid lives. During those days the idea of Castro's downfall had become so palpable that our mentioning it was the best way we had to keep the guards from abusing us; for the idea so depleted them that they lacked even the courage to be bullies.

As for Castro, he too was more himself than he had ever been as he confronted his worst nightmare. The tyrant's great suffering was not a fear of death or destruction. It was the loss of center stage. To be sure, he had positioned Cuba between the U.S. and the U.S.S.R. with supreme audacity and skill; but when things got going he became like a gnat between dancing elephants. He screamed about shaming the *yanquis* or about using the Rebel Army to defend the Soviet missiles as well as *la patria.* For once he had no audience at all. Everyone in the world was too busy watching the superpowers. When the Soviets announced they were removing their missiles, Castro had to learn about it from news reports. It galled him and made him scream louder than ever that the Soviets had taken a decision on Cuba without talking to him.

A point that observers barely noted was that the October crisis gave Castro a permanent grip on power. As everyone could see, the outcome of the crisis made the Americans feel grand and it made the Soviets feel small; but those results for those nations were not definitive. General de Gaulle keenly caught the essence of the matter when he remarked about Kennedy and Khrushchev: "They don't belong to the race of warriors." Within a couple of years both leaders were gone, while Castro had become President-for-Life.

Even then Castro couldn't stop talking about how the Soviets had mistreated him, and that was the essence of the man: taking his tremendous fortune as a given, while acting bitter and vengeful about someone having insulted him. For years he went on about the wicked Soviets until Cuba's economic collapse was so complete that he had to look to Moscow for a bailout. In 1968 he again purged Cuba's Communists, a move that always brought him closer to the Soviets; then he voiced support for the invasion of Czechoslovakia, after which the Soviets began pumping really big money into Cuba.

When the October crisis was over, news reports claimed that the Americans had promised they would leave Cuba alone in exchange for getting the Soviet missiles out. We didn't want to believe it. We couldn't accept that the Americans would fail to come to our rescue. Within a couple of months the Bay of Pigs prisoners did get their release, the Americans having ransomed those men with an enormous shipment of medicines and baby food. The day they went out, Christmas 1962, one of the older political detainees, a former Batista henchman, cried out: "Hey, they have left us alone!"

I had to laugh. "Alone, old man? How can you say that? This place is packed to the rafters!"

Of course I knew what he meant. Once those hostages were gone, the Americans could forget us. We still didn't want to believe it. Then again, a realization of this kind has to mature across time.

Even when time has passed, a light has to shine on the truth so it can stand plainly in view; and a light from a dark place, like the appearance of onrushing beams along a pitch-black road, will show the truth clearest of all.

Nearly a year after the POW release our shortwave radio – the one contraband item that prisoners everywhere somehow obtain – picked up a news item that stopped us cold. Minutes earlier, in Texas, President Kennedy had died from an assassin's bullet.

We were as appalled and shaken as anyone in the world. Even if we thought Kennedy and the U.S. had let us down, we held a deeper admiration and affection for them. Besides, we felt close to Kennedy because in some way he had concerned himself with our fate; and now the President, along with his vestige of concern for us, was gone.

Next morning, after the prisoner count had ended and the guards told us to break up, the inmate announcer in every circular called out: "Yesterday an assassin took the life of the American President. To honor his memory we offer a minute of silence."

While four thousand Cuban prisoners stood to attention, the guards went wild with cursing and screaming. In nearly five years Castro's indoctrination had produced a body of people who, contrary to Cuban instincts, loathed the United States. Those guards were among them; and they were enraged at having to stand by as we paid tribute to President Kennedy.

In truth it was the end not just of a President but of an epoch – *our* epoch – that we were marking. With Kennedy alive, we could hope that someone would snatch us out of eternity and put us back into history. With Kennedy's death our history vanished, and we felt it disappear. We had no moorings in space or time. We were trapped in eternity, alive and dead at once. And we could sense ourselves embarking on a war quite different from the wars we had known. This would be an inner, invisible war supremely difficult to fight: a war of us against ourselves.

How long could we hold out against Castro's jailers? How long could we resist their cruelties as well as their seductive offers, which were cruelties in disguise? A number of prisoners who came to be called "staunch ones" fought against efforts to rehabilitate them. At every turn the guards offered the same deal: cooperate, confess that you conspired, tell us about your activities, about the activities of others, and we will make your lives better. We will give you more food, better lodgings, the right to fresh air, conjugal visits and reduced sentences. Work with us and we will return your lives.

Many men took this course and it made sense for them – especially for innocents who happened to be serving twenty-five-year sentences just because someone had overheard them say, "The government is full of shit." That statement is of course the sovereign right of people everywhere. Castro locked up plenty of people for making it. Unlike genuine political prisoners, those people had gone to jail not for a reason but for a comment. Now they sat condemned not to months or years but to *decades* without women and children, without a meal in the company of friends, without days of sunlight or evenings of music and love. Thanks to Castro and his touchy sensibility, those comments had turned wives into widows and children into orphans. Why shouldn't such prisoners try to rescue their lives by confessing? Indeed their confessions could not harm them nearly as much as the statements that had landed them in jail.

On the other hand, many of us who had gone to jail for acts of rebellion would not rehabilitate. We were still determined to oppose Castro, from jail if need be. Giving up our opposition would hurt us more than imprisonment. I myself, rather than become a willing tool of Castro's state, had been ready to leave this life. Now that I had a new life, my main reason for living was to reject rehabilitation.

Castro's jailers took many different approaches with the "staunch" prisoners. One of these was forced labor. Forced labor for political detainees was a clear violation of law and custom. The measure affronted us. It denied our status as political prisoners, which was our badge of honor. When some of us refused to submit, we went into solitary confinement. I myself was in a solitary cell for twenty months. During a two-year struggle we were able to sabotage the work-projects, which led the authorities to break up the community of political prisoners at the Isle of Pines. Authorities took us off the isle and dispersed us to various jails around Cuba. Thereafter the lot of the political prisoner included frequent jail transfers, as well as frequent changes of cells within jails to keep us from forming bonds.

Next the authorities decided to strip us of our khaki uniforms and compel us to wear the blue uniforms of common prisoners. For us to don blue uniforms was to give up our identity. Rather than accept those uniforms, many of us walked around in our drawers. Again the confrontation with our jailers was lengthy and taxing. They returned our khakis. Like Camus's Sisyphus, we could feel pleased by a small victory that we had won at great sacrifice; but many men wondered whether the gains had been worth the cost.

At the time of the fight over our uniforms I was at Guanajay prison some fifty miles from Havana. After the return of our khakis a guard told me: "Get ready to leave your cell in proper dress."

I knew this could not be a visit. A guard took me to the prison entrance where a car from State Security was waiting. After an extremely hurried ride we pulled up to Security headquarters in the capital.

What was in store? Could it be, after I had spent nine years in prison, that they would interrogate me all over again? Perhaps they would give me a second trial – and this time they would be certain to shoot me.

They showed me to an upper floor and to a seat in a small room.

"A gentleman is here to speak with you," the guard said.

Before I could think, instinct had put me on my feet. Benjamín del Cordobés was standing in front of me.

"I am here to arrange for your release," Benjamín said.

Having aged a good deal, Benjamín was still in form; but a wistful, teary-eyed quality played against his habitual vigor.

"Benjamín, these people will not let me go," I answered.

"They want to. We have been talking with them about your case for two years. Now they are ready to deal – but please! You must give something."

Clearly Benjamín was here with the knowledge and support of the U.S. government.

"What do I give?" I asked him. "Do I wear the blue uniform? Do I talk about things I cannot talk about?"

"You must give the *appearance* of not being whole."

"What does that mean?"

"I am not asking you to break. I only ask you to let them *feel* they have broken you."

"Benjamín, why are you here?"

"Your father is ill. He wants to see you. He needs to see you."

"What must I do?"

"First: the Cuban government asks for a pledge that if you are set free you will not engage in activities against the state."

"I have no objection to that."

"Can you put that in writing?"

"Most certainly!" I said.

He gave me a paper and pen. I set the statement down in my own words and he took it.

"A guard is standing outside this door," he said. "When I call him in, tell him you have agreed to wear the blue uniform. It will only be for a short time. Also, tell the guard you have a statement to make about your activities at the time of your arrest. You don't need to name names. Just say enough so they can claim you gave something."

"If I do that, I lose."

"If you refuse you also lose. Remember what matters."

"Benjamín, I trust you as I have trusted few other people. I love my father as I have loved no one. But on those points I cannot move."

"All right," Benjamín said like the gentleman he was. "Let me see what I can do with this paper. Perhaps it will be sufficient."

We said good-bye with a firm *abrazo*. During the return ride I felt a gaping hole in the center of myself and realized I would not see my father again.

At a later date my mother was able to visit me in jail, and she shed some further light on my interview with Benjamín.

"Your *friends*, two of them, came to me after Benjamín saw you. They said that all your *friends* very much wanted you out of jail."

"Of course!" I told her. "My *friends* were afraid that if I stayed in jail I would talk."

"Well, your *friends* didn't understand the first thing about you," she said. "They told me: 'What would be the harm in his wearing blue?' They said you had thrown away the chance for a deal because you wanted to stay in jail."

I couldn't believe my ears. "They actually said I wanted to stay in jail?"

"Yes. I told them you were in jail because what you wanted was not to be a traitor."

I had to laugh. "They must have loved hearing that from a mother! You are ten times the man they are!"

"Benjamín was very disappointed and so was your father, but you did what you had to do. Everybody understood that."

"God bless you, *vieja*, and God rest the two of them."

In the sixth year of my stay at Guanajay prison, as the populace of Cuba raised glasses to its soldiers who had gone to fight as Soviet mercenaries in an African war, I received news that my father had died after heart surgery in a Miami hospital.

In jail I was a rebel, and a rebel almost by definition is someone young. It was therefore in spite of my surroundings that I grew into middle age. In another sense however I was growing old, if old age means the time at which people around you start to die. Heretofore death and I had not been strangers, but in prison we became close friends.

Thinking people have observed that political prison is a barbarity. Actually the opposite is true. Political prison represents the apex of what we call "civilization," a consummate victory over nature. In this artificial atmosphere an inflexible will dominates and everything natural disappears – especially a thing most natural for us humans, which is a feeling of hope and of love for the future. Every detail of prison routine conspires to strip away our most natural instinct, the desire to live. In certain situations guards told prisoners, "We cannot allow you to keep a pencil or a toothbrush, because you might try to kill yourself with it." Those statements were invitations to try killing yourself. Suicide was always in the air. To be sure, nature dead – a piece of flesh that used to be a man – was not something we saw every day; but every day we saw nature dying. Only those who have heard grown men cry themselves to sleep – who have heard suicides being born – can understand what a blow to nature, what a triumph of human creativity, political prison is.

My friends and comrades were perishing. Alejandro, who had taken part in the attempt on Castro, escaped capture during the "dragnet year" of 1961 but died the following year in Pinar del Río province, trying to achieve in the west of Cuba what Lázaro had begun in the Escambray.

Vladimiro, my "mole" in the Rebel Youth, met his fate in quite a different way. In the summer of 1961 Cuba received a state visit from Soviet cosmonaut Yuri Gagarin, the first man to travel in outer space. Castro took the occasion to announce one of his endless political changes. Vladimiro attended the ceremony as assistant to Félix Gálvez, the cadre from whom I had fled at Playa Girón. Some plainclothesmen showed up – nervy and inconspicuous at once, in their typical manner. Right there at the state visit they took Vladimiro into custody. Gálvez did not fail to see it and he was horrified. Not even he knew how they had their information; but I knew, and I was heartsick when my junior comrade showed up at the Isle of Pines.

During the forced-labor dispute, Vladimiro and I became a two-man phalanx against the measure. One day, for giving a rough answer to a guard, Vladimiro got the beating of his life. I was amazed that he survived, and equally amazed that after such a beating he stood up to eighteen months in solitary. Five years after that, at age thirty-one, he suffered a stroke and death claimed its due.

Death is not just a matter of physical termination. It is even more powerful and present a force when it touches a living spirit. At the Isle of Pines our backward comrade Ernesto established himself as a vocal opponent of rehabilitation. I knew something about Ernesto that other prisoners didn't. Before changing his mind, he himself had started down the path of rehabilitation and had turned informant. He had betrayed me, Vladimiro, and who knew how many others. But none of us could have hated Ernesto as much as he hated himself for having sung to the interrogators.

Whenever I crossed paths with Ernesto he glowered at me, his hatred as visible as steam after a rain. At first I didn't understand it since, between us, I had not been the offending party. I never gave Ernesto a word or even a look about his informer past; and I never told anyone, not even Vladimiro, what I knew.

After a while I saw Ernesto's hatred of me had nothing to do with me. It had all to do with him. Ernesto hated me *because* he had betrayed me. And that was just how it worked with the guards. First they were cruel to us, then they hated us. Later in my prison life I read the novels of Dostoyevsky, who said that hatred never starts as "I hate you and therefore I hurt you" but rather as "I hurt you and therefore I hate you." I was able to confirm this magnificent insight from my own experience.

I never went in for hatred of others but at times I did not escape hating myself. I had not harmed anyone in the prison; I was even polite to the guards. The ones I had hurt were my own kids. The thought of them never stopped weighing on me.

My wife was free of me. She had divorced me after my capture. That much I wanted; but I never wanted her to divorce me from my kids. Whenever I sent letters to them, it was she who answered. My parents told me they were not able to see their grandchildren; and my friend Antonio, whom I asked for help in this matter, told me Elena was giving no ground at all. I was afraid the kids believed I was dead.

In prison I read voraciously. One book I encountered was the Norwegian epic *Kristin, Lavrans' Daughter.* Lavrans is a nobleman-farmer in the 14th century, a good and proud man. He goes with some of his men on an expedition to a mountain pasture and takes along his seven-year-old girl. On their trek into the mountains they stop for lunch. The men build a bonfire to keep away savage creatures who can threaten them even in daytime. The trekkers have their feast and fall asleep. When Kristin awakes it's dusk, and the great fire has turned to ash. The others are so still that Kristin fears them dead. She hears her father's trusted steed and feels safer walking with the horse. They go down the slope until they reach a pond. A strange woman on the other side of the pond beckons to them. The horse rears up, neighs with fear and runs away. Kristin, realizing she's alone and in danger, cries out: "Father! Father!"

One night I awoke in the middle of sleep, my heart pounding wildly. I'd been dreaming of Kristin alone in the woods and I was incensed. How could her father have let her wander off by herself? And why was I so perturbed? I understood that the girl in the woods was my daughter; and unlike Kristin, whose father found her after a few minutes, my Yrene would live in the woods for years, decades, perhaps her whole life.

How could I be doing that to my children? How many chances had I passed up to change my situation? Why had I refused to make a deal with my captors, if such a deal would have enabled me to leave prison and be with my family? What did my honor matter, compared to the happiness of my parents and the safety of my children?

For a long time I had no answers to these questions; but for me it seemed that prison was like the Paris café of which people say that if you sit there long enough, everyone you have ever known will pass in front of you. The writer Karen Blixen observed that life eventually grants us not only the things we have chosen but also the things we have rejected; and in time the answers to my questions did come in a surprising way.

After the incident at the embassy of Perú, one of the signal episodes in our history, I was going in to dinner at Combinado prison with my chess-mate Arturo Alemán when he touched the back of another man, who turned around quizzically. The man wore thick eyeglasses.

"Hi Arturo," the bespectacled man said. "What's up?"

I had seen that face many lifetimes ago.

"Go on, Núñez," Arturo said. "Have a seat and say hello to my friend Félix Gálvez."

"Hello, Gálvez! I remember you well."

"Indeed," the other man said with a broad humor. "How could anyone forget that trip to the invasion beaches?"

I was amazed. In this man before me I found no trace of the arrogant cadre who had placed me under arrest at Playa Girón.

After that reunion Gálvez and I talked almost every day. Gálvez had been a man of importance in Castro's régime. As an honest Communist he had spoken within the government for reform. In 1968, during Castro's second purge of the Communists, the régime denounced Gálvez before the nation as a conspirator and traitor. He was out of politics and had to work as an assistant auto mechanic. His marriage suffered, almost none of his old friends would talk to him and he became, as he put it, "radioactive."

Twelve years later, when Castro decided to open the embassy of Perú, police rounded up a number of purged ex-officials to prevent them from using the embassy as a route out of the country. So it was that Félix Gálvez, one-time big shot, landed in Combinado prison with the status of "common criminal."

When I got to know him he told me he often wondered whether his political honesty was worth the cost to his boy. I said I had the same question about myself and my children.

"At first it's terrible," he said. "The kid is unpopular at school because everybody is calling his father a traitor...."

"Or maybe he doesn't even have a father," I said.

"Maybe not. But as kids grow up they are bound to ask questions about who their father was, what he did, what he stood for. I never wanted to be the kind of father who tries to be a nice guy and who then looks like a jerk when my kid starts asking those questions. I wanted him to find me a pleasant surprise, not a disappointment. Believe me, Núñez. When your kids grow up they are going to come looking for you, and I mean they will look for you in every sense of the word. Of course they will want to know how you felt and thought about them. Once again they will ask what their hearts have always cried to know: why you left. *But* – but – I am sure that finally, and most importantly, they will want to know what kind of man you have been. After all, they are *your* kids. *You* thought them up. *You* conceived them. Somewhere inside them they have what's in *you*, and they will come looking for that. Even in jail you are working for their benefit. You are securing their happiness because by simply sitting here, by showing yourself as a brave and decent man, you give them something money can't buy. You give them your honor, which becomes their honor. You give them the right to be proud of you and therefore of themselves. What can be of greater value?"

As I was extremely moved by that talk I decided to ask my second big question, a matter I had not yet raised with anyone.

"Tell me, Gálvez. Apart from your child, have you ever thought about other people who have suffered from your political actions and the problem of making things up to them?"

"Interesting you should ask," he said in a whimsical way. "As it happens I have thought about that one quite a bit, and it's not easy."

"Well," I replied, "it's not a question for the masses."

"And how not! I would rather say it's a question for Dostoyevsky."

"So you've read him too."

"Indeed I have. He is one of the great dialectical philosophers."

"Actually I interpret him as a religious thinker."

"So you would call this the problem of redemption, while I term it a matter of ends and means," he said without missing a step.

"That's it! Along our way, in the fight for liberty ..."

" ... or the struggle for power ..."

" ... for what I, the bourgeois romantic idealist, call liberty, or for what you, the Marxist theoretician and cadre, call power ..."

" ... we do harm to certain individuals and we expect that the outcome of our struggle will justify ..."

" ... or redeem ..."

" ... the sacrifices we have inflicted on others ..."

" ... but after what we did to those people, we lost. We sit here for political offenses ..."

" ... or for petty criminal ones ..."

" ... that may not even relate to the personal injuries we caused ..."

" ... and you want to know how we can justify ..."

" ... or redeem ..."

" ... the injuries we caused."

"Exactly!" I exclaimed.

"On this point I'm somewhere between the Marxist doctrinaire view and the Russian redemptive idea. I think it comes down to sincerity."

"Sincerity! How do you mean?" I asked, a bit surprised.

"Well, let's distinguish between sincerity and *sincerity*. The first is skin-deep. Don Juan loves one woman today and another tomorrow. Each time he is sincere. He *does* love; but he transfers love so quickly that it becomes meaningless. That's what Castro does in politics. He's tremendously committed and he expresses himself so well that people will follow him anywhere, but nothing sticks. This year it's the Harvest of the Ten Million Tons. Next year it's the miracle bull who will impregnate all of Cuba's cows. There actually was such a creature! I saw it myself. The kind of sincerity that you and I practice, may I say, is of a different order. You have followed a real trajectory in your life. So have I. Each of us has failed, but we have tried. Now we are experiencing our failure, and in its way this is also to the good. Even in jail we are becoming better men. And somehow I think this justifies, redeems, the things we have done. I am not quite sure how this works but I do believe it to be so."

"That sounds like a comment from someone who thinks about God," I said.

"My friend," he answered, "I am not yet prepared for such a conversation!"

"Ha! Neither am I!"

"Then perhaps we will do it another time," he offered.

"Perhaps we will," I said.

We never had that talk. Gálvez had been in jail for two years when the authorities first brought charges against him. At a judicial hearing in his absence, prosecutors accused Gálvez of stealing books from state libraries. The court found him guilty. That charge carried a sentence of a year and a half. Since he had already served two years in prison, the judge ordered his release.

One night the release order came down to jail in the usual random way. Gálvez must not have wanted to give the guards even an extra five minutes to think about the order, so he packed his things and ran from the prison without taking the time to say good-bye. That's how it was in the environment. You encountered people, you knew them deeply, and then they were gone.

I thought often about the Moor. From time to time, when I met a prisoner who had been in La Cabaña, I mentioned a big olive-skinned guard I had seen there. Some of the men had also seen him. From their accounts I was able to catch glimpses of my comrade who emerged as a fearsome and melancholy apparition, rather like some lone whale of mariners' legend.

After the opening of Perú's embassy I heard from incoming prisoners about a guard who created some stir when he took asylum there. Others in that crowd of refugees at the embassy had recognized him from La Cabaña. One last time the Moor had surprised Fidel Castro and left through the door that history had opened in one of its most bizarre turns. Later I heard from Antonio that the Moor was driving a bus in Miami.

That same month, April 1980, I had my forty-seventh birthday; not much of an occasion except that it brought to mind an earlier one. Twenty-one years earlier I had celebrated my birthday in the company of my friend Antonio Moreno. We were in the glorious year of 1959. The revolution was newly in power. The country had gained a fresh start. Moreno and I were prospering from our legal pactices. As we raised a glass for my twenty-sixth Antonio said: "The next twenty years are going to be the happiest of your life."

Antonio's twenty years had already expired but no matter. Of those twenty I had spent nearly eighteen in jail and the clock was still ticking.

How could I reckon my time in jail? What was the meaning of a quantity like eighteen years? Perhaps it would make sense to see it another way. It was roughly the time in which a baby is conceived, is born, wins the hearts of his or her parents, learns to walk and talk, has a period of mischief, goes to school, develops friendships, learns to read and write, to play sports or maybe a musical instrument, has a first love, gets hurt, suffers the pangs of maturity, then puts it all together and steps into adulthood.

That was the amount of time I had spent in jail.

Another curiosity: in prison the guards treated political inmates as rule-breakers. When a smaller number of us took exception to certain policies, like forced labor or the removal of our khakis, even the other political prisoners looked on us as rule-breakers.

Rule-breakers? As I reviewed my own history and Cuba's I came to a different conclusion. We staunch prisoners had been rule-*keepers* while Castro and his government had been the ones to break the rules.

Consider. In April 1980 – as a result of Castro's argument with Perú and of eleven thousand souls who had packed into that embassy for the chance to flee from Cuba – the United States government decided to teach Castro a lesson. It announced it would welcome any Cuban who wanted to immigrate. Castro answered: Why not? Anyone who wants can leave.

Cuba's prison guards threw open jail-cell doors and hollered: "Who wants to go to the United States?" The prisons emptied out as killers, rapists and other criminals – though not political detainees, of course – went hurtling toward the U.S. As Gálvez commented, this was a sheer gangster move on Fidel's part, like holding a state dinner and serving human heads for the main course.

Mental patients, the chronically ill and other so-called "undesirables" joined tens of thousands of everyday people in a massive exodus. After months of receiving Cuban refugees the U.S. agreed to negotiate with Castro; and Castro cancelled the right to emigrate as abruptly as he had granted it. Of course the emotional spigot of the exodus was not so easy to turn off, and people kept trying to get away by boat. They fell into the nets of Castro's patrols and the prisons filled up again.

A hell of an irony: Castro threw people into jail for doing the very thing that, only months earlier, he had pulled people out of jail to do.

Cuba under Castro had been replete with such absurdities. Here is what Gálvez had to say about the period after the October crisis.

"These were the years of the anti-Soviet policy. Fidel reorganized the Communist Party, which then removed economic structures of all kinds. They abolished accounting. Do you imagine? *Abolished accounting.* No fiscal planning! Foreign exchange became a fraud because the currency had nothing to back it up. All utilities, phones, buses, movie-houses, sporting events, were free of charge. Of course this was immensely popular. It was also completely irresponsible. The leaders kept talking about a 'better tomorrow' but production fell to nearly zero."

"How could Fidel ignore the laws of history?" I asked.

"Because he thought and indeed still thinks that he is *bigger* than history! And in his way he is right. He and Ché *did* step over history. They became mythical. Of course even mythical people need to eat, but Fidel assumed he could produce wealth in godlike fashion. He *decreed* that Cuba was going to be productive. He told the people: 'Now you are free. Now you can do anything and be anything you want. Here is a hammer. There is the stone. Go and be Michelangelo.' Of course it didn't happen because we could never set up a *structure* to make it happen. Fidel wouldn't think in terms of structures. He despised them and he was suspicious of them. He just expected people to step over problems as he himself had done. Many thought this an excess of idealism – in other words, a sympathetic trait. No! Wrong! This was not big-mindedness but small! Not selflessness but self-absorption! Not idealism but an excuse for being careless! Fidel was irresponsible because he never took the trouble to understand *the everyday business of being a decent person*. And that lack in him became a source of tremendous suffering for millions upon millions of ordinary, decent people."

Gálvez enabled me to see this history and the direction of my own life in a clear way. The thing I had objected to, and had gone to jail for opposing, was government by caprice. Cuba had no government. It had one man talking to and talking for the country. Official programs and policies did not exist. It was simply Castro trying one thing one day and another thing the next. We staunch prisoners were perhaps the only ones in Cuba who had the luxury of being constant in our behavior. We had refused to bend as the rules bent. We had kept straight as rails. The French call their long-distance railroads "grand lines," and I started thinking of us as grand-line prisoners. The name had another sense too: grand-line railroads extend a large distance in space, and our prison terms were extending a very great distance in time.

When I looked back along those tracks I was able to see how my life had moved, and I made the discovery of discoveries. For me, even for me, time had sped by.

Is it surprising? To anyone who has lived a normal happy life, or even a normal unhappy life, the idea of time going quickly is no revelation. I had lived an exceptional life; not good, not bad, just exceptional. Through most of it time did press heavily. Nowhere did it press as in jail, where one must work like a sharecropper to make time just a bit lighter than it wants to be. When you think about time you perceive its endlessness, and that's a notion poisonous to life. Let it sit on you for any period and you wind up wanting to kill yourself. But if you do what you can to keep this idea out of your head, the days begin to move. At first they walk, then they trot. When you have almost stopped noticing the days, they run. You almost don't remark the weeks and months. Years begin to pile up, and soon enough you don't know where the decades have gone.

I was amazed at how short my life had been; and I started to uncover the density of wisdom contained in the words, "time flies." Whoever you are, whatever you do, however long or hard the road you have taken, beware. And when you think you have enough time or more than enough, then doubly beware. Time does fly.

XXII.

LOSING AT POKER

In May 1982, quite abruptly, Mariano José Núñez Hidalgo, a.k.a. Rodrigo, got an early release from prison after agreeing to leave Cuba at once and to conduct no activities, there or elsewhere, against Castro's government.

By a curious turn the man who signed the release was the officer he had known twenty-one years earlier as the interrogator Porfirio. The man's actual name was Amarillo. A colonel who had recently become director of State Security, Amarillo granted the release after deciding from personal knowledge that Cuba had nothing more to gain by holding this prisoner.

* * *

"We have begun our final approach to Orly Airport. Please fasten your seatbelts for landing."

Unbelievable. Three nights ago I was on a cement slab in Security. The next night I slept in a hotel on the Malecón. Yesterday afternoon I was on the streets of Havana. Now I am about to get off this immensely powerful airplane and step into Paris.

Why Paris? The usual destination for an outcast prisoner is México or Costa Rica, but Amarillo said I was "earmarked" for France. I wasn't about to start asking questions. When I told the driver from Security I had no idea how to make my way in Paris, he said a reception committee would be waiting. It seems that certain people are pulling me here. The Americans? I'm sure they haven't lost sight of me but I believe they have lost interest. Who else then? I think I know.

Alighting in the terminal – an everyday scene from the industrial world, *anno* 1982 – Rodrigo found a display of beauty and abundance beyond his reckoning. He had seen many such things but in his memory they showed like a black-and-white film. A technicolor universe was exploding around him, and he remained a man from the black-and-white film.

As he looked around for his reception committee he saw he was good in his guess.

The lady's face was as fresh and alluring as when he had first seen her twenty-two years ago. It was only her hair in a bun, rather than freely caressing her shoulders, that made the difference between the mature woman before him and the girl-woman he recalled.

"Nathalie!"

"Hello, Núñez. Let me welcome you on behalf of the French people." The lady cracked a smile and said: "Are you surprised to see me?"

"And how!" *Always assure a woman she has caught you by surprise – especially when she hasn't.*

"You must be tired, and you have a busy day tomorrow," she said. "The Americans are waiting to see you."

Rodrigo also knew that must be true but for form's sake he asked: "What does that have to do with you?"

"Our office works closely with them. When we told them you were coming out of jail they said they wanted to see you."

"I will be glad to see them, but I cannot present myself like this!" Rodrigo held up the "beggar's bag" that enclosed his few possessions.

"We will find you some clothes. Then you must go to your hotel and rest. Have you eaten?"

"I could use something," Rodrigo said with understatement.

"We will eat in the city. The airport food is unspeakable."

Nathalie took him outside to the curb where car and driver waited.

"*Au deuxième, s'il vous plâit. Boulevard des Capucines,*" she told the driver.

"How beautiful this looks!" he exclaimed as they rode the highway.

"But this is only the suburban sprawl. It's hideous!"

"Bear in mind where I have come from," Rodrigo said without a trace of self-pity.

"Of course," Nathalie answered with respect.

He noted the famous Moulin Rouge. They had reached the southern *arrondissements* and as they rode onto the boulevards he was overcome by their beauty as the visitor to Paris always is, no matter how many times one has been there before.

They crossed the Seine, turned onto an immense tree-shaded avenue, and stopped in front of a luxurious department store.

A nearby *boulangerie-patisserie* forcibly struck Rodrigo's eye.

"Why don't we eat there?" he asked.

"We have better food in the department store."

"That looks fine to me," Rodrigo said, his hunger in full view.

In the bakery they sat down with some cakes and a large *baguette*. Rodrigo's communion with the food was so ardent, so intimate, that Nathalie must have felt herself watching an act of love.

After this meal and then some shopping, the car took them across that most exquisite of urban fixtures, the Place Vendôme, and stopped before a stately building which was the Intercontinental Hotel.

"When you go to the embassy tomorrow just turn right on Rivoli, there, and walk into the Concorde," she told Rodrigo. "The embassy is across the square, ten minutes on foot. Let's have a look at your room."

His heart quickened at the thought of her coming upstairs; but it was only a brief visit to give some coins to the bellhop and make sure the accommodation was suitable.

"Do you mind if I use the phone?" she asked.

"Not at all."

She dialed. "Hello? Yes. In reference to today's meeting 3:30 is fine."

Nathalie put down the phone and reached into her purse.

"Here, you need some pocket money," she said, giving him a pair of 500-franc notes. "Your appointment at the embassy is for nine tomorrow. They have your name at the reception. When you have finished, take a taxi to the restaurant *Aux Pieds de Cochon.*"

"The driver will know it?"

"It's as famous as the *Tour Eiffel.* I will wait for you there."

"Thank you," Rodrigo said.

"Don't thank me, thank the government of France! They are the ones with a budget for political asylum."

He was rather sure at least some of the money was hers instead of France's, but anyway he said: "In the absence of the Prime Minister I give those thanks to you!"

"Thanks accepted."

* * *

"At the Feet of the Pig," during the lunch hour, was a densely peopled cave that somehow gathered light from the mingled perfumes of its cooking and wine as well as from a vivid sense of the vibrantly beautiful air outside.

In his new clothing Rodrigo was far from the beggar Nathalie had picked up the day before. As he swept over to her table she leaned toward him and offered her hand galant-style. He took and kissed it.

"You look like a man on whom fortune has smiled!" she said. It was the kind of statement that tries to deflect emotion by pointing to the emotion of another.

"Well, at least I have a destination. And today I can have you as my guest."

"Thank you! By the way, I hope you don't object to the noise in here. It makes an atmosphere but one could find it disturbing."

"Actually it gives us privacy. It's the smoke I don't enjoy, but I have already seen enough of Paris to know I can't escape it."

"Well, I promise no smoke at this table. Tell me. What *is* your destination?"

"Miami."

"Of course. I imagine you will make your home there."

"What makes you say that?"

"Miami is a wonderful city – the city Havana should have been. And you must have family there."

"A mother who suffers from lung cancer, and two children."

At that moment the waiter strode up and said efficiently: "*Vous désirez?*"

Nathalie looked at Rodrigo, who said, "You order for us both."

"Onion soup and green salad for two," she told the waiter.

"What are you drinking?" the waiter asked with importance.

"A bottle of good *viognier.*"

"Excellent choice," the waiter commented. "I will find one for you."

"I am sorry about your mother," Nathalie said when the waiter had gone.

"She has had a long life, and we will be able to spend time together before the illness claims her. The hard part will be introducing myself to my children."

"They have never seen you?"

"When I left on my last mission they were three and two. That was twenty-one years ago. Since that time I have had no contact with them."

"Think how happy they will be to find you!"

"Every day in prison I used to imagine some aspect of their lives." He paused with emotion. "Now they are grown up. Whatever they have made of themselves, they have done it without me or perhaps in spite of me. I will be dropping out of the sky and landing on them like a parachutist. It's funny. I left them to enter Cuba by parachute, and now I will parachute onto them!"

"You are *much* too hard on yourself," Nathalie said. "Since your children have made it without you, they are free to adopt you. You say you are falling on them from the sky. For them it might be like looking up and finding a second sun."

Rodrigo saw once again why he had loved this woman. With all her complications, what a tender gift of insight she had!

"Anyway," Rodrigo said, "Miami is out for me as a place of residence. Maybe the U.S. is too."

"But you are welcome there!"

"As a resident, yes. As a citizen in five years' time, yes. As a person who can give something of value to society, I think not."

"Why so pessimistic?"

"It's time to tell you about my visit to the embassy."

"I am waiting."

At that moment the waiter appeared with the wine in an ice bucket. He uncorked it and poured a sip into Rodrigo's glass.

Rodrigo took a look at the wine and said to Nathalie: "It's white."

"Of course!" she answered. "With onion soup you take white wine."

"Why not red?"

"Impossible. You would make a scandal!"

"Let's see," Rodrigo said and tasted. "Huh! This is extremely good."

The waiter, who understood English when he wanted to, lifted his head with satisfaction and strode off.

"Here's a toast to my first wine in twenty-one years, and to all the wine I will drink in my next twenty-one!"

"Salut!"

"Now I will ask your permission to make a small preface," Rodrigo said.

"Of course."

"I have been in prison a very long time. That's evident. The reason I mention it again is simply this: in prison you learn to see people's masks. Everyone wears a mask. It's a necessary part of life. While I see the masks, however, I don't talk to them. I prefer talking to people's faces, and that's what I will do with you."

Nathalie gave a very broad smile. It was the best mask she had.

"In visiting the embassy I did not simply go as an ex-political prisoner seeking asylum from the Americans. The fact is that at the moment I fell captive I was working with their government."

"That is hardly cause for surprise," Nathalie said. "So were many of your countrymen."

"Yes, but you know something more about me."

"What makes you say that?"

"Earlier in our talk, not once but twice, I spoke of my last mission to Cuba. Almost anyone would have shown curiosity but the curiosity lines in your face were completely still. That alone would have told me you knew what I was talking about."

Nathalie looked at him rather gravely.

"Be certain of this," he said. "What I know about you I am not going to share with anyone. I know you are in a unique position. I know you have balanced many things. Most important, I know you have been a friend to me in spite of our different loyalties. You have confided nothing to me and you do not need to. I treat your secrets as my own."

Nathalie gave a breath-stopping smile that was no mask.

The waiter arrived with two steaming crocks of soup.

"Please have another one ready in case the gentleman wants it," Nathalie said to the waiter.

"Of course! It's the specialty of the house!" the waiter answered with an attitude verging on insolence.

The fragrant vessels overflowed with essence-of-onion and cheese. Wielding a section of bread, Rodrigo hurried to subdue the portion in front of him.

"Do you want another?" she asked when he had reached the bottom.

"No, thank you. I want to tell you about the embassy."

"Please do."

"Mostly I was in a medical exam. The doctor said I was in astonishing shape for someone with my experience."

"One doesn't need a medical degree to tell that! And after the exam?"

"I met with an official."

"Which one?"

"A Mr. Elliott, very young. He introduced himself as being from the State Department but he was clearly 'company.' "

"What did he tell you?"

"Residency and eventual citizenship are mine for the asking. No surprises there; but I did get a surprise when I asked about a debriefing."

"And that was?"

"He told me: No debriefing."

"How can that be?"

"He said the Reagan administration is still exploring the chances of an agreement with Castro. America's policies and methods of the early sixties now appear in a very poor light. People in Washington do not want to hear anything more on that subject."

"It's most ungrateful."

"I told him that I had a mass of information on Cuban matters; that I had kept my ears open in prison, which is one of the best places to hear things; and that I know the U.S. is encountering heavy problems in Central America. Those problems have a close relation to Castro."

"Obviously."

"I made clear I was not trying to give information as a way of involving myself – but because the information I possessed was bound to be helpful to other Cubans as well as to the American government, I felt I should be able to share it."

"The man showed no interest when you said that?"

"He gave me an official response. 'We are very well informed.' 'We are pursuing these matters in our own way.' Et cetera."

"I am sorry," Nathalie said.

"You know, at this point in my life I don't so much care for politics. I have come to agree with Goethe that the way to clean up the world is for everyone to sweep in front of his house. When I went into jail I was trying to change the world. In jail I worked on my house. Life has given me the right to be modest, and I am not easy to offend; but that particular dismissal *does* offend me. After all, the Americans and I worked together. I kept their secrets, not just my own, for twenty-one years. Now I have the ability to tell them things they do not know and *should* know – but they refuse to open their ears!"

As he drew to a finish Rodrigo took note of the waiter standing over him with a large plate of greens.

"Do you want more wine?" Nathalie said. "And please excuse the interruption."

"Of course!" Rodrigo laughed. "Interrupt me a hundred times. I know what my priorities are!"

A few minutes later she asked: "How did your meeting wind up?"

"Take a guess."

"They paid you off."

"The check had already been cut. Young Elliott gave me a list of banks where I can deposit it. I can begin drawing funds immediately."

"The amount?"

"Adequate. Not generous. Not close to what I would have received or what my family would have received if I had been one of their own. In that sense, too, they have not kept their word."

"How does it make you feel?"

"It disappoints me but I understand it. Those people simply cannot swallow me. They cannot accept what I did."

"Why? You honored them!"

"They are angry at me for honoring them because they did not honor themselves! Before my last mission the Americans warned me that if I fell captive I was going to break. When I got captured they wanted me out. For years they sent messages telling me to leave jail by making a deal with my captors: give a few minor secrets, wear a common prisoner's uniform, whatever. This was exactly the line that Castro's prison authorities used. If we wanted to avoid a lifetime in jail we must give in to them. Ironic, isn't it? The Americans wound up saying the same thing Castro did!"

"But it made no difference to you."

"Why should it have? If I didn't break for Castro's interrogators I certainly wasn't going to break for the Americans! It didn't make the Americans happy with me. You know, in many parts of the world the Americans fight, and fight hard, for political independence. All the same, they do not respect personal independence! They do not like or trust people who fail to obey them. And they have long memories. They have paid me not because they like me but because they want me to keep quiet!"

"No wonder you do not feel welcome."

"In prison I discovered I belonged nowhere in the world. Believe it or not, that was a good piece of news. If I belong nowhere it means I can go anywhere. The truth is, I feel lucky."

The waiter was there again. "Have you decided for dessert?" he said with his importance.

"You choose for us," Nathalie told the waiter.

"*Très bien*," the waiter said and departed in a cloud of happiness.

"Lucky?" Nathalie said to Rodrigo with a smile in her voice.

"You?"

"Yes, lucky. Maybe you haven't heard the story about the man who said he enjoyed losing at poker."

"Losing at poker? What about *winning* at poker?"

"Yes. People always made that objection. And the man told them: 'Of course! To win at poker is the greatest pleasure imaginable. Why state the obvious? The whole game is so enjoyable that as long as you play you are going to have pleasure. When you are losing at poker it means you are still playing.' "

"I see! You are still in the game."

"And what a game! You know, prison might not have been such a bad thing for me. In prison, in war, in all I have done, I have been able to see everything the human condition offers. At moments it was something horrible. At times I used to think that if I reincarnated I would not want to come back as a human. Now I know I have been wrong to think that. Being in this game any way one can is a privilege. And best of all is to know that the joy of winning is inseparable from the experience of losing."

"That's very enlightened," she said, "very *dialectical*."

The waiter put down two slices of apple tart along with two *demitasses* and went quietly away.

"That's what a well-informed Parisian would say," Rodrigo answered. "I know that in your case the word goes deeper."

"How so?"

"In the sense of playing two sides at the same time."

"Which sides?"

"America and Cuba."

"I *had* to see both sides of that. I was a journalist."

"You were also something more."

"Please! The subject is difficult." Nathalie was quite nervous.

"Don't worry," Rodrigo said. "As I have already told you, I am keeping your secrets. Anyway, it's understandable. You admired Castro. Millions of people did. The whole world, minus a few resentful ones, hoped he would succeed. With your background you *had* to like Castro. That made *much* more sense than liking the United States. I should imagine that you, like so many Europeans, were looking for a remedy to 'the God that failed.' And like so many people all over the world you surely admired a leader who had the gumption to defy Uncle Sam."

Nathalie stayed quiet and Rodrigo, who needed no urging whatever, kept on.

"In time Castro became another God that failed. It's too bad that so many people who invested themselves in him are still stuck in their illusions. I think you were too smart and too honest to go down that road. Somewhere, I would guess, you began to have questions about Fidel's version of history. After all, you did speak of Miami as 'the city Havana should have been.' That's quite a remark. It cuts pretty deep. I haven't seen Miami in more than twenty years but I did see Havana a few days ago. I couldn't imagine the decay in front of me. So many buildings in ruins, propped up by wood beams. Havana has become a city on crutches! Miami, whatever its problems, whatever its heartaches over Castro's success, is a handsome and vibrant city that Cubans have made. In prison we knew it but could never say it. If we had, Castro's guards would have fallen into an Islamic frenzy and cut out our tongues. But here you are, saying it – *you,* who used to be such a friend of Castro's."

"How do you presume to say such a thing?" Nathalie interjected.

"Because I know about you and Castro," Rodrigo said. "I know you were close. I know you helped him convince the Americans to take an action they greatly regretted. I am not dwelling on any of that. I *will* say how impressed I am that you went from being a friend of Castro's to being other-than-a-friend of Castro's. Almost everyone who tried to go that route lost everything – while you, who also had to avoid the wrath of the Americans, handled things beautifully. Please, Nathalie. Be at ease! I do not mean to pry into your life or cause trouble. I only speak of these matters because, more than anything, I believe I have something to thank you for."

"And what is that?"

"I believe you saved my life."

Nathalie had no answer.

"I can tell from your silence that I am not off the mark. It took me some years to put the pieces together. Of course the mock execution left me in a poor position to think."

Rodrigo paused as if waiting for a comment, then resumed. "There. You see? When I spoke of my mock execution you gave no sign of surprise."

"Why should I? I followed events in Cuba. I knew they had done that to you."

"The mock execution was not public knowledge. Almost no one knew about it. But let's talk about the real thing. The plain and simple fact is that by every rule of life and logic they should have executed me. People who had not done a twentieth of what I had done were dying at the wall every day. My only way to save myself was to convince Castro's officials that my being alive could profit them. When my interrogators informed me that my appeal had failed, I knew I was going to die. Next thing I knew, Castro had commuted my death sentence to a prison term. For a long time after that I was empty. I had no thoughts of any kind. But when my thoughts went back to the question of why I was still alive, I came to the conviction that it must have been you who had spoken to Castro on my behalf."

Rodrigo paused and added: "This is only part of what I have to tell you."

"What else can there be?" she asked with a perceptible tremor in the voice.

"The fact that quite unknown to you, and some time before you saved my life, I chose to save yours."

"*You* saved *my* life?" she said incredulously. "How?"

"I would rather not say exactly. Let us only say that someone had decided to kill Castro. Let us say this person had gone to a great deal of trouble to find out how and where to put Castro in a trap – a thing which, as you understand, was and still is far from easy. Let us say that with a great deal of persistence and luck the assassin got Castro in his rifle-sight, only to find someone else there too. The choice was to shoot both or shoot neither; and the assassin missed his chance because he would not destroy that second life."

"My God!" Nathalie said with a blush that showed bronze on her coffee-and-cream-colored skin. Without the need of another word, that night of rifle-fire at the river had again come alive for both of them.

"Do you see the beauty of it?" Rodrigo said. "When I saved your life I saved my own! Many times in prison I wondered how destiny would push us together again, so I could say this to you. Well, at last I've said it; and now I think I am ready to say good-bye."

As Nathalie's tears flowed quietly, Rodrigo saw what he had hitherto only known. The two of them had shared something unpredictable and miraculous: a thing far beyond those surface-to-surface contacts that pass in the everyday world for love.

"When do you leave?" she asked.

"I should probably go rather soon but I could stay in Paris a few days, or maybe take a train to Germany or Italy. What do you think?"

The waiter came with the bill and placed it before the lady. Rodrigo snatched it away. He returned it to the waiter with a number of bank notes that included a pretty generous tip. The waiter looked at the notes, pronounced "*Oui, ça va*" and withdrew.

"Oh my!" Nathalie exclaimed. "I've just noticed the time. I am late for a meeting."

Rodrigo smiled and said lightly: "You are going to see your lover."

She smiled back. "It is good for one's health."

As she stood to leave he got up and embraced her. Then she vanished from the place like the expert spy she was.

Rodrigo lingered for a few minutes at the table, absorbing all the pleasantness around him, and stepped out into the brilliant Paris afternoon.

THE END

RECOGNITIONS

This book owes its existence to the generosity of others.

Many years ago, David Halberstam did me an act of kindness that substantially encouraged me as a writer. I did not recognize him adequately at the time. So here's a compressed and heartfelt thanks.

Elric Endersby III, Dan Wedge, Elton Anglada, Daphne Abeel and Robert LeGrand also live in my memory as people who stood out from a fairly indifferent world to befriend my craft. You were great, each one of you.

Of the many people who have taught me about Cuba, first among equals are E.A. Rivero and Adolfo Rivero. Through many hours of conversation with these exceptional gentlemen, I have started to understand how one can draw wisdom, dignity and a sense of humor from the ravages of history.

I have also learned much about Cuba from Carlos Quintela, Abelardo Menéndez, Rosa Berre, José Solís, Víctor Delgado, José Hernández and Ricardo Bofill.

Karen Gantz Zahler is a samurai in literary agent's clothing.

Héctor Menéndez, *gran caballero*, intrepidly carried the banner for this book in Spanish America.

Benigno Dou, gifted novelist and poet, beautifully translated this work into Spanish.

Bob Fuller has been my daily co-conspirator – a thinker and colleague of surpassing quality.

Wakeford Gong brought this book to life through his genial artistry and design.

George Duebner, Cathy Benko, Marie and Vin Gaudenzi have been the most steadfast of supporters.

Ed Cohen read the various versions with a dedicated intelligence that my thanks cannot compensate.

Among other readers of this book I am proud to mention Harry Rieckelman, Andy Schmookler, Norberto Fuentes and Norwood Pratt.

The kindness of strangers is a piece of whimsy, like Tolstoy's happy family – but I've had more than my fair share. Special regards to Victoria Broughton, Julie Kemper, Sam Gruen, Ron Berlin, Bruce Brett, Michael Landy, Kate LaPoint, Ray Hudson, Stuart Loory, David Horowitz, John S. Carroll, Gerald Levy, S.J. Kalian, Tanya Simpson and Richard Pollock.

Dr. Mario Castejón, José de Lima, Armando de la Torre, Amalia and Cristina Quiñones, Marta Buonafina, Acelia Pacheco, Irma Price, Niurka de la Torre, Steven Hecht, Marge Silverton, Tony Russo, Robert Hart, Frank and Gerd Ziegenhorn, Anthony Cefaratti and Antonio de Oyarzábal are *siempre en mi corazón.*

Gayle Martin and Jack Henry, Sheila Simpson and Tom James, Marie-Louise Rodén, Zitta Zahor and Serban Rusu have been music to me.

Colleagues who have been more than colleagues are Bill Smith, Janine Sternlieb, Bill Lipsky, Mark Mericle, Aileen Alfandary, Lisa Rothman, Kéllia Ramares, Susan Stone, Andrea du Flon, Robbie Osman, Larry Bensky, Aaron Glantz, Phil Osegueda, Kris Welch, C.S. Soong, Matt Martin, Mary Bishop, Wendell Harper, Roy Tuckman, Brian Myers, Molly Anderson, Lisa Sellers and Matthew Burkley.

Vital editorial help came from Emma Edwards, Noah Johnson, Carol Staswick, Thanasis Maskaleris and Kathy Glass.

As this book was going to press, I sent the first pages to Robert S. McNamara. He called to say that he was "extremely interested" by the themes in play. That reaction confirmed me in my impetus to publish this book, and I am very grateful for it.

Many, many affectionate nods to my families in the New York and Tokyo areas.

Toshinori Kanemoto, Ryoya Funakoshi and Goro Aoki have enriched my life with their inimitable friendship.

My thoughtful, ebullient and tender wife Kaori is with me in everything I do.

Impossible to name are those, yet unknown to me, who may extend their appreciation to this work or to myself. In exchange for your future kindnesses, please accept this blanket tribute. You may count on me to repay by passing on to others what I've been fortunate enough to receive from you.